THE DEATH OF AN EXTE

A story of detection

by

Stephen J Ball

Catalunya 2019

Staverley stared at the postcard. He read the short message for the third time. He tried to remain calm and not to think about what it meant. In any case he realized he did not know what to think. His moral compass had spun and fallen off its spindle. All of the things that had happened and all the things he had done over the past two months had profoundly shaken his sense of what it meant to be an academic and his sense of himself. He now knew things about himself and about others that were difficult to deal with. He had thought himself pretty ordinary, a regular law-abiding person who strove to be honest and truthful to the best of his ability. He now knew that he was not. He had done things that he never thought himself capable of, he had done things he had never thought about at all. He put the postcard carefully on the mantelpiece and despite trying not to he started to go over everything again in his mind, and what he could have done differently, what he should have done differently. But he could not change anything now. What was done was done and he was who he had become.

Summer 1983

CHAPTER ONE

The Social and Economic Sciences building near the back of the Watermouth
campus, a 15 minute walk from the station, was a recent addition to the
university's property portfolio, as the Vice Chancellor liked to call the buildings.
The reduced funding of higher education by Margaret Thatcher's penny-pinching
government meant that the experimental concept architecture for which
Watermouth was known had in the case of Social and Economic Sciences been
replaced by a primary emphasis on cheapness, drabness and flexibility. The
triumph of function over style was one thing, the triumph of austerity over
function was another – at least for those who had to teach and learn in the
buildings. The nearest equivalent architecturally, for those who gave it any
serious thought, was mid-60s British Rail. The effect was somewhere you might
go to, if you really had to catch a train, but you would not want to linger there
and would probably want to a good wash later. The university cleaners worked
long and hard but the building always seemed grimy, everything was chipped
and marked although it had only been open a few months. It was inventively and
artfully down-at-heel and constantly smelled of an exotic mix of floor polish,
disinfectant and damp. All of this made the architect's reputation and got him a
permanent place on Channel 2's late night culture programme sofa.

Staverley stood outside the building for a moment and stared up at the eleven
stories. No cardboard milk cartons filled with water were being dropped from
the postgraduate lounge today. There were no telltale splats on the concrete
steps. Once inside he contemplated the two lifts and decided they were not
worth waiting for. The porters sometimes made a point of holding the lifts in the
basement for long periods when they were most in demand and given the
current state of pay negotiations between the university and the campus
workers the lift wait this morning might be a particularly fruitless one. He
hustled up the seven flights to his department, arriving out of breath but very
pleased to have made it without stopping.

Wednesdays at the university were mainly devoted to administration and sport. Which for teaching staff usually meant committee meetings, which could occasionally be mistaken for sport. Committees were not Staverley's favourite pastime, although when he had first been appointed to Watermouth he had been a keen university politician and prepared carefully in advance for meetings to make sure his views were taken seriously. He engaged enthusiastically in lobbying colleagues and certainly got a buzz from seeing his proposals accepted in the face of opposition. But he soon tired of these 'boys games' and now limited his efforts to the bare necessities or to issues he felt to be of real importance, of which there were surprisingly few. Most things of real importance were never even considered for discussion, which was frustrating. In practical terms, of real importance meant things that were likely to affect him directly but there were very occasional matters of principle to be defended or administrative atrocities to be opposed. He still found the micropolitical process interesting, but for the most part he now preferred to watch, to stand on the terraces so to speak and analyse tactics and assess the relative skills of the players - their grasp of the game and ability to make a decisive pass or crunching tackle. He could recognise now the playing out of behind doors deals and trade offs, 'smart moves' and countermoves, the long game and strategic sacrifices, as against the hapless pleading and rampant stupidity of those players who lacked committee nous. As a spectator sport university politics is an acquired taste but in terms of tension and inter-personal rivalry it has snooker and darts totally beaten. Staverley thought he might write a book about it someday.

When he entered the large seminar room fourteen of his nineteen department colleagues were already seated around the large square of wooden tables, papers to hand but the meeting had not yet begun. He looked around at the spare seats and made his way to the far side of the room to sit next to his friend Pauline Oriel-Hay - an ardent feminist, excellent scholar, vivacious blonde and all round good person, Pauline also had a wicked sense of humour and could lighten even the dullest meeting with her double-edged whispered witticisms. They smiled at each other and he sat down.

'Looking forward to a thrilling morning.' He whispered in her ear.

'No – are you?' She didn't seem to be joking now.

'What's up?'

'Oh, I had a session with Lionel this morning about my leave of absence and we ended up growling at one another again. I will end up strangling that man.' Lionel was their much unloved Head of Department.

'That's ok, strangling fools is justifiable homicide. Do you want to talk about it after and plan a counter attack?'

'I don't know. I'm too upset. Maybe. I'll see.'

'Can we make a start people,' Lionel spoke loudly to quieten the various conversations going on.

'Not a long agenda today but let's get going and not waste time.' Lionel was very much against wasting time, the room fell silent and people turned their attention to the papers in front of them. Staverley thought he could detect a communal sigh but it was probably his imagination.

The business of the meeting flowed by without much irrelevant discussion or comment - which made a pleasant change. Most academics love to discuss. Whatever the topic any group of academics will eagerly seek out all the possible positions, views and interpretations and rehearse them in detail and at inordinate length given the slightest opportunity. As a chairman, as in his office, Lionel was not normally keen to offer such opportunities. He did not value discussion and preferred nods and other non-verbal signals of assent that allowed him to have his way and avoid debate and dissent. As in other areas of his work as Head of Department he tried to avoid confrontation whenever possible. He particularly detested displays of personal or political commitment. He also had an awkward social manner, which made any kind of frank exchange of views painful and fraught. In meetings with colleagues he liked people to speak quickly and briefly and dispassionately and interrupted when he had heard enough. He always gave the impression that he wanted you out of the room as soon as possible and that you were wasting his valuable time by wittering on. He did not see it as part of his role to mollycoddle his staff and he hated any kind of personal revelation. His usual responses to any of these things were either noisy bluster and irritation or blatant lack of interest. But he always seemed to have an uncanny knowledge of other peoples work and to have read almost all the journal articles published by members of the department – admirable, if foolish but also a little worrying.

Duncan Cleeves, the Deputy Head of Department, sat next to Lionel and between agenda items made a couple of his usual desperately unfunny jokes and practiced his schoolboy laugh, much to everyone's embarrassment – Duncan was never embarrassed. Archie Rankin, the department's other full professor, and Staverley's erstwhile mentor, sat directly across the room glowering out of the window, he appeared studiedly uninterested in the proceedings. Alistair Dupin, the department's specialist in cultural studies, a relatively new and rather mysterious area of academic endeavor that involved 'reading' everyday objects as texts, made a couple of typically pedantic interjections, including one to correct a minute from the last meeting which had inaccurately recorded a previous interjection in which he had corrected an earlier minute - all much as usual. Staverley sometimes despaired of his colleagues. Were they deformed by the academic life or did academia attract people with peculiar personality characteristics who could not function in the real world. Perhaps he was as strange as they were but just unaware of it.

'Ok item 7'. Lionel announced: 'the appointment of an external examiner for the new undergraduate major in Applied Social Sciences.'

This related to the department's new teaching initiative. The university Senate had at last, after much debate and delay, approved a re-designed, updated undergraduate degree course – Applied Social Science - based entirely within the department. Previously ASS, as it was usually referred to, had been taught in joint programmes with other departments. This new course meant university recognition of the rising national standing of the department, especially its research record and its reputation for good teaching. The latter was a mystery to Staverley who felt that most of his colleagues could not teach their way out of a wet paper bag. The choice of an external examiner, meaning someone from another university, who would act as arbiter and monitor of academic standards, was particularly important for a new programme like this. A lot seemed to hang on getting the right person. There had been numerous informal discussions about the various possibilities and Staverley was under the impression that a general consensus had already emerged, although it was one he had not contributed to. Indeed he thought the choice that was likely to be made was not just a mistake but a retrogressive move, one which would give quite the wrong signals about the department and the discipline. He had yet to decide whether any airing of his views would be worthwhile. It was sometimes better in the long run to stay silently disgruntled rather than voice opposition and lose the argument. It was left to Duncan to make the formal proposal. As usual he took the opportunity to make a rather pompous speech.

'I think we all recognize the enormous significance of this appointment. I don't need to spell out to you the long process of canvassing and writing and re-writing that has gone on into the preparation and final acceptance of this degree programme.'
But he would spell it out, he would.
'I have been personally involved at every stage and as a chairman of the degree working party I have endeavoured to use all my influence and all my contacts and goodwill in the university as a whole to ensure that our proposal would be well received.'
This self -agrandisement was all part of Duncan's bid to be next Head of Department and for a personal chair – to be made a full professor.
'I have also taken the initiative in discussing with colleagues the best possible candidate for external examiner. We have looked at the field long and hard. There are many considerations to be borne in mind. We have to be very aware of the implications and ramifications for the reputation of the department and for the recruitment of students.'
Lionel cleared his throat very noisily and glared at Duncan. Clearly his tolerance of Duncan's speech making was coming to an end.

'And not least the possibility of a productive working relationship. We need someone who can help us refine and develop the course, to make it the envy of other universities.'

Duncan was enjoying himself, he grinned broadly.

'I think that the requirements all point in one direction.'

Can requirements point Staverley wondered. Lionel sniffed loudly and intensified his glare.

'I would like to nominate Professor Sir Alan Layton, as external examiner for the BA in Applied Social Sciences.' Duncan grinned again and looked around the room as though expecting a round of applause. There was a moment of silence, followed by a strangled groan from Archie and a loud collective intake of breath. Archie half rose from his chair banged both fists on the table and stuttered.

'I, I, I am, I am appalled, I don't believe this.' He stopped. He was clearly not one of the people Duncan had consulted, which was a strange and somewhat insulting omission. Archie was extremely flustered and distressed, he was shaking and very red in the face. He scattered his untouched committee papers across the table like an angry child. He clearly wanted to say more but only emitted further groans. Lionel spoke from the chair, trying to restore calm.

'I fail to see why you should be appalled Archie. The obvious and strategically sensible choice I would have thought.'

Archie actively disliked Lionel, although so did most of the department, but Archie took particular pleasure in derailing Lionel's plans whenever possible, especially in open meetings. This was beginning to look like one of those possibilities, although Archie normally went about his demolition work with careful obstreperous argument rather than stutters and groans. Something very different was going on now.

'I am appalled.' Archie repeated a little more calmly. 'I am appalled.'

He was still unable to find any other words to express himself and his problem with Layton, the phrase hung in the air. He was rarely at a loss for words and was normally adept at marshaling careful arguments and criticisms to great effect. Not now. The enormous effort that he was making to control himself was clear to everyone. He tried again.

'I am appalled that we as an innovative department in a new university should want to appoint one of the senior citizens of the discipline. A man who has retired from his own university, who has dominated the field for thirty years by using tactics of bullying and deliberate exclusion and unfair practices. Members of this department have suffered professionally by this man's hand.'

'I think that's a little strong.' Lionel interjected.

'It may be strong but would anyone dispute it. The man is quite unacceptable here. He will foster the wrong image, the wrong impression, and the wrong political context for this course. He is far too close to the present government. He is domineering, dogmatic and far too conservative. I oppose, strongly oppose. I am sure many others would agree with me.' That sureness might be misplaced today Staverley thought. Archie's face was even redder now and he was trying to control his breath.

Professor Sir Alan Layton was all the things that Archie had said and probably more. He was widely disliked and feared and admired by his colleagues in the social Sciences field all in equal measure. He regarded himself as the intellectual leader and arbiter of the field. He felt able to define the boundaries of the specialism, acceptable methods of research and forms of analysis in his writings and would brook no dispute over these. Dissenters were subject to vicious criticism and hounded out of the field where possible, out of the academic profession if necessary. And crucially he was the founder and senior editor of the *British Journal of Applied Social Sciences, B.Jass* for short, the journal of record for the social sciences in Britain. This was a powerful instrument of community control. Those who did not fit the Layton mold were simply not published. In Layton's own papers, which appeared frequently in the journal, attempts by others to extend or re-define the field were ridiculed, dismembered and patently misrepresented with total impunity. The victims of these academic assaults rarely found an outlet for their replies. Several promising careers had been thus blighted or destroyed. Hints of malpractice on Layton's part, of tampered-with data and even of plagiarism all went unanswered. Even in retirement his various honorific positions and vantage points meant that Layton remained an influential and effective maker and breaker of academic careers. He continued to exercise his *Droit du seigneur* through appointment boards, reference writing and quiet 'words in ears'. Sometimes it seemed as though Layton was everywhere, manning every bastion, sitting on every important committee, commenting on every new appointment.

Staverley had seen Layton in the flesh only once, giving the keynote address to the annual meeting of the British Social Science Association. The man's appearance was as dramatic and daunting as his prose and his personality. He was a large man, in all respects. His frame carried enough weight to define others as fat, but did not embody fatness, just over-bearingly large, dauntingly large. When he spoke, his head was thrown well back on his shoulders giving him a perfect angle for keeping his eye on those around him, although it must have made it difficult for him to tie his shoelaces comfortably. His hair was now perfectly white and long enough to create a leonine effect and to attract attention in any social gathering but not long enough to seem unkempt or avant garde. Even his features were large, his nose in particular spread high and wide across the centre of his face, causing his eyes to be compressed, creating a permanent look of quizzicality and suspicion. He apparently always dressed in the same way, in large misshapen black suits, the style of which was barely apparent but hinted at sort of thing Robert Mitchum wore in early nineteen-fifties gangster movies. The person sitting next to Staverley at the conference explained that only the colour of Layton's ties changed according to the degree of formality of the occasion. His voice did not entirely match his persona it was low and reedy, wet with saliva. You would not want to stand too close when the man was angry.

Given the fundamental difference between his own research style and Layton's, Staverley had paused on several occasions to consider the intricacies of Layton's mind and think about how the world looked to him through grids of numbers, correlations, variances and effect sizes that constituted his research as against the lives and loves and travails of the people these numbers claimed to represent. It was the flawed and complicated visceral individuals, with all their foibles and convoluted views and obstinate peculiarity that Staverley sought to make sense of, but they were rendered by Layton into statistically significant relationships between variables. It was the outliers, those who were uncorrelated or statistically unrepresentative, who were always more interesting to Staverley and he actively sought such people out in his research. Nonetheless, it was Layton's magic numbers that were considered 'important', and that were used by government to identify and define social problems and their remedies. Not that those remedies made much impact on the problems they were addressed to, except on occasion to immiserate further the lives of those subject to intervention. Numbers offered simple stories to politicians who did not want to hear that the social world was actually rather complicated but were instead interested in quick fixes at low cost. In this respect Layton was their man. He was a kind of social scientific gradgrind. 'Its facts that count my boy, facts' he would chant as his research closed down one social issue after another.

Staverley often pondered how he had got as far as he had in the midst of this academic feudalism. He had a permanent post in a relatively respectable university without ever having had to bow his knee in Layton's direction or curry favour with Layton's vassals and courtiers. Perhaps his topic – tourism – was below serious consideration, enabling him to make his way relatively unnoticed through the by-ways of academia, which was fine with him, although there was a delicate balance and sometimes a powerful line between not being noticed and making your mark, between not being bothered and not getting on. Staverley is ambivalent about getting on and if he were honest with himself he wanted to be recognised and rewarded as a worthwhile scholar without actually having to make special efforts to draw attention to himself. Not easy and probably not likely in the long run. He owed a great deal of his current security and opportunity to Archie who had mentored and sponsored him in various ways, for reasons he remained unclear about, but for which he was extremely grateful. Archie, who was now so distraught sitting across the room from him, and we have digressed.

Archie's opposition if it continued and if taken seriously could be a real problem. The room was now silent and several people wriggled nervously in their chairs as they began to deal with their embarrassment and to think about the possibility of having to take sides. It was at this point in committee meetings, Staverley thought, that the sense or the weight of opinion was cast. The next contribution could be crucial. And it was Roger Campion who spoke.

'I see Archie's point.'

As ex-graduate student of Archie's he often did. He normally supported Archie in committees and expected his support in return. Roger was one of the cleverest, but most insecure and difficult people that Staverley had ever met. He was capable of brilliant critical insights but found it extremely difficult to commit his ideas to paper. He had published a couple of excellent papers in his early days as a member of the department, which had been read by Staverley and others with admiration, but despite these positive responses even the most minor critical comment would drive Roger into a raging despair. He had been known to tear up copies of his papers in public. Each new piece of writing carried some hint of Roger's cleverness and his unusual grasp of complex theoretical ideas. But overall they were more technically efficient than incisive or groundbreaking – a triumph of form over substance and were never completed. He now devoted most of his energies to other preoccupations, including for the moment long-distance running. His thin, fragile body, his nervous energy and his manic determination meant that he was ideally suited to this.

Roger continued: 'I can see the argument, but the department must think carefully about its future. We are launching a new initiative during a period of crisis in higher education. Expediency must supersede morality here, I think. With Layton's support for the degree, as our external examiner, and the increase in student numbers, we will be virtually immune from drastic cuts in the next round of the university budget. And there will be cuts. I guarantee it.'

In Roger's case his personal insecurities had it appeared won out against his loyalty for Archie. This as an act of betrayal was apparent to everyone, people avoided looking directly as Roger, and Staverley thought he detected a hint of a smile on Lionel's face. Across the room Archie was close to tears whether as a result of the sentiments expressed or the humiliation of Roger's public disavowal was unclear. And as Staverley expected the tenor and direction of the meeting was now firmly set. Alistair added his voice to the emerging consensus.

'I have little time for Layton's epistemological position personally, and would be dubious about letting him too near my Policy Text Analysis option, but I see the force of Roger's argument. It must be Layton.'

Archie moaned loudly again and was writhing in his chair. Heto not care that he was making a spectacle of himself in front of his colleagues. His distress obviously cam from some inner turmoil and he had lost any sense of the conventions of meeting behavior. Duncan was staring at him with a look of undisguised hostility.

Pauline now spoke. 'Layton is an out and out chauvinist, an academic sexist of the worst kind. I agree with Archie. And would propose that we resolve to appoint a woman external as a matter of principle.'

Staverley would have been very happy to support Pauline and a different line of opposition in other circumstances might have made some impact but committee tactics were not Pauline's strong point. To agree with Archie on his own terms might have had some impact, but to link the attack on Layton with the issue of sexism was likely to be counter-productive. The department sexists, and there were plenty of them, would now rally to Layton almost by instinct. Staverley now had to decide whether he should speak or not. Two things suggested to him that he should not. First, he was trying to cultivate a safe and peaceful identity as a neutral in the department's politics. He was fed up with the factionalism and wanted to distance himself from the canvassing and alliance building that went on in anticipation of almost every issue or decision of any import and many of none whatsoever. He had even been practicing a new facial expression for meetings, which denoted a studied indifference combined with deep and careful consideration. He tried it now and attempted to see his reflection in the newly cleaned window to see if it worked but could not. He had the feeling that it was not coming out right. The second reason for not speaking was his relationship with Archie. What had been a close and warm friendship generated out of Archie's support for Staverley's work, and a lot help in getting his book published, had recently deteriorated. The change had begun around the time of

Staverley's divorce, his ex-wife Liana and Archie had got on well and Archie dealt with Liana's self-centredness with a gentle good humour that she accepted and enjoyed. Archie had made it very clear at the time that he blamed Staverley for the marriage breakdown. This mystified and hurt Staverley. More recently Archie's calm and stable personality had been displaced by a new Archie who was dour, withdrawn and touchy, and he appeared to have lost interest in his own work and no longer asked Staverley about his. Encouragement had been replaced by resentment and Archie had made various very uncharacteristic and petty critical comments at a recent department seminar where Staverley had presented his work in progress. And a recent decision by Staverley not to include a paper of Archie's in a collection he was editing seem to have set the seal on the breakdown of their friendship. The paper Archie had submitted was based on data more than ten years old whereas the main claim and point of the collection was its up-to-date-ness. Archie just did not see that. 'If the paper's good it should go in', he had kept repeating in a long and disastrous Sunday afternoon telephone call. Staverley did not have the courage to say that he also thought the paper was not very good.

'Its too old Arch, it won't do your reputation any good to publish it.' He had kept repeating in response.

'What about some newer work, something from that stuff you have been doing on the impact of microprocessors on office work practices.'

Staverley was unsure how far this idea for new research had actually progressed given they were no longer exchanging work ideas. The conversation went no-where and Staverley got the strong sense that Archie now regarded him as some sort of ungrateful upstart, who was getting above himself. Nonetheless, he knew he should say something because he agreed with both Archie and Pauline and despite what Duncan had said he felt sure that the appointment would send out the wrong message about the department but he was equally certain that further objections would be pointless. He was saved from the final decision as to whether to speak or not by Archie himself.

'I really cannot understand this.' Archie sounded desperate. 'I appeal to you.' Don't do this.' This was also unusual, appealing was not Archie's style.

'I could not stand by and allow you to appoint this man. I would find it impossible to work with such a person.'

Now he was going to do his well known and often very successful prima donna bit which had carried the day in many a meeting, but the recent absence of publications and research activity had undermined Archie's once high standing in the department.

'As a professor in this department I would find myself definitely compromised by such a decision. I would have to consider my position very seriously.'

Such vague threats had often worked in the past and people rallied around to reassure him that he was a valued and respected member of the department, far too important to lose over some minor matter and he would get his way. More recently though someone, usually Lionel or Duncan, would call his bluff. That was what happened now. Duncan clearly saw his opportunity to do down his rival to replace Lionel as Head of Department. He smelled blood.

'I am sure if that is the way you feel the department would not want to stand in the way of an heroic gesture on your part. Indeed I would not deny that I would have some admiration for such a bold decision, particularly in current economic circumstances. But equally we should not let Archie's rather idiosyncratic views on this matter sway us from the sensible course. We must appoint Professor Layton. To ensure our position, to confirm our future.'

Duncan began to sound like an American Presidential Candidate. He had once spent a sabbatical term to the University of Chicago.

'If we want to see this department growing stronger, getting fitter and becoming a significant player in the wider university, and I am sure that we all do. Then we must stride towards the horizon grasping Professor Layton's hand firmly in our own. Making our intentions clear and our aspirations undeniable.'

Staverley stifled a chortle just about enough for anyone but Pauline to hear. Duncan again swiveled his head around the room beaming his gummy smile.

It was evident that Archie wanted to speak again but his emotional distress had produced a total loss of the power of speech. Only ragged exhalations of breath emerged, he was close to sobbing. Lionel now moved in for a decision.

'While Duncan may have overstated the case somewhat I think the options are clear. Do we need a vote on this one?'

It appeared that we did not. No one spoke. Archie's head was bowed, almost resting on the tabletop. He was a tall man, bony, sharp edged, but he was now crumpled like the agendas papers on the table in front of him.

'Good. Now, any other business? I have none.' Lionel looked quickly round the table. Duncan or Alistair could usually conjure up something arcane at this point but even they seemed to have realised that something significant had occurred, something more than a simple decision about external examining, and that further business would be inappropriate.

'Meeting closed then.'

Lionel collected up his papers quickly, and hustled toward the door. Duncan followed one hand raised.

'A point Lionel, a point.' They left the room together. Several others left more slowly glancing back at Archie's bent form and speaking in whispers. One or two hesitated and appeared to want to stop and speak to him but did not. Roger remained in his place rubbing his hands together nervously, staring into space. He then stood up suddenly and rushed out of the room without a glance at Archie. Only Pauline and Staverley were now left. She looked at Staverley.

' Do something.'

'What?'

'Something, I don't know.'

They approached Archie together. He had still not raised his head. Pauline squatted at his side, her head level with his.

'Arch.' She said softly, 'Arch.'

Archie did not respond.

Staverley felt his heart pounding hard. He was suddenly both angry and tearful. He put his hand gently on Archie's shoulder.

'It can't be that important Arch, it can't be.'

Archie recoiled when he recognized Staverley's voice.

'Leave me.' He said hoarsely.

Pauline and Staverley looked at one another. Pauline shrugged her shoulders.
'Would you like us to get you a cup of coffee?' Staverley asked, trying to sound
normal and unemotional. He thought coffee was the solution to most problems.
'Leave me.' Archie said again very slowly and deliberately, he sounded
exhausted.
Pauline stood up and they left the room together.
'What on earth was all that about.' She said as they went down the corridor.
'I have no idea.'
'What's wrong with him? Why is this so important to him that he should become
so distraught? It can't just be academic differences surely?'
'I really have no idea,' Staverley said.

CHAPTER TWO

The 'Archie incident', as it came to be referred to was quickly and firmly
entrenched as the main focus of department gossip and speculation and
insinuated itself in various forms into virtually every conversation during the
next few days. Everyone was ill at ease, almost as though expecting further
ructions. Professional and personal feelings were misaligned. Despite his
occasional prickliness and his confrontational style Archie was well liked. He was
always the first to come to the support of a colleague in difficulty. But people did
not seem to know how they might support him now. Staverley and Pauline were
rerunning their own analyses of what had happened in the meeting the following
week as they sat on steel and leather chairs in Pauline's office eating a sandwich
lunch. Pauline had a thing for Eames and had bought her own chairs to replace
those supplied by the university. Staverley was attempting to explain Archie's
behaviour based loosely on a French psychoanalytic interpretation of the male
menopause he had read by accident in a journal he found left open on a desk in
the library while waiting for a shower to pass. It sounded good but did not help.
It certainly did not explain Archie. They were both still struggling to make any
sense of what had happened and what was happening to Archie.

'Well, just think Althusser went crazy and strangled his wife, and Poulantzas threw himself out of a friend's window. Maybe it's exactly the same sort of middle aged social scientist crisis thing?' Staverley ventured. These were two French Marxist philosophers, one now dead and the other in a mental hospital.

'I trust you are not serious.' Pauline said, with her own very special, very Oxbridge, you are a total idiot, tone of voice.

'Not really, but we've tried everything else - his marriage, his kids, Valerie and the girls are fine I think. Sure, his career is not so great at the moment I will admit but what's that got to do with Layton. What has upset him so much about this appointment? I've seen Archie angry before and he can give short shrift to people he thinks are fools but never anything like that. It must be something else. I don't think he even knows Layton.'

Pauline sniffed and bit into her tuna and red pepper sandwich. 'Isn't that a bit unusual.'

'What do you mean, unusual?'

'Well I would have expected that someone like Archie, having got where he is in the field would have had to have crossed paths constantly with the grand old man, at conferences, society meetings and that sort of thing.'

'I'd never really thought about it.' Staverley was chewing noisily on a Stilton and salad granary roll. 'I suppose they must have. It's just that Archie only ever mentions Layton in the abstract, not as someone he knows and usually only attached to some kind of jeer, or his 10 minute diatribe version of "the corrupt bugger with a royal ring through his nose". I can't think of any time that Archie has actually talked about meeting him, but you're right he must have done.'

Pauline's telephone rang and she got up from the armchair to answer it, showering crumbs over the floor and her tailored red suit as she did so.

'Hello, Oriel-Hay.' She always used her surname on the telephone. 'Yes, he is.' She turned to Staverley. 'It's Lionel, for you.'

'How did he know where I was?'

'Come on, you know that we are now the object of department gossip.'

Staverley laughed 'Silly man, why didn't he come in here, why did he telephone from the other end of the corridor.'

'He probably expected to find us entwined in naked passion on my authentic berber rug, far too embarrassing, here, take the damn thing.'

He stood up and took the receiver. He deliberately straightened his face and assumed an unnaturally deep and serious voice.

'Lionel, it's me, what can I do for you?'

'Have you seen Archie since the departmental meeting?'

'No, I haven't, why?' his voice had returned to normal.

'I've just had him on the phone for 45 minutes, 45 minutes of drivel and what sounded like tears. Tears mind you. I think he might be having some kind of breakdown. I won't put up with it. The man's a liability.'

'But tears about what?' Archie was very aware of Lionel's rabid dislike of emotions, he knew better, or used to.

'About Layton of course, he doesn't want the man here. It seems he will do anything he says to stop him coming, ranging from resigning, to reporting us to the union, to volunteering to take over a research tutor. All we have to do is drop Layton, which is out of the question now of course.'

Staverley thought that Lionel might actually be relishing Archie's pain.

'Why not drop Layton if it is so important to Archie?'

'Don't be ridiculous and in any case it's too late, I dictated the letter straight after the meeting, we need to have the thing settled before the end of this term and then, if Layton accepts, set up an initial course team meeting here before the start of next term, so we can begin to plan for the first student intake.'

'If that's the case why tell me this now?'

'I want you talk to Archie, make him see sense or find out what on earth is bothering him. I don't want this dragging on until Layton arrives. I certainly don't want him to get wind of any opposition to his appointment. Do something. You must see we will all lose if something untoward happens.'

The last comment sounded like one of those deeply embedded threat/bribe statements that psycholinguistics like to spot. But Staverley let it pass.

'I don't think I'm the right person Lionel, I am not on best terms with Archie at the moment but I will think about it ok!'

'Ok, but don't take too long. I will be expecting you to sort this. This is important, hear me?'

Staverley did not like to be expected to sort things out, especially by Lionel. He replaced the telephone receiver very gently and very slowly.

'Trouble?' Pauline asked.

'Trouble.' He confirmed.

Everything was very quiet and the whole department ominously calm, people kept to their offices or just stayed away more than was usual. The coffee corner remained virtually unvisited. Even the students seemed to sense that something was amiss and stayed away, writing their essays or sleeping. Staverley was also maintaining a very low profile. He had heard nothing more from Lionel and had done nothing about the telephone conversation. He was still thinking about what Lionel had said and thought that he would continue to do so until the whole thing was forgotten.

Like his colleagues Staverley was maintaining a low profile and keeping mostly to his office, with the door closed. He crept in and out surreptitiously and went to teaching sessions or the library using the back stairs. The library was a good place to hide and there were plenty of journal back issues to keep him occupied. He liked his office. It is basic but comfortable. Big enough to have a rather old and worn armchair, a South American rug on the floor, a battered wooden desk he had re-varnished and several unmatched and overfilled bookcases he had found abandoned in the basement of the building with the help of Ernie the porter. He maintained a good and useful relationship with Ernie via their shared interest in football and in particular the travails of The Rovers, the local team that had finished the season uncomfortably close to the relegation zone of the second division and had just that week sacked their fifth manager in three years. Staverley reminded himself that he should seek out Ernie to discuss this latest development. Ernie had seen many a manager come and go from his regular spot standing on the terraces of Seaworthy Lane, The Rovers tiny ground. Staverley enjoyed talking to Ernie more than he did many of his colleagues, many of whom who were as much uninterested in football as they were the social sciences. He worked mostly sitting in a hard, reclining swivel chair, found abandoned in a back alley and there was a separate small desk for the new and very unreliable

BBC microprocessor which now glowed and hummed in the corner. The light flashing on the screen indicated as usual that there was something amiss. The BBC was really a glorified word processor but Staveley was determined to master its idiosyncrasies and learn to write faster than he did on his much cherished, AEG Olympia de Luxe Traveller S typewriter. There was a different department on each floor of the Social Sciences building and the offices were distributed similarly in each case, a central core for the admin staff and head of department with academic staff rooms and offices on five sides. In the early days of the university such an arrangement had symbolized cooperation and openness. It now stood for and offered infinite possibilities for surveillance and being constantly disturbed and for timewasting. Everyone knew who was 'in' regularly, and who was not, who kept their students waiting or turned around their tutorials in short order, who spent time in whose office and who had visitors, visitors were always of interest. Fortunately the faculty offices had been left in a state of plain simplicity by the architect - white painted bare bricks walls and a pin-board if you were lucky - a bare canvas for the academic imagination, or lack of it. The result was a startling variety of individual décor. Most people took matters into their own hands, and some basic do-it-yourself skills and weekends of painting done with spouses, with varying degrees of artisanal talent, produced some weird and pleasing effects. Walls were subject to rococo paint effects, wallpapered, layered with cork, graffitoed and muralised. One or two bolder spirits with money to spare had commissioned interior decorators. Lionel's room had no decoration, no posters, no colourful prints – but he did have a lot of pot plants, although most looked dead or dying.

Staverley had retained the white painted bare block walls in his room but had added a liberal sprinkling of posters and prints. Some were intended to soothe, like Picasso's saucepan. Others to stimulate, like the cinema posters of a young Katherine Hepburn. A few had been specifically chosen to annoy particular colleagues, like the anti-Contras Sandinista poster, and Staverley enjoyed their discomforts. Alistair Dupin viewed the combinations and juxtapositions on Staverley's walls as theoretically disturbing and challenging to his frequently and tediously rehearsed theory of political bricolage and Duncan Cleeves, regarded the political content of some of the posters as 'unfortunate', as he liked to put it. He sighed and grimaced every time he came to Staverley's room. It transgressed his ingrained belief in the necessary objectivity of the social sciences.

Duncan's room was neat, overwhelmingly and oppresively neat and sought to capture something of a private school headmaster's study. He would have liked to have had the walls lined with wooden paneling but the cost had proved prohibitive. Duncan referred to his own work as policy evaluation and repeated nauseatingly often the need 'as I see it' for social scientists to cultivate and practice 'democratic detachment'. His paper on 'The Need for Democratic Detachment: a way forward for the social sciences' had been regarded for two or three days in the mid-seventies as a seminal contribution to the value-freedom debate. Alistair now mostly used the hundreds of offprints, which Duncan had ordered from the publisher at the time, as textual analysis exercises for his first year students. The decoration of Alistair's room was unstable; it was repainted at least once a year but always with some attempt to be Parisian. Out of term time Alistair spent his time on the Left Bank, in cafes and going to lectures at the College de France. He had once accidently bumped into Michel Foucault in the Café Flore and cherished the moment and on his return had frequently showed the bruise on his shin, he was devastated when it faded. Staverley particularly enjoyed his morning coffee when Duncan and Alistair were in the corner together. They both felt it necessary to speak; to be minimally sociable but it was as though they were speaking in different languages. Their conversations, if that is what they were, were punctuated with 'sorry' 'pardon' 'say again' and facial contortions of confusion and frustration and much head shaking. Each thought the other totally mad and a total waste of academic space. But their encounters were as entertaining to others as they were pointless to the participants.

Between seeing students the requirement for regular doses of caffeine meant that eventually Staverley had to venture out of his office and creep past Lionel's door to the department kitchen to wash up a mug, he had re-used it several times already and it was looking distinctly unhealthy. Jean, the department administrator was already there. Staring out of the window with a perplexed look while she waited for the kettle to boil.

'Hello you.'
'Hi' said Staverley 'what's the problem?'
'What problem?'
'I don't know you look as if you had a problem.'
'I always have problems working with you lot. You are all problems. You all produce problems, universities are machines for problem proliferation. Every day new problems for me to sort out for you lot.' Jean was clearly not happy.
'Not so much of the "you lot", administrative grade person. Without our problems to keep you busy you would be out of a job.' They both laughed.

Staverley and Jean conducted most of their conversations in this sort of silly banter, they both enjoyed it and usually got along well, unless Staverley was late with his marks sheets or needed some secretarial support, which was always in short supply. Jean was efficient and absolutely dependable in running the department, and in the grand scale of things Staverley was only a relatively minor maker of problems. There were others who were worse, much worse.
'I was looking for you yesterday.' She said.
'Sounds ominous. I was working at home, I told you. I was reading MA chapters and writing the exam papers for my undergraduate course next term, as required by you tomorrow, and generally slaving away on behalf of my ungrateful employers and even more ungrateful students.' Staverley always felt the need to justify himself to his colleagues when he worked at home. But he found it difficult to do any sustained reading or writing at the university, there were too many distractions, too many knocks on his study door, too much busy work to be done. And he didn't mean it about the students, or at least not all of them.
'What did you want? Much valued colleague.'
'Lionel wanted to see you to talk about the allocation of department responsibilities for next year and the Research Tutor position.'
Staverley felt himself pale slightly.

'What. I'm finishing my three-year stint as the MA course director this year. It's accepted that everyone has a year free of major responsibilities after that. Anyway I thought that was all sorted out at the last steering group meeting?' He could feel a sense of raising panic. Jean looked peeved.

'There's no need to get excited at me. I'm only the hired help around here. You lot are the big shots. I don't get a year free from responsibilities do I.'

The agreement in the steering group meeting had been that Alistair take over from Duncan as the Research Tutor, being responsible for overseeing the work of the department's twenty odd research students. They all had personal supervisors so it was not a massively onerous task. And Roger would take over the MA work from Staverley. But Archie's histrionics seem to have upset what had been a relatively straightforward reallocation of roles, or was there something else. Staverley paled a little more. 'What exactly does he want?' Staverley wondered if this was a ploy of Lionel's to ensure that Staverley would do something about Archie, another threat.

'I don't know really but I think its not just about jobs for next year, its something else. Lionel was climbing the walls yesterday. I had to go and do photocopying about ten times to get away from him. He was unbearable. And he wouldn't let me go early like usual for my evening class.'

'I did speak to him about it last week. He said he forgot.' Staverley said. Staverley sometimes tried to intercede on Jean's behalf when Lionel got into one of his terrorizing moods. He would try to point out diplomatically that Jean was too valuable to lose and worked twice as hard as most of the department secretaries in the university and needed some consideration. Sensitivity, especially towards women, was not Lionel's strong point but 'what would you do without Jean?' usually had the desired effect at least for a time.

'Do you want me to speak to him again?'

'No it's ok. I actually think that after two years I am beginning to learn how to handle him. Yesterday was just a very bad day. Next week I am going to leave a note on my typewriter and go at four-thirty and if he doesn't like it he can stuff it.'

'I shouldn't worry he will have to stuff it. He can get away with almost anything in the department but upsetting you would produce a revolt of the peasants.' Said Staverley.

'And the peasants can be very 'revolting' she said. 'But you do need to talk to Lionel, all of this kerfuffle with Archie and Layton has thrown things into disarray, Lionel is in a huff and Duncan keeps grinning at me – but I did not say that, loyal and obedient subject that I am. You as far as I can see are now the nominated voice of reason, the sorter, the mediator, the chosen one, go talk to Lionel.' Jean could be very commanding when irritated and it was clear that she was about to be irritated with Staverley, and was already with Lionel and Duncan and Archie, just about with everyone really.

'Okay imperious leader I will go, right after the exam board, I am yours to abuse and command. But I shall expect recompense, some secretarial time from one of your minions to type up some of my new research interviews.'

'You will get what you are given, go, now, go, be off with you.' At least Jean had not lost the taste for silly banter. She took her cup of tea and walked back to her admin pod – as it was quaintly called. The banter was all very well but Staverley definitely did not want to talk with Lionel about Archie, or to talk with Archie on Lionel's behalf. He did not want to be a mediator or a voice of reason. He wanted to be left alone.

Staverley had often visited Archie's home in the town and ate dinner there a lot after his divorce and Archie's wife Valerie had been particularly supportive despite Archie's disapproval. He had spent a lot of time talking with her about Liana. He really did not understand why his relationship with Archie had been going steadily down hill. One theory, of which he was rather ashamed, was that Archie resented the modest success of his book. Its publication did seem to highlight Archie's own recent lack of productivity. A lot of time spent advising a series of workers pressure groups involved in disputes with their employers and writing a pamphlet for them critiquing Thatcher's industrial policies appeared to have sapped Archie's energy and undermined his enthusiasm for academic work. It was not unusual for aging professors to go into paid and employed retirement, resting on their laurels as they say, but Archie's inactivity did not seem to be like that. It was more a kind of fugue state, a constant resentment of others and an uncharacteristic irritability in his social relations to which Archie's family where the only exceptions. He was spending more and more time at home. His relationship with Staverley had now reached a stage that could be roughly described as strained verging on cold, occasionally leaning towards bellicose. The next stage was likely to be unconcealed hostility. The whole thing caused Staverley a good deal of pain and a lot of perplexity.

Tourism is Staverley's area of specialism, that is tourism and its social and economic impact and effects, good and bad, on the lives and livelihoods of the unsuspecting and unprepared who find themselves in its way or those seeking to make their fortunes by turning their town or house or garden into an 'attraction'. He had written his PhD thesis on the effects of the building of a massive holiday camp on a small south coast seaside resort. It was based on interviews with local residents and business people and a lot of time spent in local cafes and attending council meetings and the local business roundtable. Staverley was good at this kind of research, he was good at getting people to tell him things and he knew when to keep quiet and listen. He sometimes thought of himself as a professional listener. For some reason he was not sure about people enjoyed talking to him and often ended up saying more than perhaps they intended. His demeanour created a space of interest within which they could tell their stories. Many times his interviewees ended by saying that the telling had been a good experience and how unusual it was to find people who really wanted to know about them and their lives. He was also careful in his analysis of data - the stories - matching and comparing accounts, following up omissions and discrepancies, separating the mundane from the important. Attention to detail in this way was a cultivated talent. He worked hard at it. He broke his data down into the smallest units of analysis and categorized or labeled them – using file cards which were spread across the floor - and then joined everything up again to make a narrative that made sense of what was going on. It was not the only sense that could be made but it was more often than not plausible. It was this that had got him his job. The department needed someone to teach qualitative research methods.

The thesis when turned into book form, with Archie Rankin's help, had much to Staverley's surprise sold quite well. As manufacturing industries moved their production to Asia, tourism was becoming a major foreign currency-earning sector of the British economy and Staverley was now regarded as an expert on its development and consequences. But this was a very small, very low status field in the social sciences. He continues to research and write papers in the area, he also contributes pieces of popular journalism to newspapers and trade magazines and once or twice had spoken on radio discussion programmes about tourism. He had recently been promoted to Senior Lecturer as a result of all this but his career could hardly be described as meteoric. The social implications and changing patterns in British holidaymaking was hardly the stuff of academic stardom. Most of the time career as such was not the driving force in Staverley's life. He regarded his research as important for its own sake and in terms of the general awareness it could create about the untoward effects of what he called 'big tourism' - the big money multi-national leisure companies that were increasingly dominant in the British tourist industry and elsewhere. At the same time he worked hard to be some kind of rounded human being with ordinary interests and a life beyond the petty squabbles and ambitions of academia, but on the whole he was not very successful at being rounded.

If the seriousness of everything or the pursuit of career for its own sake were allowed to dominate entirely then it was all too easy to burn out early or to develop ulcers or other stress related ailments like madness, or just get fed up. Staverley found it too easy to become manic and driven, spending hours in the evenings in front of the unreliable word processor tapping out a new research paper or book chapter and he tended to want to accept all the invitations that came his way to give talks and seminars, write conference papers, and become an external examine. He realised his weakness, that he was flattered by the interest in him and his work and he also worried that if he said no too often, and he did sometimes, that the interest would wane. And doing all of this stuff was certainly the route at some very distant point in the future to 'a chair', to becoming a professor, but the costs also had to be counted. There was squash, which he enjoyed and tried to play once a week, but was not very good at. He used to play with Archie but he now claimed that shoulder problems had ended his squash-playing days. There was football, he did go to a few Rovers matches, sometimes catching a pint with Ernie before or after, and he regularly watched Jimmy Hill extolling the virtues of his hometown team on Match of the Day. There was the cinema – Fanny Hill and Betrayal being the most recent excursions. Both good but both flawed, he thought. And there was walking. There was the coast and plenty of countryside around. These 'interests' also filled the gap left by Liana, to whom he had been briefly and painfully married. He and Liana had met as postgrads at the University of Middle England and married as soon as they had both finished their respective PhDs but once married the balance between companionship and argument that made up any close relationship quickly tilted heavily toward the latter. The arguments, at least as Staverley saw it, were mainly precipitated by Liana's unprincipled and single-minded pursuit of academic fame and fortune, which was heavily based on her use of feminine wiles to accumulate favours and patronage from men in senior positions which made him uncomfortable. She had had five different jobs since finishing her PhD, three of them during the time the two of them were together, in three different countries, which at least meant breaks between arguments, and then she left him for an Indian economist working at Princeton, who was being touted as a future Nobel Prize winner. But she was now back in England working in a little-known research centre of some sort in the midlands, which was odd, definitely not part of her often talked about and carefully planned career trajectory. Staverley was not really sure what she was researching now or why she had left the United States or what had become of the economist and how she had ended up at the Poppleton University, and did not really care any more, but she did telephone him regularly which was disconcerting. Her account of the failures of their marriage would probably be very different from his and would understandably focus on Staverley's many shortcomings – at least some of which he knew were very real. But he did not really want to hear that account and oddly during the more recent phone calls she spoke to him with an infuriating bland affection – as though he were a maiden aunt or distant cousin rather than an ex-husband. The calls always left him feeling uneasy and used, although he did not quite know why. He realised more and more that he did not really know Liana very well despite their marriage and the incessant arguments and exchanges of barbs and put-downs. If asked he would struggle to describe her personality and her wants and needs other than her general driven-ness and uncompromisingly self centred pursuit of academic advancement. What he did know was that the marriage was a huge mistake and that actually he did not like her very much. But ex-husbands, at least as far as Liana was concerned, still had their obligations and uses and he was willing to maintain some kind of a basic relationship, even if it was on her odd and opaque terms.

All of that leads inevitably to the question of relationships in the present. There was Pauline, a departmental colleague, she was very attractive and very desirable for sure, but she was also a good friend and sometimes painfully upper class and married. Can you have a sexual relationship and a friendship at the same time? He doubted it, but it might make a good starting point for a film. The university was full of attractive women students, some of whom had no compunction about flirting with their lecturers, but they were definitely off limits for him, although some of his colleagues were not so scrupulous. Otherwise the future as far as sex and romance were concerned seemed barren. Maybe he was just not good at relationships with women. Apart from Liana none had ever lasted more than six months and usually he found himself getting bored after two or three months. Perhaps he was just a not very likeable or lovable person. He needed to consider that seriously.

Staverley stood in the centre aisle of the crowded, slow moving train, and as usual he used the 11-minute morning journey to the university to think. He enjoyed thinking, most of the time, and after all there is a general expectation that someone like him, a university lecturer, an academic, would and should do a lot of it. Thinking was the job really. But, he wondered, was it the quantity of thinking that was important or the quality? Did he think differently from the man in the street or was the difference that he got paid to do it? Staverley always carried a notebook, just in case some significant thought came along but it was also useful for making lists of things to do. There were always things to do, always lists of things to do. For now though the particular thoughts with which he was engaged were focused on Archie and Lionel's directive and the various responses and reactions of his colleagues to the 'Archie Incident'. Academics did not normally do emotions and more than anything Archie's behavior had resulted in general embarrassment and speculation about his mental health. Staverley also resented being chosen as Lionel's intermediary. It appeared that despite their work being organized around talk and measured by their fluency that when it came to it academics found it very difficult to talk to one another as people with flaws and feelings and personal problems.

Staverley made an effort to think about something else and curb his resentment. He looked around the carriage at his fellow passengers, almost all of them students. Summer always brings out the most sociologically interesting forms of dress – male and female – although the young men do not so much adapt what they wear to the season as just wear more of less. One young woman was wearing a long white linen skirt and matching blouse. The effect, cool and elegant, reminded Staverley of his ex-wife Liana, she wore a lot of linen, summer and winter, and such a reminder initiated some less pleasant unscholarly thoughts. They were not the kind of thoughts that he was willing to submit to on a bright and fresh summer morning close to the end of the university term. He allowed a slight curling of the corner of his lip to register his displeasure and thoughts of Liana were shoved unceremoniously into his unconscious, or was it his sub-conscious – anywhere dark and deep and musty and infrequently visited would do very well.

Of course, he thought, what he should be devoting his thinking time to was not Liana but the other difficult and dangerous woman who was beginning to loom large in his life – Margaret Thatcher. Now, on the basis of her post Falklands landslide election majority, she was poised to take Britain apart and remake it as a national corner shop just like the one her father used to run. It was clear that Britain was about to change, she was going to change it, to make it a different place. Staverley felt all of this as a sense of unease and foreboding more than fully understanding what was about to happen. It felt like the end of something,

something worthwhile - flawed but worthwhile. And that was unsettling in all sorts of ways. Things that he had grown up with and that were obvious and important and good, like the welfare state, the NHS and universities, were now out to question and had become political problems, sites of dissent and wastefulness, regarded with suspicion and in need of reform – whatever that might mean. Staverley was a child of the welfare state, he had grown up with free orange juice and milk and dental care. He had served several stints as milk monitor while at primary school. It literally made him who he was. The history of the welfare state was written into the fillings in his teeth. A means-tested student grant had enabled him to go to university and the national research council had funded his PhD. Was all of that now bad? It seemed so, according to Thatcher and her New Right cronies. If things were about to change, he thought then he might also be changed in the process and was beginning to think that he would not like who it was he might become.

When the train arrived the business of getting off and passing through the narrow ticket barrier of the one-man operated country station took as always a ridiculously long time. The mass of travellers, several hundred, squeezed through the single file exit and then waited patiently to cross the busy road or in some cases darted between the speeding cars. Eventually they all disgorged onto the university concourse. Staverley hurried on through the arch of the triumph of the proletariat, he was late for a meeting - there was always a meeting to be late to.

The course committee was brief and relatively painless, the people attending were somewhat wary, and less talkative than usual, perhaps as a leftover from the previous week. It was almost as though there was an expectation and dread that someone else would burst into tears or rant and rave – no one did. That left about an hour for writing memos and replying to the three-day accumulation of post before the next meeting, the research student planning group.

As a new academic Staverley had envied the gigantic piles of correspondence received by his more senior colleagues, especially those envelopes with exotic foreign stamps or official looking logos. Did they contain invitations to exotic conferences in Kuala Lumpa? Offers of lucrative summer school teaching positions in Canada? Or appointment to the editorial board of a prestigious journal? Sometimes they did but more often they were letters of application from Nigerian students who had no money or from American post-graduates who had read a paper you had written years ago and who wanted you to clarify exactly what you mean by the 'tension between post industrial community and pre-industrial tradition'. The big problem with post was that every third or fourth envelope usually required that you do something, something boring or onerous or both, and inevitably time consuming. Then there was always another committee agenda and another meeting to attend, a course evaluation form to be completed, marks due in, examination papers to be set or a long and messy resubmitted doctoral thesis to read. In this pile there was a note from Jean, the department administrator - 'a visitor from Poland would be pleased to talk to you between 2.25 and 2.55 on Thursday October 15th about recent developments in the analysis of the impact of tourism on traditional communities'. He sighed heavily. Perhaps he could pretend he had not seen the note and could be elsewhere on October 15th. Stoically he wrote the time into his diary.

With all of this self-doubt and circumspection fresh in his mind he stared quizzically again at the daunting pile of envelopes on his desk and decided to leave opening them until later. That was a good discipline in itself – deferred disappointment. Instead he got up from his desk and emptied the dried up filter paper from his coffee maker, collected the set of stained coffee mugs from various places around the room and made for the department kitchen. He finished washing his mugs, tidied the kitchen, as directed by the large notice on the wall, and returned to his room to make a cup of coffee to take to the meeting. He liked good coffee, which was hard to find around the university. Most people settled for the abomination that was Nescafe but he avoided instant coffee in all its forms and if that was all there was on offer he would rather go without. By the time the machine had gurgled and seethed through its preparation cycle he had his papers for the meeting ready and some work to do in case it got too boring, but he was now a couple of minutes late.

During the meeting, which was much ado about nothing, Staverley began to wonder if he should speak to more of his colleagues about Archie and his issues with Layton. Maybe someone would know things that he did not, things about Archie's earlier career or his personal life that might explain his violent reaction. If he was going to have to speak to Archie about what had happened then it was best to be prepared. Staverley always prepared carefully for his research interviews, which often led to variations in his questions and questioning style in relation to the person to whom he was talking. He was trying to think about what he would ask Archie in the same sort of way.

After considering various possible people to approach, and given he had already talked several times to Pauline, and much against his better judgment, Staverley decided to discuss Archie with Roger Campion. Roger had spoken at the fateful meeting and had known Archie slightly longer than Staverley. Staverley had liked Roger once, or thought he had. He still tried to like him sometimes, but with ever declining success and sincerity. From Staverley's point of view Roger was an infuriating and unstable mix of brilliant, prickly, insensitive and vain. He enjoyed putting people down. And worse, he was good at it. He was a talented social scientist but wasted his talent on uncompleted esoteric projects and curious personal diversions. He now preferred to produce bitter criticisms of other people's work than publish original work of his own. Staverley had come to realise that he resented Roger both for his fickleness in social relations – a close friend one week was the object of pitiless and barbed gossip the next – and for his wastrel dissipation of his ability, which Staverley felt to be more fundamental and penetrating than his own. Roger's diversions covered a whole variety of endeavours – apart from the long distance running, there was learning the clarinet, learning Japanese, and recently computer programming. Each involved the same kind of total, and isolating commitment and required hours of preparation, practice, mind-numbing repetition and a constant pushing against self-set standards of excellence. And each appeared to be intended, coldly and deliberately to demonstrate personal virtuosity rather than substantive interest. It was not that Roger liked to show off. Rather he liked to talk about what he was doing, how far he had got, what standard he had reached. He kept a record of everything, each milestone and accomplishment. These were recorded in a black leather notebook, bought from a specialist stationers in London, that he carried with him at all times. He was constantly consulting the book and adding notations in his tiny neat handwriting. He would also scour the university community for other long-distance runners or Japanese speakers and engage them in long technical conversations about speeds, training sessions, esoteric grammatical constructions or minute issues of pronunciation. Staverley came to dread and avoided the sandwich lunches in the coffee corner during which Roger would recount in minute detail these conversations with his fellow devotees. Last week he had explained to Staverley and several others who had been unable to escape quickly enough his latest preoccupation with writing haiku in Japanese. 'Alan Wyler in chemistry has had several of his haiku published in Japanese poetry magazines, very interesting stuff. He's been attempting to recapture the style of the pre-European period, quite successfully, I think. Mind you I did find a slight grammatical error in one of his most recent attempts. I am surprising myself but I do think I might be pushing beyond the kind of linguistic plateau that Alan has reached. I've started to read some contemporary Japanese housing economics and there is some good stuff there which has been totally neglected in Britain but has a lot to say to the inner city crisis. I've been thinking of doing a review paper on Fujita's recent work for the *JBass*. Perhaps paralleling it with a paper in Japanese for publication over there. As well as the haiku of course.'

Staverley sometimes wondered if other people saw Roger in the same way as he did or was his jaundiced view really just based on his envy of Roger's intellect. Did anyone share Staverley's view of him as a sad and screwed-up person? There were several smiles and a couple of glazed looks but nothing that could easily be interpreted as hostility or pity. Not for the first time Staverley put his own reaction down to some kind of perverted professional jealousy. Not being able to speak Japanese or play the clarinet surely made him a lesser person. But look at Roger's body language. Did anyone else notice the constant flickering eyelids, the tensing and relaxing of the hands, the nervous foot tapping or the chewing of his moustache?

Staverley knocked on Roger's door and tried to elicit his take on what had happened at the meeting and what was happening to Archie but it was very quickly evident that any proper discussion was impossible and pointless. Roger was unwilling to take 'the Archie incident seriously' and made it very clear that he was no longer interested in or felt in any way beholden to Archie. It was as though their previous relationship had never existed. Archie been supportive of Roger's appointment as much as Staverley's and had encouraged him to write up sections of his PhD as journal articles but Roger did not enjoy or appreciate being mentored. He found this demeaning.

'Admit it, Archie is a has-been, a dinosaur who doesn't know that his time has past. He hasn't published for ages, he's doing no proper research; he's obviously threatened by Layton. Just ignore him. With any luck he will take early retirement and grow rhubarb. He's just a silly little man.' Staverley sighed and said nothing more. Roger was not going to be of any help and Lionel's veiled threats loomed. It was clear that one way or another he would have to talk to Archie. It was not going to be easy.

CHAPTER THREE

By leaning out and looking left from the window of the attic room he used as his home office Staverley could see a small slice of sea, just. He was leaning there now half in a tired daze and half in studied contemplation. Like a good academic and scholar should Staverley did his fair share of contemplation, it went with the thinking. They were related but not the same. Thinking had a point, a focus, contemplation was more vague and open-ended. The range of his contemplations extended all the way from the problem of world peace to the possibilities for supper. The latter often required more effort of contemplation than was the case for most hungry people, Staverley was en route to being vegetarian, he was not there yet but now only rarely ate meat and never when he was at home. Vegetarian cooking had always had a sort of strange aura of the intellectual attached to it, but not necessarily in a good way – he was thinking a stuffed marrow. Having dealt with the supper problem his contemplation revolved around the conversation he would have, or was supposed to have, with Archie – it was one of those circular contemplations that never seem to progress anywhere. He had slept badly while his mind whirred round a variety of possible gambits and openings for the conversation. None were right and the more he thought about what might happen the more anxious he became and even frightened a little. If Archie got angry Staverley would probably leave the room. He did not do well with angry.

As a result of the bad night most of his morning had been devoted to a drowsy attempt to finish a book review. He enjoyed book reviewing and the sense of power over others careers that it gave however fleeting. But mostly he enjoyed the phrase making that was involved. The need to say something informative and sensible in eight hundred words. This book however was the reviewer's worst case. Many academic books are boring but nonetheless good. This was both boring and bad. It was supposed to be a study of British holiday habits, relating type of holiday and destination to occupation and the sexual division of labour in the family. For the most part it appeared to be an attempt to baffle the reader with alternative interpretations of dubious statistical data. Fully aware of his own biases against crass statistics Staverley had tried harder than usual to be fair. When he read back the printout from the word processor he thought he had probably been too fair. He added some veiled equivocations. Apart from the review he had also typed two letters and two memos and had begun to rework the seminar programme for his Masters option course for the autumn term - a thrilling morning's work.

Staverley's home office was built under the roof and had two gabled windows. It was lined on three sides by book cases, on the fourth side in front of one window was his trestle desk, two saw horses supporting a sanded door, next to it at right angles on a wooden cupboard sat another BBC microprocessor, more or less as unreliable as the one in his office at the university. The university had paid for one, he the other. To one side of the desk the wall was lined from floor to ceiling with cork and pinned to this were dozens of cards, papers, notes and photographs related to his research. The whole room produced a sense of busy disorganisation, which he liked, just the right mixture of clutter and orderliness. Staverley usually knew were to lay his hands on any piece of paper or book however buried or hidden in the numerous piles, box files and cardboard boxes that covered the desk and part of the floor. Those times he could not he became quickly desperate and angry with himself. The missing item would be found days later in some obvious place he had forgotten about. Most frustrating of all were the times when he put down a sheet of notes or papers one moment and was unable to find them a few seconds later. Inexplicably these escapees would bury themselves deep into the swathes of other papers on the desk, camouflaged among their compatriots in some kind of motiveless bid for freedom. It could sometimes take as long as ten minutes to track down the errant pages, during which time Staverley's blood pressure would have risen to ridiculously high levels. At these times he would resolve to get more organized but really did not know what that would mean in practice, more boxes and files did not seem to help, but he liked buying them. He has a thing for stationery and love to browse in shops that sold such stuff. He had acquired many quirky folders and notebooks, which he never found a use for but believed would come in useful one day. Staverley now stood in front of the lightless and silent microprocessor and tapped absent-mindedly on the dead keys hoping it would show some signs of life, which it eventually did. But it was time to make lunch.

Lunch at home always meant the same thing as far as Staverley was concerned: a sandwich and a large mug of coffee made with freshly ground beans. Today he chose brie and black olives with mayonnaise. A new Italian delicatessen had opened just off the seafront and this had introduced a whole new set of sandwich possibilities. He made and ate it while listening to Gardener's Question Time on the radio. He had no interest in gardening, and had no garden, but found the obscure knowledgability of the experts calming and distracting even if he did not have the faintest idea most of the time what they were talking about. What did a begonia look like? He then washed up the lunch and breakfast things. A fifteen minute nap felt a good idea before trying to work through the rest of the afternoon. At five he would walk down to the gym on the seafront and go through his exercise routine with the weights and machines while one of the young women trainers followed him around urging more reps and better body shape. At least it made him feel virtuous but it also made various bits of his body ache. He was not entirely convinced that exercise was healthy. The nap was beginning to have its way with him when the telephone began to ring. Deciding to answer or more accurately not to answer was always tricky. Who could it be? The wrong decision could put a swift end to a productive afternoon. Jean always knew when he was at home and would only ring if it were something very important. It could be Duncan again in which case it would be better not to answer, but that was unlikely. It might be a student but they tended to ring in the evenings, usually in the middle of a decent film on television. Having run through these possibilities the telephone was still persisting. That probably meant it was someone who knew he was at home. He got up and dashed up to his study.
'Hello.'
'Its me.' The caller said. It was Liana. Staverley thought he should have finished his nap and left the call unanswered.
'Hi there! How are you?' He tried to sound bright and friendly.
'Did you see it?'

'See what Liana?'

'The review.'

'Yes I saw it. I thought you would be pleased.' Liana's new book had just been reviewed in the most prestigious journal in her field, health policy. He had been alerted to look out for it by a previous telephone call.

'He seems to have liked it.' Staverley was trying to be non-committal. Liana's reactions to others' evaluations of her work could be idiosyncratic and even violent at times. He did not feel entirely safe in such conversations even at the other end of the telephone. He hoped for the best.

'Yes, I was quite pleased. He did an ok job considering he's a bit of a wally. He did not grasp the subtlety of some of the analysis but he conveyed the general drift at least. It should help nicely with my CV.'

'I thought he was quite effusive towards the end' Staverley said. 'Bright young star and all that, ground breaking study.'

'Well that's only right really, its important stuff, I clearly identify the need for changes in the way that funding is allocated, and more local budgetary autonomy and more monitoring of the relationships between funding and treatment outcomes. I'm working on a follow up. I've already got two chapters on the machine. The publishers are hot for it and Ronnie thinks it could be better than this one.'

All of this sounded to Staverley disturbing like the sorts of things that Thatcher's ministers and advisers had been spouting – reforming the NHS. Staverley did not know or remember who Ronnie was and was not going to ask. He was almost sure that her new husband or partner or whatever, was Dirk, a Dutchman, who was teaching, he had thought in the USA, at Cornell, a molecular biologist of all things. Liana visited him there once a month she had explained in a previous call and was actively looking for positions in the States.

'I've been invited to spend the summer at Leyland University in the US by the way, teaching on a summer school, with the possibility of a full time position later in the year. I'm not sure I really want it, but it would be closer to Dirk and it's good to be seen around the circuit. It's not exactly in my field of course but I could probably talk them into it. Unless it turns out to be a backwater.'

'There are some good people there.' Staverley managed to squeeze in.

'I think they definitely have their eye on me. I did a couple of seminars there the last time I visited Dirk and they've asked me to do a faculty lecture. And a guy from the Accountant General's Office took me out for dinner. That could mean some big research money.' Liana had the knack of conveying lots of information very quickly.

'I might be down your way weekend after next. I am speaking at a Department of Health symposium on health policy at the Prince Regent. A weekend do, all expenses, best hotel and all that. Busy though, I want to tie up the details on the collection of Elliston's papers I have been invited to edit with Rosby.'

Staverley's mind was truly boggled. As ever Liana managed to amaze and confuse him. Patrick Elliston had been the major figure in the field of health policy in Britain. He had died recently and Staverley knew that Liana had given a paper at the memorial seminar; but to be invited to co-edit the man's papers with Rosby, another leading and long-established figure, was incredible for a relative newcomer like Liana. Knowing her methods invitation was possibly the wrong word.

'I didn't know you knew Elliston?'

'Yes, of course, Pat was organizer of that seminar series run at University College last autumn. I shall probably edit those too now he's gone. Goodness, I'm due at a meeting, I must get clear. I'm flying to Frankfurt tomorrow. Just phoned for your reactions to the review really. Ciao.' She hung up.

Staverley was left receiver in hand. As usual he was both befuddled and depressed by Liana's call and as usual she had failed to ask him how he was or what he was doing or basically anything about himself. Liana was a lost cause he thought. For about two weeks during their two-year marriage he believed that he understood her and what kind of person she was but he was wrong. He soon found out how wrong he had been. She was unfathomable. Each year she became more self-absorbed and more calculating in her bid for academic fame and fortune and at the same time less and less likeable, at least by him. Her strategy was to attach herself to a series of important and influential men who could further her career. She was able to dazzle them with her combination of flirtatious behavior and sparkling intellect. Almost everything she did was done with one eye on her CV and the other on a more prestigious post and a more prestigious university. He could now hardly recognise the woman he had married. He wondered again why she still bothered to phone. Did his opinion really matter to her? Was it important to her to tell him the things she did or was it some form of revenge for having taken up two years of her life and slowing down her advancement? He really did not know and really did not want to worry about it or think about Liana at all.

Staverley decided to ration his time carefully for the rest of the afternoon. Ninety minutes on student draft chapters, thirty, probably pointlessly, skimming the latest issue of the *BJass*, and thirty making notes of things to say to Archie. Perhaps a useful and painless way of getting into the Layton thing would occur to him. He rang Archie to make a time to meet in the evening half hoping that Archie would be busy or out or just unwelcoming – he wasn't.
'Come then if you must.' He said.

The night was crisp and clear and very still, unusually so for a seaside town. There was usually a breeze at least off the sea. It was a perfect night for walking, even walking to Archie's house. He passed the rows of neat and elegant Victorian villas that dominated the seafront in this part of the town, then turned inland and uphill for a couple of hundred yards until he stood in front of Archie's house. The house was a particularly large semi-detached Victorian villa, framed by an ancient unruly wisteria, now slightly, but only slightly, down at heel. Archie spent a great deal of time every summer painting and repainting the vast exterior walls and multitudinous windows but he could never quite eradicate the down-at-heel-ness. He always said that he enjoyed the process rather than the outcome. The house had probably been built with pretentions it could never quite fulfill. Perhaps down at heel was the 'in' style for 1877. The date was embedded in an elaborate plaster molding above the front door. At one time Archie had talked to him a great deal about his house, his family life - his wife, Valerie, the several children, all girls, and Wally, the enormous, shaggy, over friendly dog. Staverley had been a frequent visitor to the house for family meals and evenings of talk and laughter. All very well and good, and all very much in the past. As was the case with Liana, someone who he thought he knew and understood, had turned into an enigma. He wondered, as he often did, whether he was the problem and not them.

Despite the house and his position at the university Archie carried his working class origins – shared in part by Staverley, like a heavy weight. He was never quite sure whether he wanted to celebrate or distance himself from his class history but it was always there in one way or another. Archie rarely spoke about his family or childhood, although had once suggested vaguely that he had suffered from rickets as a child. Staverley did not take that seriously. It was like a kind of sociological one-upmanship rather than a political statement of class affiliation. Staverley countered with his maternal grandmother who had been born in a workhouse. Like Staverley, Archie clearly sometimes felt himself to be out of place at university events, a professor yes, and one of some standing, but not quite a proper professor. There was something not quite shared with others for whom the university was their natural habitat, part of their heritage. It was as though they did not know the secret handshake or did not walk in quite the right way, had not read the right books, or had read them but had not understood them properly, they did not bring the necessary casual discernment to the reading. These were things below the surface, unspoken and unspeakable, but generated a constantly lurking sense of difference, which at some moments made themselves apparent in acts of gentile humiliation and exclusion. Staverley had been invited soon after being appointed to a tea for new staff members and after a brief chat cum interrogation of his education, family and personal history, a woman professor of French literature had commented how refreshing it was to hear a demotic accent about the place. He was put in his place or at least reminded of it, and that place was somewhere else. He was an outsider, an interloper. He should have been cooled out and directed elsewhere at some point in his education but by luck or cunning had avoided the cull. He was one of those outliers that so interested him in his research. He was confronted with further evidence of his social inadequacies when he and Liana, still then man and wife, were summoned to one of the VC's dinner parties, at which the VC sought to 'get to know' some of those who labored under him. Evening dress was required, which meant a visit to Moss Bros and a first and rather expensive encounter with a bowtie, wing collar and cummerbund. He tried to spend the evening imagining he was James Bond and the phantom bulge of the Walther PPK beneath his left armpit was a great consolation as the social vetting progressed. He could always use, he fantasised, it to terminate the other dinner guests with extreme prejudice. Liana, daughter of a Scottish fishing family, should have felt like him but loved the whole thing, was very much at ease and in her place, and made a great impression on the VC, Sir Wallace. Staverley got a strong sense as the evening wore on, and wore him down, that the academic knight – services to government as advisor to a committee charged planning the future of the coal industry– would have much preferred to have had Liana appointed than Staverley himself. He drank too much as compensation, the wine was very good, and only just managed to avoid embarrassing himself. He got a stiff talking to afterwards from Liana about needing to making a better impression. The whole thing felt deeply uncomfortable but he enjoyed wearing the dinner jacket even so.

Staverley now stood motionless staring at the panel of coloured glass in Archie's front door. He was still nervous. It was foolish but his stomach was fluttering and he sweated slightly. Perhaps this was not such a good idea after all. Maybe he could telephone from the call box at the end of the street and feign illness. Archie sometimes had the effect of making him nervous in academic settings, a sort of contagious unease, but not usually in social ones. Perhaps the indeterminate status of this meeting was the problem. The transition from job applicant, to junior colleague, to friend, to something else unspecified, is never easy. The element of judgment, of evaluation, of social asymmetry embedded in the mentor-mentee relationship is difficult to leave behind. Staverley often felt even now, four years on, that Archie was still judging him, wondering perhaps if he had made a mistake in supporting his appointment. And yet, Archie was not a judgmental person. Indeed he rarely expressed judgments on other's academic work. In the early days of their relationship this had exasperated Staverley when he needed some reassurance that he was doing okay, reaching the appropriate standard, but he also wanted some critical guidance, he wanted to be pushed and challenged. That wasn't what Archie did. His support and encouragement was subtler, more indirect. He had the ability to make students and colleagues feel that they could do things for themselves, that they were capable of producing good ideas without his direct input. That was a special gift but a difficult one, one that Archie himself was not always happy with, it sometimes made him redundant when he wanted to be needed, or perhaps that was just a load of psycho-twaddle. It did delay the moment of ringing the doorbell for a little longer.

The judgments that Staverley felt subject to came as part of the relationship package, were not usually conveyed in what Archie said, or did not say, they were embedded in his manner, in his mood, his emotions. When Archie was talkative and laughing Staverley knew that his work was good. When he was withdrawn, moody and argumentative Staverley got the sense that his work was not up to scratch. But more recently even this interpretation of Archie's view of him, and of others, was not right. Staverley was coming to the horrifying view that it was not the standard of his work, which had influenced Archie's mood, but Archie's mood, which had influenced and affected his view of the work. That was deeply disturbing.

In an effort to pull himself together Staverley ululated quietly and circled his shoulders for a few seconds as he has required to do as part of his warm-up at the gym. The ululations echoed along the deserted street and then faded into the night. He poked hard at the large doorbell. It did not work. He lifted the heavy iron knocker and let it drop but it made surprisingly little noise. Perhaps he should leave now, the omens were bad. He resorted to tapping on the door with his knuckles and there were noises of movement inside, the exterior light came on and the door was opened. It was Penny or Susan or Sarah, one of Archie's many and seemingly identical teenage daughters, all of whom were delightful but sometimes disconcertingly adult and knowing.

'Oh' she said, Penny or Susan or Sarah, in a not very welcoming tone. Things were not starting well. Staverley waited, looking expectant. Susan or Penny or Sarah turned away and yelled, 'Daaaaad, he's here.' She then retreated inside and left Staverley standing on the doorstep. He, the traitor awaits at the gate. He tried to imagine what was being said inside.

'It's that slimy shit Staverley. Why did you allow him to come here?' Hopefully not. Archie's face appeared around the door. He looked both stern and preoccupied but not overtly hostile. 'Hello, come in, come in.'

Staverley went in and was confronted with Wally. In the old days Wally would casually mob him, leaving him heavy with hairs, licks and garden mud. Now the dog eyed him suspiciously, sniffed and turned away into the kitchen. Another bad sign. 'Let's go upstairs' Archie said. No family greeting then, no kiss on the cheek from Valerie, Archie's wife. Valerie was a very beautiful woman, even now in her late forties, she was fourteen years younger than Archie, and Staverley had always liked her, and he had thought, she liked him. When he and Liana were still together they met Archie and Valerie for drinks quite regularly and Valerie was one of the few people, certainly one of the few women who got on well with Liana. She and Liana were at ease in each other's company which was not normally the case with Liana and other women and they often exchanged quiet confidences of some sort while Staverley and Archie talked social science or football. But Valerie was nowhere to be seen this evening. She might not be at home or hiding in the kitchen to avoid him. This was really not going well.

Upstairs meant Archie's study, although the word has to be used in its loosest sense. It was probably one of the world's most untidy rooms. It raised untidiness to unprecedented heights. Not dirty as such but in a state of total disorganisation and disarray that made Staverley's own workroom seem like a paragon of order. The floor was covered almost wall to wall in dusty and yellowing piles of papers, books were piled in untidy and tumbling heaps against the walls and in the grate of the fireplace. Back issues of journals tottered precariously on top of the papers, and some of these piles on piles were topped off with teacups and odd souvenirs from visits to overseas universities, including a sword and several elaborate paperweights. Offprints and union pamphlets and books, old and new, dozens of them completely engulfed the large Edwardian solicitor's desk rendering it useless as somewhere to work. Apart from this paraphernalia of academe the room as always contained an assortment of family ephemera. This time part of Archie's ancient butcher's boy bicycle was perched precariously in the middle of the floor, its chain hanging loose, a wooden paint splattered step ladder lent against the fireplace and very oddly a baseball glove lay on top of one of the piles of books and papers on the desk. There were also three chairs in the room. Archie collected the papers which covered one of these and ushered Staverley into it. He sat down on a monstrous teetering double pile of papers by the fireplace and leaned back against the wall. Perhaps Archie's lack of scholarly output was not a loss of momentum but rather a loss of space for productive activity or an inability to find anything. Why did he keep all this, all these papers? What were they for? Archie had once confessed that he still had his secondary school essays tucked away in the loft, Staverley had not believed him at the time but latterly had become convinced that they were actually up there moldering away.

Where to start? How to start? Clearly Archie had no intention of making this any easier, he was saying nothing. He crossed his arms and stared fixedly at Staverley over his half frame glasses. 'Archie.' Staverley said.
'Yes.'
'Archie.' He repeated.
Why not try to be straightforward, speak from the heart, be honest'.
'I feel very uncomfortable about this.'
'Yes.' Clearly Archie was not going to help.
'Yes. Lionel wanted me to talk to you.'
Archie made a peculiar throaty chortling noise that he often managed to produce when Lionel's name was mentioned.
'I want to talk to you, well actually I don't, but Lionel is, he feels, that is he thinks, he asked...' This was not going well, perhaps he should try another tack, Staveley was so not enjoying the role of ambassador.
'I was, I am worried about you, the meeting. You were so distraught. Your reaction was so out of place, so over the top, so not you. I don't think people understand why you were so upset. I didn't understand.'

Staverley realised he had slipped into an odd stuttering staccato but he building a momentum.

'I don't like Layton any more than you. He's a bully, but it's all politics. We, the department, we are only using him really. Playing him at his own game. He will accept the position of external examiner because he always does. But he never does the work these days. We will use his name and do what we want to do. All that will happen is that he will make his royal visit, say some arrogant things, shake some hands, make even more people dislike him, overcharge for expenses and go away again satisfied that he is still in control of the discipline. But he's not, it's slipping away from him, its changing, everyday it's becoming something new, something exciting and challenging. But we need the name, his name. You can see that. It is just expediency. If we could do it any other way I would be the first to support you but it's just being realistic and it really doesn't matter. He still has enough influence with the funding council and in the university to stymie us if we just snub him but in reality there will be no compromises. It is the course we want just as we designed it. He will not be able to change anything.'

To Staverley it all sounded logical. He had half convinced himself at least. He did not like the idea of trading with Layton but he could live with it, it was realpolitik. He really did not see that it mattered that much and did not understand why Archie could not see that it did not.

'It's a matter of principle.' Archie announced.

'What principle?'

'We, I cannot accept Layton under any circumstances.'

'All right, okay, you've registered your disapproval. You did that at the meeting. But Lionel said that you went to see him. What exactly is the principle? What are you defending? What's at stake?'

'He shouldn't have told you that'. Archie said, his lips tightened into a sort of ugly sneer, not a normal expression for him.

'What?'

'That I went to see him.'

'Well he did, sorry, I did not want him to tell me, I'd much rather he hadn't, but he's worried about you. He said you were emotional.'

'Lionel should keep his mouth shut, what is said between us in his room is confidential. I was discussing some possibilities for departmental responsibilities in relation to the external examiner appointment.'

Staverley did not want to say this, but his relationship with Archie was probably already irrevocably damaged. There was no further point in being careful.

'He said you cried.'

Archie was silent. He closed his eyes and rested his nose on his fingertips. He breathed deeply and produced a painful sigh. There was a long, a very long pause and then he spoke again.

'It is a matter of principle. I will take it to wherever I can, in what ever way I can, to have Layton barred from being our external. Perhaps you and Lionel are not used to people having principles they stick by.' Staverley did not like the idea of being a person like Lionel.

'That's a petty mean sort of comment.' He said. He had never talked with Archie in this direct way before. He had never said what he felt. Never spoken without thinking first, without holding back. It was frightening but also a bit refreshing. 'Mean or not I am sticking on this one! And I have influence. I can speak to the VC, to the Registrar, There are ways.'

Staverley now confronted another area of self-censorship in his previous relationship with Archie. His heart was beating hard but he decided to press on. 'Come on Archie, you have no real influence with the VC or the administration. Not anymore anyway. They see you as a nuisance. If you had any real influence you lost it years ago. If you had any now you would have been made head of department last time around instead of Lionel. I'm sorry but you must know how you are perceived in the university. You've pursued too many lost causes, too many foolhardy campaigns. You've blown up in too many university committees. They don't want to hear you and they won't hear you on this!'

Archie's expression had not changed but when he spoke his voice was strangely deep as though he were making an effort to keep it under control. 'I think you have said enough, you better go now. But I am not giving this up. I will not have that man here.'

Autumn 1983

CHAPTER FOUR

Staverley never found out what Archie did or did not do after their talk, where he took his matter of principle or to whom but whatever happened over the summer Layton had been invited and accepted the role of external examiner and he was coming. With the new term a few days away a preliminary meeting of the new course exam board was arranged – 9.00am Monday September 26th - to confirm the curriculum and assessment structure for the degree programme. The agenda was set, a room booked and Layton's hotel sorted, an appropriately and expensively smart one. Staverley had no idea whether Archie would turn up for the meeting, they had not spoken at all since the disastrous visit and Archie had certainly not put an appearance in the Department. Staverley had reported to Lionel that he had 'spoken' with Archie and Lionel sounded satisfied, or at least he did not press Staverley further. Staverley spent a couple of weeks cycling around Normandy staying on small campsites and the rest of the summer doing writing. The cycling was very wet but the writing had gone well. He was almost looking forward to the new term and the new year.

Layton had requested an early start, Staverley was not very good at early starts, but there he was standing in the meeting room, coffee cup in hand, slightly befuddled and wanting to be somewhere else – preferably back In front of the microprocessor watching the green cursor pulsate. On the other hand, he would be meeting the great man in person, and seeing the grand wizard, the ogre of social science in action first hand. The room was full now, papers laid out neatly, water glasses in position, university coffee jugs at the side – horrible stuff, brewed at 6.30 and left to stew for the rest of the day. Staverley had made his own. The start time came and went, but there was no Layton.
'We will wait.' said Lionel to his colleagues. 'Probably transport problems.' A taxi had been ordered evidently.
More time passed with whispered conversations and quizzical looks eddying around the room. Most of the conversations were still about Margaret Thatcher's

landslide victory in the General Election in June and what it would mean for university funding, although from what Staverley could over hear Alisdair and Roger was more interested in the latest episode of BlackAdder. After an awkward 20 minutes Lionel spoke again. 'There is obviously a problem, I will call Sir Alan's hotel.' He left the room and returned quite quickly.

'Bloody hotel say they wont disturb him, he was quite clear about that evidently, but has not appeared for breakfast as yet.' He hesitated. 'Someone will have to go.' He hesitated again and looked around the room. 'Staverley, you go.'

'What, sorry.'

'Hotels, your thing, who better. Pauline will drive you.' Staverley had no car.

'Will I?' she said. 'Ok, Ok.' She put her hands up, 'let's go.'

So he was it. So up close and personal with the beast of *B.Jass*.

Pauline's red Beetle was parked right behind the Social Sciences building. The early start had meant that very unusually she had found a space in the small adjacent car park. On a normal day her car would have been on the edge of campus a good 10 minutes walk away. She drove fast and they did not have far to go, less than 15 minutes and Staverley was dropped off outside the main entrance of the Paine Place Hotel – the name a reference to Tom Paine, who had lived in the town and worked there as an Excise Officer there before emigrating to America in the 1770s. Staverley had been to the Hotel several times in relation to his current research. A young woman in uniform was at the desk.

'Sir Alan Layton.' He said, 'a guest, he is late for a meeting and we are worried about him.'

'I am very sorry, he left very clear instructions that he did not want to be disturbed.'

Staverley sighed, but he could see her point.

'I better talk to the Manager.'

'Of course sir, he's right here.'

She disappeared through a door behind her and a tall man in a neat dark suit replaced her at the desk. Staverley recognized him immediately.

'Nicolas, Nick, of course, good to see you.' They shook hands.

'And you, how are you, and what can I do for you?'

Nick Fell was the Manager of the Paine and he and Staverley had met several times at meetings of the local hoteliers association and Staverley had interviewed him over a drink for his research. They had got on well and Nick was a useful source in relation to the politics and economics of local tourism and shenanigans in the town council.

'I am well, but I have a problem. We, the university that is, have a guest here, Sir Alan Layton. He is here for an important meeting, it was to start at 9.00 but he hasn't showed up, and we are worried. He's not young and this is not like him, he's a stickler about obligations, and anything could have happened up there. Can we check the room?'

Nick thought for a second. 'Of course, if anything where amiss then we would not want to be seen to be obstructive.'

That was one way of putting it Staverley thought, but he could understand Nick's dilemma. What would be in his guest's best interest? Very hotelier.

'I will get a pass key and come up with you.'

'Sounds good to me.' Staverley was relieved that there would be no arguing and no more delay. Nick collected the key from his office and together they walked up the old and very wide main staircase that creaked and groaned in a reassuring way, as it had done for the past 200 years. Layton's room was on the first floor.

'This way.' Nick led the way down a much narrower but equally creaky corridor and stopped at the fourth door, number 17. He cleared his throat, tidied his suit jacket and knocked gently.

'Sir, the manager.'

No response.

'Sir, is everything OK?'

No response.

'Sir, may I come in?'

No response.

Nick edged the key into the lock and turned it as quietly as he could. He opened the door enough to peer round into the room. Nothing appeared to be amiss. He drew his head back.

'Can't see much, the curtains are drawn, the bed looks empty. Perhaps we should go in together.'

He opened the door wider and Staverley followed him in. The room was in semi-darkness. Nick tiptoed across the room, it was large enough to have a sofa and coffee table, which was well covered with various work papers, a large desk diary and an overflowing ash tray, he pulled back the curtains. Staverley had heard that Layton was a heavy smoker. In full light it was clear that the bed was empty and had probably not been slept in although someone had laid on it at some point, the cover and over pillow were lightly indented. They both looked around the room but could see nothing untoward. Nick braced himself again and moved to the bathroom door, which was fully closed. He knocked.

'Sir, sir, sir are you in there?'

No response.

Again he opened the door wide enough to peer around it, he withdrew quickly and his hand covered him mouth.

'My God'. He said. He was clearly very shaken.

'What, what is it.' Said Staverley. Nick took a moment to respond.

'I think he's dead.'

'What do you mean?'

'He's in the bath, not moving, not awake and in a terrible state.'

This is above and beyond the call of duty Staverley thought.

'Uh, should we check?' He asked.

'You do that.' Nick said, 'I will call an ambulance.'

'Oh Thanks.' Said Staverley.

Nick moved to the telephone on the bedside cabinet. Staverley very slowly pushed the door of the bathroom fully open and there was the great man. Not a pretty sight, as they say. Layton was half immersed in bath water, not moving, certainly not conscious. He had vomited and the discoloured bathwater had splashed over the floor and up the walls. His face was locked in some kind of grimace of pain and his eyes were red and weeping. The smell was awful. Staverley was actually not sure how you tell if someone is alive or not in such circumstances but as he had seen it done in the movies and very reluctantly he moved across the room and tried to feel for a pulse in Layton's neck with two fingers. There was nothing but very cold, rather unpleasant and rough skin. He took his fingers away quickly. There was certainly no sign of life that he could discern. Staverley noticed how oddly green the bath water looked and noted the vivid reddening and roughness across Layton's chest and arms. Probably goes with dying while wet he thought. Maybe it was a heart attack of some kind. Layton had certainly experienced some kind of catastrophic seizure and by the look of him he had not been in good physical shape to start with and was certainly not now. Staverley really had no idea what he was supposed to do now. He wanted to leave and be done with this. He thought he might be sick. He glanced around the room. It looked like any other bathroom in an up market 200-year-old hotel. A bathmat on the floor, slightly rucked, a white-toweling robe over the back of a chair, and some usual bits and pieces of toiletries by the sink. Nick reappeared at the door but did not come in. He looked like Staverley felt.

'I think he's gone. Dead I mean. But what do I know, let's get out of here, please.' Staverley said.

'They're coming. It wont be long, the ambulance station is only on the edge of town. Let's wait in the bedroom. And I think I need to call the police.'

'Really, is that necessary?'

'It would be the usual thing, death in a hotel room, indeterminate cause. Hotel manager's good practice manual page 4.' Nick lightened the moment a little.

'Should I wait?' asked Staverley. 'I suppose I should.' He added quickly, answering his own question. 'But I'll phone the university. I better do that down stairs. I promise not to wander off. Can I use your phone?'

'Of course, ask Mandy.'

Staverley returned to reception and explained quickly and was shown into Nick's office. He called Jean.

'Jean, you better get Lionel for me.'

'What is it, is something wrong?' She said.

'Better get Lionel.'

She sensed the urgency and put the phone down, a couple of minutes passed.

'Yes.' It was Lionel, slightly breathless.

'Lionel, I think he's dead.'

'What?'

'I said, I think he's dead, Layton.'

'Think?'

'I am not a doctor Lionel but it looks that way. If not dead then very close.'

There was a moment's silence.

'That is really very inconvenient.'

There was another moment of silence.

'So, at least Archie will get his way.'

Staverley was astonished. Lionel could be really, really obnoxious and crass when he tried hard but this was extraordinarily insensitive and inappropriate even for him.

'I suppose I should postpone the meeting and we need to start thinking about a replacement for Layton.' His mind had quickly reverted from shock to practicalities. The external examiner is dead, long live the external examiner. Clearly, there was little left of the student-teacher relationship Lionel and Layton had once had. Or perhaps this was Lionel's way of dealing with the shock. Staverley wondered about giving him the benefit of the doubt but decided to stick with obnoxious. But he did wonder about that relationship.

'I have to stay a while, the police coming'. Staverley explained 'I will tell you more later.'

Lionel is a terrible person he thought. In the lobby Pauline was sitting in an armchair in the bar area, looking calm and elegant, she was glancing through a country living magazine of some sort.

'So where is he then, what's the excuse, let's get going, for goodness sake.' She said.

'He wont be coming, he's dead.'

'What?'

'Why does everybody say that? He is dead. Or I think he is. They will tell us.' He pointed as two ambulance men came in at pace through the front door of the hotel and followed the direction of Mandy's pointing finger, up the stairs.

'Dead?'

'It looks like it, we found him in the bath, cold, wet, very messy and I am almost sure, not breathing. I had to touch him, horrible. You would not believe the state he was in!'

Pauline blinked and swallowed hard. 'Well.' She said. 'Well.'

'Exactly. It's incredible. I think I have to stay a while. The police are coming. What do you want to do?'

'I'll stay with you. Let's order some coffee. It is ok here? Are we allowed?' Pauline knew well his coffee prejudices and firm views about where it could be drunk and where it could not.

'Surprisingly good here actually. Let's get a pot, I could do with it, I'll ask Mandy.' As Staverley returned from ordering, a uniformed constable and another man in a suit, presumably a detective, walked through the lobby and strode two steps a time up the stairs, creating a cacophony of creaks. The coffee arrived but before they had time to pour the constable was back.

'Mr. Staverley?'

'Yes, that's me.'

'Constable Grace, Wessex Police, Sergeant Mellmoth asked if you could stay sir, he needs to speak with you. He'll be down soon.'

'Of course, not a problem I will be right here with my coffee.' He gestured to the pot. The constable returned upstairs. Mellmoth, Mellmoth, an unusual name, and one that rang a bell for Staverley. Not a name to forget, and as he watched the Sergeant come down the stairs a few minutes later he remembered. Mellmoth approached them with a grim smile.

'Mr. Staverley?'

'Doctor to be precise, but it doesn't matter. How can I help?'

'If we can have a word in private?'

'I will take my coffee over there.' Pauline volunteered, 'you stay here' and she moved across the lobby to another armchair with her coffee cup and magazine. Sergeant Mellmoth sat in the chair she had vacated.

'Now Dr Staverley, if I may, a couple of questions.' He took a notebook from his jacket pocket. 'Mr. Layton, what can you tell me?'

'Sorry to be a pain, its Sir Alan Layton.'

'Oh, good to know.' Said Mellmoth 'Sir Alan, noted.' He did make a note.

'Well, he was here on University business, for a meeting. But he didn't turn up this morning so Pauline and I', he gestured across the lobby, 'were dispatched to find him. I spoke to Nick, the manager, I'd met him before, and we went up together to the room. Nick knocked but there was no reply, so we went in, there was no one in the bedroom, then Nick looked in the bathroom and there he was. He looked dead and Nick asked me to check while he phoned for an ambulance. To be honest I had no idea what to do, so I felt for a pulse on his neck, and there was nothing there. Not that I would really know.'

Staverley raised the fingers in question and noticed the green tinge on their tips; he rubbed them on the napkin, which had come with the coffee.

'I didn't touch anything else but the floor was wet and Layton was in a terrible state, I have never seen anything like that, I hope it didn't disturb anything, anyway Nick waited in the room, while I came down here. I phoned my Head of Department to tell him what was happening and Pauline and I waited for you and ordered a coffee while we waited. That's about it. I think.'

'That seems very clear,' Mellmoth said 'and tallies with Mr. Fell's account. We need confirmation from the police surgeon, he's on his way, but it certainly appears that Sir Alan died sometime during the night - obviously. At the moment it could be something quite straightforward but we must wait and see what the police surgeon says. And Layton, did you know him personally?'

'Er, no, I had never met him as such, I did hear him speak at a conference once, I was just sent to collect him because he was late. He's very well known and some of my colleagues knew him personally.'

'I may well need to speak with your colleagues, we will see, and I may need to speak to you again and I would be grateful if you could be circumspect as regards sharing anything in detail about what you saw with your colleagues or anyone else.'

'No problem, of course, whenever, and yes I will be careful, and I'll tell Pauline that also, shall I?'

Mellmoth nodded, closed his notebook and stood up to leave.

'One thing Sergeant.' Said Staverley, and Mellmoth paused.

'I may be wrong, but I think we have met. I did my first degree at the University of Middle England, and there were two seconded police officers on the course, and I think you were one of them.'

Mellmoth smiled. 'I wasn't going to say anything but I thought I recognized you too. That's right that was me, there was me and Inspector Gideon from the traffic division, he's a Chief Superintendent somewhere now – meteoric career. The Worcestershire force used to send two officers each year for several years to do social science degrees at Middle England, until budget cuts put a stop to it. I enjoyed my three years at UME and I remember you from lectures and seminars and we had a couple of beers over the years I think. You were one of those to overcome the general suspicion of the filth.'

Staverley flushed slightly. There certainly had been some resentment about the police students, not surprisingly given what was happening in student politics at the time but it faded slowly as people got to know the two officers, who proved to be eminently sociable, and they were able to bring some rather different experiences to bear on discussions in seminars and did not take up the sort of stereotyped positions on social and political issues that many people expected, quite the opposite sometimes. How odd that Mellmoth should be here now.

'And you? Career progress?' Staverley asked.

'Well, after the degree I moved across to CID, then up to Detective Sergeant, then recently here, and in a couple of weeks I move up to Inspector in CID, just waiting for the paperwork to clear. So I have done alright for myself. And you, PhD obviously, Doctor Staverley, presumably you teach at Watermouth?'

'I do, yes, I been here nearly 5 years. It's Ok. I've done alright too I suppose. Look when the formalities are out of the way and I am no longer a witness or whatever what about getting together for a drink, catch up and talk about Middle England and our riotious student days.'

Mellmoth smiled again. 'Good, yes, great idea, I'd like that. Let's do it.' They shook hands and Mellmoth went back up the stairs.

Back at the university there was an endless series of further "Whats" from various colleagues that Staverley found increasingly irritating and he soon tired of telling his story, a minimalist version as Mellmoth had instructed. He retreated to his office but found it difficult to settle into any work. It was a very unsettling day to say the least. He kept thinking back to the sight of Layton in the bath and the smell in the room. He pottered about and fiddling with various tasks but got very little done before lunch. He needed a nourishing sandwich to perk himself up but before leaving thought he would try Nick Fell for an update. The ever-present Mandy put him through.

'Nick, it's Staverley, what's happening there?'

'Well he's gone now thank goodness. Poor man. The ambulance has just left. The place has been chaotic all morning, having to explain to guests, making arrangements about the room and whatever, we seem to be getting back to normal, but.' It sounded like a big but. 'The sergeant tells me that they are treating it as a suspicious death.'

'What?' Now Staverley was doing it.

'Its suspicious until they determine cause of death evidently. The police surgeon was uncertain, and someone else came with a big black bag, but not a heart attack by the sound of it, I assume they will conduct a post mortem. Isn't that what happens?'

Staverley did not know. His knowledge of police procedures and suspicious deaths was limited to what he had gleaned from watching detective series on the television.

'You probably know as much about that as I do, but it sounds as though we might be learning more about what happens first hand. Anyway, thanks for the update, I'll keep in touch.'

The front page of the next evening's edition of the local newspaper made it clear that suspicious had turned into something else much more dramatic. 'University Examiner Murdered' the headline read. The article explained that the police had made public the death in suspicious circumstances of Sir Alan Layton, a well-known and respected academic, in a local hotel.

Another call to Nick was probably a good idea.

'Nick, sorry to bother you again but I was reading the Gazette.'

'Yep. It looks like they are treating it as a murder. They were back this morning to interview me and the night staff about Sir Alan's and comings and goings.'

'Comings and goings?' asked Staverley.

'You know did he leave the hotel, did he have dinner, did he have visitors?'

'Did he?' Staverley could not help himself.

'Did he what?'

'Leave, dinner, visitors?'

'Leave, we don't think so, he checked in around 4.00, dinner, yes, with a young woman, visitors, at least one, a man who asked for him at the desk and went up to his room.' Nick explained.

'Do we know who they were, the young woman and the man visitor.' Staverley probed.

'We do not.' Nick replied 'Who ever we are.'

'We are the ones who found the body.' Staverley said. 'We need to know these things.'

'You may need to know, but I have a hotel to run and that running is being disrupted by the murder of your examiner person.'

'OK, point taken, but do we know what the man visitor looked liked or what he wanted?'

'He said he wanted to speak to Layton, who asked for him to be sent up.'

'Any clues to who he was – a description?'

'The police asked that of course.' Nick said. 'I was off duty, but William who was on reception said nothing obvious like a scar or tattoo. He was in his forties or fifties perhaps, but wore a cap and a scarf which partly covered his face, let's see, clean shaven and very pale skinned and soft spoken, may have had a slight Irish accent but Will wasn't sure about that. He said that there was something odd about him but didn't know what that was. I think that's it but I'll keep asking.'

'That sounds very precise for someone who has a hotel to run.'

'Maybe, I just wanted to know what William had told the police. A good manager needs to know everything that goes on, hoteliers manual of good practice page 28.'

Staverley laughed. 'In that case, the young woman?'

'A bit vague again I am afraid, no one saw her arrive and she was sitting with her back to the waitress during the meal. Yvonne, the waitress, said she was attractive, I don't know how she could tell, perhaps women can sense such things. She ordered a cocktail evidently, but something a bit exotic for us and she settled for a gin and tonic and they had wine. Yvonne said the dinner had been tense rather than convivial, the talk was stilted and the young woman hardly ate anything, then there was some kind of kerfuffle and she left abruptly. Oh, and she was wearing a very expensive perfume according to Yvonne. No one else had seen her come or go, a bit odd that really but it was a quiet weekday night and the maitre'd was mostly backstage, he saw nothing at all. Oh yes! After the woman left Professor Layton asked Yvonne for a sticking plaster for a cut on his hand.'

'Times?' asked Staverley.

'You know you ask the same questions as the sergeant, are you contemplating a change of career?'

'I am a social researcher Nick, and that's what we do, ask questions. Remember when I interviewed you for my research. Questions.'

'I guess, and as you say, you and I both have a sort of vested interest here, as gruesome as that may be. The young woman came around 7.45pm, Layton was already at the table, and she left a bit before 8.45pm. Layton went up to his room before 9.00pm and the visitor arrived around 9.30pm but only stayed for about 10 minutes – I wrote all of that down when I spoke to my staff.' Fell explained.

'You are being very precise again.' Joked Staverley.

'My staff are very reliable and very observant, they have all read the hoteliers good practice manual and I test them regularly.' They both laughed.

'Does that help you?'

'To be honest I don't know. I don't really know why I am asking you all these questions, but thanks Nick. This is a major thing in the world I work in. Layton was significant, if you know what I mean. His dying will change a lot of things for a lot of people, and murder, well that's going to make things even more fraught. I have already had to explain umpteen times to umpteen people what I saw and what I know but I am keeping all that to a bare minimum like Mellmoth said. Anything you share with me will go no further I can promise you that.' Staverley explained.

'I can understand, and I know you will be discrete, like you were with all the council stuff I talked to you about. Its my first murder too, so its appalling and intriguing in about equal measure, we did have a suicide once when I was assistant manager. I want to know what's going to happen as much as you do. And I am also thinking about what impact the news coverage will have on hotel business, but so far, at least today, there has been quite a spike in our bookings for the next week or so. It might be journalists, although we may be too up market for them, or maybe its ghouls or a convention of amateur detectives hoping to solve the crime. Anyway, I will tell you my news, if you will tell me yours. If there are developments at your end, alright?'

'You're on.' Staverley said.

There was a development or two. The first was that Archie phoned Staverley at home. 'I need to talk to you.' Archie said abruptly.

'I thought you weren't talking to me.' Staverley countered.

'Well now I am. It's important. Look, I know I have been difficult. I will be civil, I promise. I will try to be more than civil. Will that do?' Archie asked.

'Civil is a good start Archie, it really is. When and were.'

'I am at home and the family are scattered to the winds, could you come now? I'll make a cup of tea and Valerie has made rock cakes.'

'I am on my way.' Staverley said, he put down the phone and picked up his keys. The other was a further headline in the local paper and more relevations about Layton's death. The paper claimed that an unnamed source had revealed that the police were concentrating on a bar of soap as the murder weapon, a poisoned bar of soap. Thinking back to what he had seen, and the state Layton had been in, Staverley thought that poison made a lot of sense, although he did not understand how you could be poisoned by soap. He would have to ask.

CHAPTER FIVE

Archie opened the door of Alleyn Villas with a smile of sorts or an expression that meant he was trying to look a little less stern and annoyed than he had been at their last meeting.

'Tea first?' he said.

'And a rock cake please, I was promised.' Staverley replied.

They went into the kitchen and Archie went through the full tea making ritual with leaves, teapot and strainer and large gaudy cups announcing his status as the world's best Dad, that looked like presents from the girls. He handed Staverley a large rock cake on a plate, which he began to nibble and enjoy. Valerie was a good at baking. Archie sat down across from him at the kitchen table with his cup between his hands and blew on the surface of the tea as he always did.

'Well', Archie began 'this time I am the one who needs to talk, I have to explain myself to someone, and like it or not, you are it.' He paused. 'The police have been to interview me.'

Staverley spluttered a shower of crumbs from his mouth over the table and quickly began to gather them up.

'Sorry, you took me by surprise. Define interview.' He asked, cleaning up as best he could.

Archie sighed long and deep 'They wanted to know why I had visited Layton on the night he died and what had happened.'

Staverley did not have a mouthful of cake this time but spluttered anyway, he was struggling to make sense of this. He could not think of anything to say and closed his eyes for a second, trying to think.

'You were the visitor?' He managed to say.

'I was, how did you know about it?'

'It's not important. So why did you?'

'Why did I. Well I wish I hadn't. I needed to clear the air about things, with him. I have known him a long time or a long time ago anyway, and there was something I wanted to say to him. I said it. He didn't like it. I left. That's it.'

'But I didn't know you knew him well, and what thing did you have to say, and what did the police say? And how did they know it was you?'

'I told them. A constable came to the department the day before yesterday to talk to people who were involved in inviting Layton and organizing his trip and those who had known him personally. I explained that I did know him but had not seen him for a long time and called on him at his hotel on the night of his death. This morning I got a telephone call asking me to go down to the police station to make a statement, which I did.'

'And what happened?' Staverley asked.

'Well, they listened to what I had to say, asked questions and they sent me on my way, but said they might need to speak with me again. They wanted to know why I went, and to pin down precisely when I left home, when I arrived at the hotel, how long I stayed, what we talked about and when I got back. It was all very civilized but not a good experience. In fact I think it is only the second time in my life that I have spoken to the police. Isn't that incredible? But I am worried, and a little frightened to be honest. It seems I was the last person to see him alive… Apart from the murderer of course', Archie added hurriedly. 'That's what people say isn't it.'

'It is I guess.' Staverley agreed.

'But its true, it really is.'

'I don't doubt that,' said Staverley 'not for a second. But why were you there? What did you tell them about why you were there and what you said?'

'I lied.'

'What?' Staverley spluttered again. This spluttering was becoming a habit.

'I lied.' Archie repeated. 'I told them that I had known Layton since we were teenagers, that we had been at school together, which is true, and that I called into to say a quick hello before the meeting in the morning. As old school friends do. But that is not true.' Archie took a long sip from his tea. 'I have decided, I don't know why exactly, to tell you what really happened, and why I really went. I think if I don't tell someone I will go crazy or do something stupid. And I have done enough stupid things already. I've had this stuff in my head for so long, I thought it had all gone away but the last few months have been unbearable. And

I know I have been unbearable. And I don't want to be. So I thought telling you might help, and that you might help me. Do you want to hear?'

Staverley surprised himself by hesitating. Did he want to hear? Sometimes not knowing things is better. Ignorance can be blissful. What would he do with knowing? How was he supposed to respond? Why him? How was he supposed to help?

'Of course I do.' He said.

'Right, this is a long story. If it is going to make sense then I have to tell you about myself, put things in context as we say in the social science business. I guess it's a sort of explanation of who and what I am, bearing in mind, as we also say in the social science business, that we narrate ourselves and our histories from who and where we are now. There's no simple access to how things really were in the past and what really happened and I am not sure what 'really' means. This is how I remember it now, polished and twisted during long nights of bad sleeping and repeated bouts of could things have been different? Sorry, this is beginning to sound like the start of a lecture to undergraduates. What I am trying to say is that there are different versions of who I am and this is one, one that I may not like very much but one that I realize I have to own up to and that made me what I am now. Ok Prologue over.

I think I did tell you that I was born and brought up in rural Gloucestershire, in a small town or big village anyway. My father was the village baker, an old fashioned artisan who owned and ran his own shop, he worked in the back with his ovens, my mother served behind the counter and kept the accounts. She talked to customers all day and he worked in a busy silence, except when the deliveries came. We are hard to place in sociological social class terms. Petit bourgeois doesn't seem right. My parents owned the business yes but it was almost always a matter of getting by, always being susceptible to customers whims, competition from big shops and the price of flour. It was my father who taught Valerie how to bake. They spent hours together trying out recipes for different styles of bread and pies and cakes. He always worked hard, but never talked much. He used to get up ridiculously early to get his bread in the ovens and went to bed early. He had no spare time for hobbies or friends or holidays.

An occasional pint in the evenings and listening to the radio with my mother were his only distractions from the grinding round of hard work – it took its toll on him over the years. Sometimes now when Valerie bakes bread the smell when it comes out of the oven makes me cry, it's like going back to the times I used to sit and watch my father kneading dough and pulling loaves with his oven paddle. My friends at home and the school in the village were sons and daughters of other men like my father – tradesmen as they were called. The local carpenter, mechanic, the postmaster, farrier, people like that, all one-man businesses, all with a valued skill, all part of a tight knit community on whom they depended and who depended on them. They all had their place in the village pecking order, separate from the professional men above and from the employed men, the labourers below. They were the people who kept the village fed and watered and dry and moving. My closest friend was Luke Sansom. His father was landlord of the Drayman's Arms, the local pub, or one of them. It was in many ways an idyllic childhood, a sort of Laurie Lee childhood – plenty of countryside to play in and explore, trees to fall out of, rivers to fall into, apples to scrump, sticklebacks to catch in bottles, you know the sort of thing. Scabby knees and muddy shorts and uncombed hair, but all with a smile. My parents made a decent enough living, we weren't poor but there were good and bad times, but people always need bread and cakes. My father was kind and gentle like I said, a bit distant but always interested in me. He liked to know what was happening at school and always went to the concerts and nativity plays, my mother was more attentive, more hands on, she was a bit of a cliché I suppose, she 'wanted something better for her son', you know a Jackson and Marsden mother. My father never showed me how to bake bread, although I asked more than once, but my mother taught me to read when I was very young – *The New Path To Reading primer*, it was, I can still recite bits of it – and I moved on from there and became a reader. I loved books. Which meant of course I did well at primary school. Sorry I am going on, we're getting there.

I was no prodigy but just devoured books and that made most schoolwork easy – except arithmetic, which I was useless at. I came somewhere near the top of the class in most subjects, except Maths, I hated those mustard yellow mental arithmetic books. My great rival was Jennifer Appleyard, whose parents ran the toyshop. I often wonder what became of her. Sorry. So primary school was great, good marks, good friends, I always looked forward to school. Then the 11+ came along, I did predictably well and got a scholarship to the Grammar school in the nearby town. That meant saying goodbye to most of my friends and climbing trees was replaced by homework, a school uniform and Latin. No one had mentioned Latin – that was a shock, a disaster. From being a good pupil with supportive teachers I become a struggling nonentity. Anyway there I was a tradesman's son surrounded by the offspring of doctors and solicitors and charter accountants and school changed from somewhere I looked forward to, to something I began to loath and dread. I was out of my depth amidst all of the cultural capital that my classmate's families had accumulated over several generations of grammar schools and universities. They could read the school and its rhythms and routines, it was all so natural to them, they didn't have to make an effort to fit in. This was for them, their entitlement. I even started to resent my parents because they could not help me with my homework. I changed in one year from a happy child whose life made sense to a morose and miserable pre-teen who didn't understand what was happening to him. And at the Grammar, I was fair game. I was the baker's boy, the village oik.

And this is where Alan Layton, God rest him, enters the story, my story and my life. If things were not bad enough he was about to make them worse. Its familiar stuff, you know it, let's pick on the outsider etc. etc. And Layton was a most inventive picker on of vulnerable others. He was several years above me but he spotted me, he seemed to recognise that I could be a source of endless amusement for him and his mates and overtime he wanted to make picking on me his life's work. Almost everyday there was something, some small humiliation, and some not so small humiliations. Lots of jokes and name-calling related to bread, there's plenty of good material there. My uniform was regularly ripped, my books went missing, my homework ruined. I tried to keep a low profile, to be invisible but he would always seek me out, he was always ready with some new sarcasm or demeaning epithet. But as we grew to become proper teenagers there was a new and very potent source of potential humiliation –

girls. Our school merged with the local girl's grammar and we had to learn to be around girls, to take them into account, and more importantly get them to take us into account. Layton was good at being taken into account, I wasn't. School, the bus home and homework left little time for girls. I thought about them of course, a lot. But then who would believe it, I had a girlfriend and my life began to feel a lot better. Sian, she was Welsh, very shy, sort of pretty, not a stunner but I thought she was great, and we sort of matched. She was good for me. He father worked in an office, some kind of accounts clerk I think. Her shyness and my moroseness worked. We got on. We went for walks, to the cinema in the town sometimes, to the café, it was all very innocent and tentative. But Layton noticed. He always noticed everything about me no matter how much I tried to avoid him, how invisible I tried to be, how quiet I was. He was always there watching and noting and stocking up for his next offensive. He noticed Sian and I am sorry to say, Sian noticed him. He started to be nice to her, a girl he would not normally have paid any attention to. He started to talk to her. I would see them sometimes at break time, talking and laughing. Sian was spending less and less time with me and her attitude toward me had begun to change. We never got very far in terms of teenage petting but we had our moments and we were both okay about taking things slowly but she began to say that she didn't want me to touch her and we started to bicker and sulk. And then one evening on the way from school to the bus stop she said it – 'Alan has told me about you'. I didn't know what she meant. 'Told you what?' I said, and then she sneered, I had never seen her sneer, I never thought her capable of a sneer, but her face distorted into this horrible thing and I knew it was bad. 'He told me that you prefer boys, that you're one of them, a fruitcake' - it would be a different word these days. When she first said it I didn't know what she meant but then it dawned on me. I had heard jeers and jokes and sniggers about men who preferred men but it was not something I understood. I did not know what to say. I could not respond. This was supposed to be my girlfriend. I think now, didn't she see a slight inconsistency? Apparently not, I don't think she really understood what she was saying either. It was a way of getting rid of me and pleasing Layton at the same time. But it was cruel. 'So stay away from me Archie Rankin, and I have told the other girls' she said. And she had. So that was it. I went from an outsider to absolute ostracism, an outcast. It was no longer just Layton and his friends who were mean to me. I was shunned, by everyone, called names, attacked and beaten up more than once. My nightmare turned into horror. I was 'Archie the pansy', 'the baker's fruit', that was Layton's particular epithet for me.

I had to spend the next two years like that before I could leave. I couldn't explain it to my parents. I couldn't bring myself to tell them what was being said about me and done to me. But they had to put up with it too in a way, with me, my desolate moods, my desperate attempts to avoid going to school. They couldn't understand what was happening. In a lot of ways that is what I resent most, what Layton did to my family, to my life with my parents - I hate him for that much more than the name calling - the tension and silences and their disappointment. I never recovered the closeness I had had with my mother, even much later when she was very ill I had the sense that she was still struggling to make sense of what had changed me all those years before and what had become of the young boy with so much promise and so much joy in his heart. She was always proud of me I know that and she lived long enough to see my career take off, my first book published, overseas travel and all that, and she was pleased, but it was as though she was on the outside watching, rather than part of it all as she had been at the beginning. I could have killed Layton just for that, very easily, with great pleasure. But I didn't. I never really thought of killing him. I thought about some kind of revenge but something that involved humiliation rather than actual violence. Much later when he reappeared in my life I spent hours imagining situations in which at some public event I reduced him to a sniveling wreck having exposed his fraudulent research or him coming to me to offer a groveling apology that I would reject, although that would never have been enough. I always wanted more, I wanted people to see what he was, to recognize him for the callous, evil bastard he was. When I went to see him at the hotel I just wanted to confront him, to say here I am, I survived, I survived you, I am happy, I have a family, you did not destroy me, you failed. But it didn't happen like that. He didn't care. I was of no importance to him. I am not sure he even remembered what he had done, what he was responsible for. I was dismissed. I got to say nothing, all the words I had practiced so many times just stayed in my head. The best I could do was to insult him, like a schoolboy, like him. I told him he was fat. Would you believe that? Pathetic really but it was better than nothing I suppose and when I left I did feel better. It wasn't one of those great moment of catharsis it just felt good to see him looking old and unwell. But the important thing is that when I walked out of that room he was alive, although from what I have read in the papers that might not mean anything.'

'So how did you get away?' Staverley asked.

'From the hotel?'

'No from him, at school.'

'Oh, one thing that came from my pariah state was that there was little else for me to do but schoolwork. My friends in the village had moved on. Even when I didn't go to school I was still reading, studying. I spent hours in the school library. I read half the books in there. It was a refuge. I even managed to come to grips with a bit of Latin. I was still rubbish at anything that involved numbers but anything that involved words and concepts, anything that involved reading I could master on my own. So much to the surprise of my teachers, most of who had dismissed me as a waste of time, I did rather well in my O-levels and could have stayed on. The headmaster asked to see me, and that was the first time I had ever spoken with him, he tried to convince to stay, but I left and moved onto the local Technical College, which confused my parents no end. It was a new start for me and it was a different kind of environment, more modern, obviously mostly technical subjects but I was able to put together a set of courses that reflected what I liked and what I was good at. I even made some friends, people a bit more like those from the village, more like me, and that gave me more confidence, and it made me realise how unfair and exclusionary the education system was, how divided it was, how much talent and energy and promise it wasted. Those divisions ruined people's lives. For a lot of us, for different reasons, the Tech was a second chance to make something of ourselves. Anyway you more or less know the rest. I did my exams, did well again, I worked for a couple of years in tedious office jobs looking for some sort of career, a future as my mother would say – and that made my parents feel better about me – and then there was the war. Somehow, in my early twenties, I found myself in an intelligence unit, nothing James Bond like, just analyzing documents, trying to make sense of enemy radio traffic, debriefing field agents. But I was working with other people for whom words and concepts were important and gradually the notion developed that maybe when the war was over I could go to university, like they had, and read even more books. That was something I had never imagined doing, but with some help from people in my unit, a lot of them knew their way around the higher education system, I got into the University of Rummidge And the rest is history, as they say, and here I am.'

'But that wasn't the end of you and Layton?'

'No, it wasn't. Didn't I have to choose an area of study that turned out to be his fiefdom? I knew nothing of him while I was an undergraduate. I thought I had seen the last of him. It was when I had my first higher education job at Batley Canalside College and was doing my PhD part time that I saw an article with his name on it in a journal. At first I thought it must be another person with the same name, but I asked around and it was him, my nemesis. My first reaction was to run, I even thought about moving abroad somewhere to start again. I explored the possibility of becoming a schoolteacher. I even visited a monastery. Now that would have been a place to hide. But then I thought no, he can't do that to me, I'll just keep my head down and avoid him and pursue my career in my own way. I was making myself invisible again. I couldn't avoid him entirely of course, he was too central, too much involved in everything, but it's surprising how easy it is to just be another face in the academic crowd.

At conferences I made sure I was never a speaker if he was going to be there, I avoided small scale events where I was likely to meet him face to face, I turned down invitations to participate in things if he was also involved. I know it had an impact of my work and my career, I missed out on things, opportunities, challenges that interested me, but I was willing to do that to ensure that I never had to look him in the eye. I was a coward I guess, and I don't know that he even knew I existed, or that the social scientist I had became was his schoolboy victim, or that any of what happened was of the slightest importance to him. But I didn't want to take the chance. And when I went to his hotel room that night I was still not sure that he really knew who I was, I think at the beginning he thought I was bringing a message from the university, and then that I was some rude, deranged person who had wandered in off the street. I hope not really, I hope he realised. I hope he understood that I survived him. But I will never know now and I do like the idea of him being dead. I like it very much. It makes the world seem like a better place. So that's it. That's me, or that's him and me. That's who I am, and how I became who I am. Not very edifying but here I am, I did survive and I will go on and he's dead'. Archie could not summon up much enthusiasm for his triumph.

What do you say to that? Staverley thought. He felt the weight of Archie's life and his pain settling in his chest. He knew he would carry Archie's story with him and that he was also changed by what they now shared. The balance of their relationship was altered, for better or worse, he did not know.

'God Archie, don't be hard on yourself – what a sad thing to say, sorry. What I mean is you are right, you did survive, in fact you flourished, you became someone. Not someone famous and hated but someone well known who is liked and admired. You are a good man Archie, someone worthwhile, we all know that, your colleagues and your friends. You have a reputation. You fight for good causes. Ok, so you've been giving us a hard time lately, you're not a saint, not even close, but you are a significant other for a lot of people. You have your place, your family – and they are great – and you have your colleagues, and you have Lionel and Duncan to battle with and crusades in the university to wage. Yes, you can be a prima donna but so what, you do the right things, most of the time, anyway, more often than most of us. That's good enough for me, more than good enough. And I really hope it's good enough for you.'

'Maybe, I know what you're saying and you're partly right. And now at least I can be a bit less of a pain around the place, unless I end up in prison of course. That was not part of my career planning.' Archie smiled wryly. Something Staverley had not seen for quite a while. 'But I have to be realistic, I am a suspect, I could well end up being charged with Layton's murder.'

'That's not going to happen.'

'I don't know, think about it, I would have had motive and opportunity, I hated him and I was there, means I don't know about, I don't know what the means were. Do you know how he was killed?'

'No I don't,' Staverley said 'but you not knowing is a good thing, if you don't know then you couldn't have done it, could you?'

'Sure but that's only what I say isn't it, I could be lying again, pretending not to know. I lied to the police, I could be lying to you now.' Archie responded.

'What does Valerie say?'

'Ah well, I have not quite spelled it all out yet, I don't want to worry her and the girls if I don't have to, I just said the police questions were routine, that they are speaking to everyone.'

Something occurred to Staverley.

'One thing that I don't understand is why the description that the young man on the hotel desk gave of you was so off. It doesn't fit you at all. Were you trying to disguise yourself?'

'I didn't go to the desk, no one saw me, I went in through the car park entrance at the back, I know my way around the Paine, we've had several university visitors put up there over the years, I got the room number beforehand from Jean's desk, she made the booking. I snuck up the stairs and snuck back out. I am sure no one saw me.'

Staverley was puzzled. 'That means then that there was another visitor, you were not the only one. What time were you there?'

Archie thought a moment. 'Around ten, just before perhaps.'

'Rats!' Staverley exclaimed, 'that means you were there after the other visitor. Didn't the police ask about times?'

'They did' Archie said 'but it was all a bit vague, I was being vague, remember I was telling lies.'

Staverley thought again. 'Didn't they ask you how you got in, about going to the desk?'

'No they didn't, they must have assumed that I was the visitor that you are talking about, they never asked how I got to the room, and I didn't elaborate. It didn't seem like a good idea to tell them that I sneaked in the back entrance if I was calling on an old colleague to say hello.' Explained Archie.

'But it does raise some interesting new questions, not the least we still don't know about the other visitor, who was that?'

'Well I don't know do I, although we must have only just missed each other by a few minutes. That might have been an interesting encounter.'

Staverley was now in researcher mode. 'It really all hangs on the cause of death, which we don't know about. Maybe I should try and find out.'

Archie looked askance. 'You shouldn't get involved, it's my problem, I will manage. I am sure the police will get their man, or their person. At least I sincerely hope they do.' He was trying to sound confident.

'Well, it's beginning to feel like my problem as well, Layton is a problem for all of us, and I found the body after all. I am sure I will have to answer more questions as well.'

Archie had a pained expression. 'From what I picked up from the interview they have been asking questions of lots of people at the university, Lionel for example, as Head of department, who invited Layton, and I think, I am not sure, that Lionel may have dropped me in it. I can imagine the exchange 'Professor Lewis can you think of anyone who might have had a grudge against the deceased?' 'Well Sergeant now that you ask, one of my colleagues ...'

Staverley could imagine it too. Lionel would have no compunction. Something needed to be said, Lionel could not be allowed to get away with that.

CHAPTER SIX

Staverley left Archie in a better mood than he had seen him for a long time, despite the dire possibilities of more police interest hanging over him. Staverley walked straight to the station, caught the train to the campus, and headed for Lionel's office. He did not really do angry. He sometimes felt that a lack of anger was a character fault, that being angry at least sometimes, was healthy. But he was not good at being angry. He felt many other emotions and tended to cry more often than normal for a grown man, especially at the cinema. But now he was angry. Now he wanted to shout and swear and wave his arms around and very specifically he wanted to shout at Lionel. He wanted to make Lionel regret what he had done. It was quite exhilarating; he could sense the adrenalin surging through his veins.

Lionel was in. Staverley knocked and walked in, taking him be surprise clearly.
'Uh! Yes, what, were we meeting?'
'We were not, we are now.' Said Staverley.
'Look no time now, sorry, see Jean.' Lionel commanded in his usual imperious manner and wafted a hand. Staverley ignored him and pressed on.
'I need to ask you a question, and you are going to answer me honestly and straightforwardly Lionel.'
Lionel was clearly taken aback by this forthrightness, this was not the Staverley he was used to. The Staverley he was used to got his way by persistence and clever argument not by raising his voice and addressing him formally. He did not quite recover himself to manage a response.
'Tell me', the new strident Staverley said, even going as far as pointing a finger, 'tell me what you said to the police about Archie?'
Lionel was further taken aback and as much to his own surprise as Staverley's he answered. 'As little as possible, I felt I needed to ensure that the members of my department did not come under undeserved and inappropriate suspicions. I told the police that there are been some academic opposition to Layton's

appointment, but nothing out of the ordinary in the circumstances. I did not single out Archie as a particular mover in the opposition, although of course, as we know, he was. My view is that there is no need to share departmental issues with the police that are clearly irrelevant to the matter at hand, and Archie could no more have been responsible for Layton's death than you or I. So rightly or wrongly I kept the events of last term to myself, or gave a truncated account of them and I shall continue to do so until it seems to me that they become pertinent. I hope Duncan did the same.'

He stared hard at Staverley and it was Staverley's turn to be taken aback. This was not what he was expecting to hear. The anger he had stocked up and the adrenalin that went with it dissipated, like air from a punctured balloon. He was now at a loss for something to say. This was not how the encounter with Lionel was supposed to go as he had rehearsed his shock and disappointment and dismay on the train. This was Lionel the protective leader of his group, fending off dangers from the outside, circling his wagons, or something like that.

'That,' Staverley hesitated, still struggling for a sensible response, 'that is, exactly what I was hoping to hear. I am pleased to know that Lionel. That's great, excellent. Thank you, well. Good. Sorry for bursting in. I got a little agitated there with all of this going on. I am sure you feel the same. It's a difficult time for us all. And it's good to know you are there for us Lionel'.

He was getting carried away and running on, sounding ridiculous. 'So yes, I will leave you to get on, sorry to have disturbed.' He backed out of the room and closed the door gently behind him, leaving Lionel looking perplexed and a little unsure about what had just happened. He went back to his perusal of the Department's monthly budget sheets.

Staverley stood outside Lionel's door leaning on the wall, breathing heavily, and feeling very stupid. He scrubbed his face with his hands and tried to think what it was he was intending to do with his day. He started to walk toward his office thinking about what Lionel had said, and then he realised, maybe he was haranguing the wrong person. The anger was still to hand and now it had a new focus. He had been wrong about Lionel but 'I hope Duncan did the same' he had said! Duncan the smiling weasel, what had he said? Duncan the underhanded boy scout, the do-gooder. Had he used the opportunity to gain some kind of advantage over Archie? Staverley turned, moved a few steps along the corridor and knocked on another door. Again he walked in without waiting for a reply. Duncan was staring out of the window and may have been picking his nose. He jumped when to the door opened and quickly picked up a pen from his desk. Staverley thought this time before speaking and adopted a more round about approach. 'Duncan', he was working at sounding calm, 'I understand that you have been spoken to by the police, and I may have to do the same. Any pointers, any advice? How did you respond?'

Duncan appeared to think that this was a quite reasonable question and it deflected him from wondering why Staverley had suddenly appeared in his office. 'Just be honest, that's my view. I told them what I knew, that's it, that's what I would advise.'

'And what did you know that you told them?'

Duncan made no attempt to avoid answering. 'I told them about Archie's out burst of course, his ridiculous and unfathomable opposition to Layton, and his threats.'

'Threats?'

'Yes, that he had said he would go to any length to stop Layton coming. I am not for a minute suggesting that he had anything to do with what occured but one has to be frank in these situations, no good covering things up, they come out in the end. I was just the same with Connelly and Rawlins. I thought the police should know about them. In any case they would anyway in due course. For an academic Layton had accumulated more than his fair share of enemies. Strange man, I never liked him much myself but you have to admire him and his role in the discipline. His contribution has been immense, his methods, his rigour, all admirable. We wont see his like again, as they say.' Duncan was launching into a eulogy and distracting Staverley's attention.

'Wait, wait a minute, who are Connelly and Rawlins?'

Duncan sighed as though confronted with an ignorant child. 'You know about Rawlins, he of the scandalous review. His patently misguided attempt to discredit Sir Alan's work in the review he wrote in some obscure journal of other. It did him no good of course, derailed his whole career in fact. Failed his probation, couldn't get his work published. Ended up in the Poly sector if I am not mistaken. He surely hated Layton, even more so I think after losing his university post. Before your time I suppose but for a few years he would turn up at conferences and waylay Sir Alan, and cause disturbances in sessions with wild accusations and groundless criticisms. I was embarrassing but Sir Alan handled him well and he stopped coming eventually, haven't heard about him for years now but I had to mention him, it would have been wrong not to. And the police should know that Archie was not the only one who had a problem with Layton, although for the life of me I still don't know what Archie's problem is, or was.'

Staverley vaguely remembered Rawlins now, or at least he had heard the stories, his attempts to confront and challenge Layton had become part of the folklore of the discipline. The popular version being that Rawlins was a sort of demented gnome to Layton's golden knight, who vanquished his challenger and lived happily ever after. Staverley suspected that quite a few of the spectators at their encounters were silently hoping for a different outcome.

'And Connelly, I don't know about him. I am assuming it's a him.'

Duncan was beginning to relish his storyteller role, carrier of the sacred texts of the social science community.

'Well that's different, a bit more low key but in some ways no less dramatic. Connelly was a research student at Poppleton, and Layton was chosen as one of his examiners. A mistake on the supervisor's part really because Connelly was doing theory, can you imagine. He has been reading some of those French fellows, what do you call them, post-structuralists. Hardly proper social science at all. Why on earth would anyone think that Layton would take a positive view of that? The story goes that it was Connelly who wanted Layton. A bit full of himself, he thought he could stir the old boy up, make him a convert, bring him into the post-structuralist camp, show him what theory had to offer. Difficult to know what planet he was living on. Layton, Sir Alan, tore it to shreds, eviscerated it one person said to me, in the exam he reduced Connelly to a quivering heap, who was evidently quite beside himself by the end. Sir Alan would not even contemplate rewrites, resubmission – a straight fail. Connelly and his supervisor launched an appeal, and things dragged on for a couple of years, but to no avail Alan Layton had passed judgment and no one was going to query that. There was even talk of a legal challenge I believe, but it came to nothing and Connelly disappeared, no idea of what became of him. Architect of his own fate in many ways, should have found a theory friendly examiner willing to offer some latitude, there are a few about here and there, and it might have turned out differently. But theory is dangerous stuff to my mind, a matter of blind faith rather than evidence, no basis for proper objectivity.'

Staverley's anger had been over taken by his fascination. He wanted to be angry but Duncan didn't seem worth it, he probably would not notice and he had given Staverley and the police some other possible suspects. Perhaps Archie was off the hook, perhaps Rawlins or Connelly, or some other victim of Layton's vitriolic largesse would turn out to be the other visitor and the perpetrator. Staverley knew he now had things to do, to follow up, research to do, things that might help Archie.

'Helpful Duncan, I will bear in mind your advice, sorry to have bothered you.'

Duncan now was obviously pleased with himself. 'Glad to be off help. I wonder what the funeral arrangements will be. Will you go? Sad for the family of course, for the daughter anyway, wife died some years ago. Suicide I believe. Anyway we shall see.'

Staverley was surprised again. 'Daughter, I didn't know he had a daughter.'

'Yes, yes, just the one child, she's also some sort of academic I think, natural sciences I think, I know nothing more of her.'

Staverley left quietly, Duncan did not seem to notice he was gone and continued staring out of the window and went back to picking his nose.

As Staverley approached his room he saw a young man in a well worn suit waiting outside the door. Clearly he was not a student, although you never could be sure.

'Waiting for me?'

'Yes sir.' Certainly not a student then. 'Detective Constable Barnaby, working with Sergeant Mellmoth, I need to ask a few questions, if I may?' He held up his warrant card for Staverley to see. Staverley looked at it, he had never seen one before.

'Sure, no problem, let's go in.'

Staverley unlocked his door, and ushered Barnaby in. He took off his jacket and they both sat. The constable took out his notebook and shuffled thought the pages.

'I'll launch in then.' He said, and he did.

'I know you have spoken with the Sergeant about the discovery of Professor Layton's body and we may have a few more questions relating to that, but I am here to ask some more general questions about the Professor and the run up to the unfortunate events.' This all sounded like something he had learned by heart. 'So, first and foremost I need to clarify your whereabouts on the night of the events in question, a matter of elimination, I am sure you understand.' Staverley got the sense that Barnaby was new to this. He had also been expecting to be asked this question.

'Well not a very satisfactory response I am afraid. I got home from work, from here, late afternoon and I did a couple of hours on my microprocessor, on a paper I am preparing for a conference. About seven I went out for a beer and I had fish pie in the Rising Sun in East Street, they might remember me, it was a bit quiet when I got there. Then I went to the cinema, the Regent – to see The Big Chill. Have you seen it?'

'I'm afraid I don't get to the cinema much, sir.'

'You should go, it's a good film.' Staverley said, but he didn't think the constable would go.

'Very good sir, and did you go alone, can anyone confirm your attendance?'

'Alone yes, sorry.' He did not quite know why he should be sorry. 'It was just me, it's a regular habit, solitary visits to the cinema. Again, like in the pub, I wasn't a particularly busy night, not many people there, so they might remember me at the ticket desk. But of course I might have bought the ticket, gone in and then left again by one of the side doors. So it wont help much if they do remember me, will it?' He really did not know why he said that, although he assumed that the police would quickly work it out for themselves.

'I can't do any better I am afraid. I left at the end of the film. I could run through the plot for you, but then I could have seen it at some other time, so that wouldn't help you, or me either, would it?' He was doing it again. 'Then I walked home, it was dark of course, very few people about, I didn't speak to anyone or see anyone I knew. I got home about 10.30 and went to bed, also on my own, and that's it'. The constable was scribbling away in his notebook. Staverley was answering questions he had not been asked.

'Thank you sir, all very clear.'

'But it doesn't add up to much of an alibi for me, does it?' Staverley said.

'Well, that remains to be seen, sir.' Barnaby gave Staverley a pitying look.

'Just one or two other things, if I may, about the run up to the Professor's visit.'

'Sure.'

'Were you involved in making the arrangements for the visit?'

'No I was not. But I knew where he was staying, when he was coming.'

'But you were party to the decision to invite the Professor to be...', he consulted his notes, 'external examiner'?'

'I was, in a rather non-committal way. He was not my suggestion but in the end I was not particularly opposed to him being invited. I would have preferred someone else, but I am not sure who that someone else might have been.'

'Right.' He scribbled again.

'But I understand that some of your colleagues were quite strongly opposed.'

Here it was, Staverley could now choose between a Lionel type response and a Duncan type response. It was not a real choice for him.

'There was some debate and differences of opinion, Professor Layton is not a very popular man with some people in our field as you may already have gathered, but it was the usual sort of university disagreements. We thrive on disagreeing, it's the basis of much of what we do here, it's the lifeblood of the academy.' Staverley thought he sounded ridiculous, but obfuscation seemed like a worthwhile tactic to deflect the constable.

'Some of your colleagues have suggested that things got a little heated, that emotions were running high?'

'It's all a matter of perception I suppose. People play games on these occasions, to get what they want, emotions can be a ploy, and sometimes that can work rather well, sometimes not. But some of my colleagues are not so good at reading the subtleties of committee tactics and get easily misled. Which is the point of course. It was all the usual mundane to-ing and fro-ing, a bit of posturing and then everyone going along with the majority view.'

'And no one took a very strong opposing position in all of this? There was no dissent.'

The constable asked. Dissent, interesting word Staverley thought.

'Not really, Archie Alleyn wasn't keen, Pauline Oriel-Hay was against I think, one or two others had doubts, like me. I can't remember everyone who spoke. It was not a memorable meeting.' Staverley was sure that some others, Duncan at least, would have recounted the meeting very differently, and would have remembered it very vividly. At least he could muddy the waters a bit. It then occurred to him that if Archie had had the intention of murdering Layton then he would not have also opposed his appointment. But then he might have wanted to be seen to oppose Layton, knowing that the appointment was likely to go through. Or he might have planned to kill him once the appointment was made – as the opportunity arose. Or it may have been a spur of the moment thing, something Layton said that provoked Archie. He was thinking about this as though he thought it possible that Archie had killed Layton, but he didn't think that, he knew he didn't, but if he thought about things as the police might, he could perhaps steer them in other directions.

'That is helpful, sir.' The constable's politeness was a little grating.

'One last question, you told Sergeant Mellmoth that you had never met the Professor, at least not before time you found him in his bath. Can you confirm that for me?'

'I can. I knew of him of course, everyone who works in the social sciences does, but his area and interests and methods are all very different from mine, and so I don't come across him directly in the normal course of things. I heard him speak once, but only as part of a large audience. To tell you the truth, I was intrigued by the prospect of seeing him in action first hand, and finding out whether he was the ogre that everybody says he was. But when it came to it, given the circumstances, I would have been much happier not to have encountered him at all, not given the condition he was. It was horrible, it really was. Not something I am going to forget, unfortunately.'

'I can imagine from what I have read, horrible.' The constable adopted a face of concern which looked as though he had learned it at police college. He then closed his notebook and tucked it away in his jacket pocket. He thanked

Staverley for his time and left. Staverley sat and wondered whether he had done the right thing, and whether he had said the right things. He was, he hoped just one of several people who could not provide themselves with an alibi for that evening and also that he had done enough to play down the idea of opposition to Layton's appointment. In the meantime he wanted to find out a little more about the people Duncan had talked about. Did they have alibi's he wondered? He turned back to tackle the various tasks accumulating on his desk.

CHAPTER SEVEN

Feudalism was alive and well, even in the relatively young and thrusting discipline of social sciences. Barons and lords, like Layton, and a rare Lady or two, exercised their feudal rights over the careers and lives of their villeins and vassals, occasional anointing chosen ones to join them, repelling upstarts and usurpers and when necessary exacting bloody revenge on those questioning their divine rights. All of this begot fear and loathing and apparently vendettas and blood feuds. Staverley pondered how he came to be where he was in all of this cut and thrust – with a permanent post in a relatively respectable, if relatively new, university – beholden to no one, apart from Archie perhaps. He had never once crossed paths, or swords with Layton; he had never had to bend the knee to him or any of his courtiers. Perhaps that was down to his topic – tourism, a field of research considered unworthy of serious consideration by many in the social sciences. But that lack of seriousness, combined with a sense of quaint originality, enabled him to make his way fairly unobserved and unattended to by the social scientific establishment, which was fine with him. Operating in an unfashionable backwater had its advantages. Nonetheless, there was a delicate and sometimes painfully fine line between not being noticed and making your mark, between not being bothered and getting on, although Staverley was never quite sure that he wanted to get on, but that was perhaps another of his many character failings. Some days he felt ambition throbbing through his two finger typing on others he just wanted to do something useful and make the world a better place – naïve or what?.

Archie's confessions and the encounter with Duncan had provided Staverley with much food for thought. He felt certain that he wanted follow up in some way on the possibilities that Duncan had raised and the misunderstanding left by the police's failure to question Archie about his movements at the Hotel – and therefore who the mystery visitor might be. It would also be worth talking to Layton's daughter he thought, she might be able to add further to the list of

Layton's enemies. There was no shortage of potential murderers out there in the nether regions of higher education. Such were the meanderings of Staverley's ruminations while the undergraduate exam board stumbled tediously on. He tried to pay attention.

'Now perhaps we can review the 2.2/3rd class borderline and consider those cases which currently fall just outside of the required marks. Would anyone like to make a case for reconsidering the classifications for Ms. Westby or Mr. Blundell – yes Dr. Dupin.'

Staverley knew that he should be attending more closely to the niceties of the degree class borders, and to social class injustices attendant upon them. But in the current circumstances the long term implications of a third as opposed to a lower second was relatively unimportant over and against the issue of Layton's death and its many implications, both what it might mean for British social science and its practitioners and more immediately for Archie's future. One set of futures over and against another set. Staverley could imagine both celebration and mourning in different factions and institutions, not so much the king is dead, long live the king, rather hail the republic, an uncertain future with new opportunities and possibilities. The status quo was up for grabs.

'Dr. Staverley one of your personal tutees I see, any views here?'

Oh God, views on what? He shuffled his papers hurriedly and a subtle finger from Pauline sitting next to him identified Fiona Christie.

'Yes Chair, Fiona is a good student, solid and competent, not outstanding but well worthy of a 2.2, let down by poor marks in one course – social statistics, which…'

Which what he thought, Fiona Christie was a blurry figure who had been in one of his seminars and who he had met with twice as her tutor. He extemporised.

'Which coincided with personal difficulties and a family illness, I believe, I think we have something on record.' Or was it another student entirely he was thinking of. Was Fiona the one who wore the Che Guevara beret or the one who always wore corduroy Dungarees? There was a general scrabbling through papers around the table.

'I can see nothing here but if you are sure.'

Staverley wasn't sure but had also struggled with statistics as an undergraduate and had been supported, there might be a better word, by a friendly maths student, with whom he had also shared a chilly, desperate and rather dispiriting term in a bed and breakfast arranged for them for the University when all the live-in accommodation proved to be filled. Debts needed to be honoured.

'I would hope that we could consider Fiona's overall profile of performance and her steady progress and improvement and,' he was getting into his stride now, 'see her as a serious 2.2 student who has made the most of her undergraduate opportunities despite difficulties at home.' He thought she might be the redhead who always wore a full-length denim skirt and work boots and lisped. There was a murmur of support and some vague harrumphing around the table, a nod or two, and 'I think we are in agreement then, Fiona Christie, a 2.2,' from the Chair. Staverley could return to his reverie, Layton's death and the future of the social sciences, but he did reorganise his papers to find the right page, just in case there was another Fiona on the agenda.

Why look a gift death in the mouth? Archie sat across the committee room apparently firmly focused on the business at hand. He was an aficionado of exam broads, an eager devotee of the tricky case, the deserving underperformer and the tragic star student, talented but flawed. He rarely missed an opportunity to explore mitigating circumstances, unfair treatment and psychological quirks that led to exam failure or essay paralysis but this morning he was quiet. Not surprising really he had much to worry about and the possibility of a knock on his door by the police at any moment.

'Dr. Staverley, Eric Scudder?' Not again, Eric who? Grubby parka and red jumper full of holes? 'Yes, Chair, can I draw you attention....'

The Board as usual lasted what seemed like forever, but the displays of feigned exasperation and intellectual posturing that sometimes came into play as potentially failing students were subject to scrutiny did not materialise. That meant that Staverley did not lose entirely the will to live and felt his own students had been fairly done by. Throughout it all Archie continued to remain silent, appeared to be totally mesmerised by the papers in front of him, merely nodding occasionally to signal agreement. During the break for coffee he quickly disappeared and returned a moment or two after proceedings recommenced. Staverley could not find an opportunity to catch his eye and as the meeting ended Archie was gone before Staverley could circumnavigate the large table and discarded chairs.

During his musings in the exam board Staverley had realised that everything he knew about Layton was either via general academic gossip – academics loved to gossip - or anecdotes of various kinds, of which there were many, although these tended towards hyperbole and fulmination rather than information. Layton emerged from these accounts like a character rather than a personality, but perhaps that's all he was, a thin man, an ego, a political animal with little human substance. Staverley was, he realised, beginning to think about Layton as a research problem, and data was needed, multiple perspectives, triangulated accounts, to bring Layton back to life as someone real rather than a mythical figure of folktales and fables. At the same time Staverley knew that making sense of Alan Layton's life and death, was not what he should be doing with his time. He had assignments to mark, a paper to finish writing, another to revise in response to some rather stern and challenging reviewer comments, a research proposal to draft, yet more committee papers to read for the Humanities and Social Sciences Planning Group on which he sat as department rep, and a trip to organize to a conference in Copenhagen at which he was presenting, chapters from two PhD students to work on and a pile of unanswered post that would probably generate even more things to be done. Evenso Layton and his death had become more pressing and more real and important than arcane academic disputes about the interpretation of key concepts in research papers. He decided he would do what he could to keep his own work going but also find time to work on the Layton problem. Perhaps he owed that to Archie and himself, he had no alibi after all. His talk with Duncan presented three obvious places to begin – Connelly, Rawlins and the daughter, but he could not imagine why any of them would be willing to speak with him nor how he might convince them to. If this was actually a piece of research then ethics would have to be considered - good practice, transparency, informed consent – but the more Staveley thought about it the only way forward seemed to be to lie. Who would write the inevitable flood of obituaries and tributes he wondered? Maybe that would be the way in? He might present himself as someone writing an obituary. In fact he was involved slightly with a small group of younger academics who were discussing launching a new research journal as an alternative to the established ones that might be a starting point. But first he needed to find Connelly, Rawlins and the daughter, and to find more background material on Layton. An hour in the library turned up plenty of stuff on Layton's career and the name of his daughter – Monica.

There was a lot of material on Layton from newspapers, the journals and a sycophantic biographical sketch in *B.Jass* to mark his retirement. From all of this, and some with imaginative reading between the lines Staveley gathered that after Oxford Layton had been appointed to establish the first inter-disciplinary department of social science at a large northern university. This had been the base for his academic empire for the next twenty years. This was just after the Second World War and while establishing himself in the forefront of the discipline, Layton had written a series of dull analytical commentaries on the social consequences of Britain's post-war economic and technological development. Then in the late 1950s he had been seconded to the Ministry of Labour as a researcher and adviser and became identified with a series of government measures which made him deeply unpopular with the Trade Unions. He garnered his first royal honour for services to government and re-entered academic life with a well established network of friends and contacts among the politically powerful and socially influential and continued to spent as much of his time heading or advising key policy committees, ministerial think tanks and royal commissions as he did on university based work. Nonetheless, he found time to write his definitive social Sciences textbook, *The Elements of Social Sciences*, and to found the *B.Jass*. In 1968 he was knighted and moved to a Fellowship at Judas College, Cambridge. He had formally retired two years previously but was no less active in the discipline and elsewhere than before. If anything, freed of his administrative responsibilities, his influence in the academic field of Applied Social Sciences became even more overbearing. He continued to maintain his hold over the key positions – both human and intellectual – although the recent import of ideas from Europe and the US were beginning to establish a foothold in the various nooks and crannies of academia into which Layton's pernicious influence did not carry.

During the late fifties and early sixties Layton fostered and shepherded the development of social sciences nationally. With the expansion of higher education new departments were set up in new universities. He was frequently called in to advise on senior appointments and in many cases was able to place his own ex-students as Heads of Department. To be a Layton graduate in the 1960s was invariably a route to academic success. Lionel Lewis had certainly found this to be the case. He had worked with Layton for a time at Judas College. Layton graduates were also liberally scattered in key positions in politics and journalism. But apart from the opportunities it offered for imperial expansion Layton did not find the 1960s a conducive decade. He was totally opposed to the liberalisation and expansion of Higher education, he spoke out forcefully against the anti-Viet Nam war movement and anti-authority student politics, and was intellectually ill at ease with the resurgence of various forms of Marxist scholarship and even more so the emergence of feminist perspectives in many areas of research. He worked hard to exclude all such work from the *B.Jass*. In 1969 he sat on a committee of inquiry into the student sit-ins at the LSE and in a minority report he identified a cell of Trotskyite academics as the root cause of the troubles.

In retirement he updated his textbook, for the seventh time, to include a stringent and vituperative critique of all the competing texts. In doing so he made enemies of several of his own students. He continued to oversee the daily business of the *B.Jass*, seemingly vetting every paper with the aid of a coterie of eager graduate students and young lecturers who slavishly reproduced his version of social sciences through their own work and thus sought to make their way up the slippery slope and have a career in his wake. In 1978 Layton published a highly regarded research study called *The Progressive Effects of Industrial Development* which argued, using many tables and graphs, that we were all made healthier, wealthier and generally better people by the positive effects of the multinational corporation on daily life, our social relations and the planet in general. The book was described by one brave and foolhardy reviewer, obvious not in Layton's journal, as 'an apologia for capital'. That was Rawlins. The review produced a long detailed response from Layton accusing the reviewer of 'a politically motivated attack based on misplaced ideology and rank ignorance'. The book effectively re-launched Layton as a public personality. He gave a series of Reith Lectures on the radio, was involved in a television documentary series on *The Face of Industrial Britain*, he regularly appeared alongside politicians on tedious question and discussion programmes and became a regular contributor to 'election special' broadcasts, in which he was encouraged to pontificate on the consequences of voting patterns for the state of the nation and the economy. All of that rounded out the things Staverley already knew about Layton from general gossip, and he hoped it would prove helpful background to his conversations with Connelly and Rawlins and the daughter should he manage to have them.

Rawlins and the daughter proved relatively easy to track down. Duncan's mention of science led him to the appropriate citation index and there she was – two published papers on lithium-ions, whatever they were, and her institutional affiliation, Fisher College, Cambridge where she was a Research Fellow attached to a lab doing inorganic chemistry research. He did not know what that was either. He would ask. Staverley already knew that Rawlins worked at East Battersea Polytechnic and the library held a brochure detailing courses with the relevant addresses and telephone numbers. Quick calls to the College and the Poly provided direct line numbers for both the daughter and Rawlins. So far so good. Connelly was more of a challenge. Four calls to the University of Poppleton enabled Staverley to identify Connolly's erstwhile PhD supervisor as a Dr. Ian McBride and Dr. McBride was in his office when Staverley called.
'McBride.'
'Good morning, my name is Staverely, I don't think we've met but I heard you speak at a seminar a couple of years ago.' The first lie.
'Oh, where was that?' This is where good preparation proved its value.

'It was at Foxe College, Oxford I think, a roundtable on the problem of translating theory from French to English.'

'Oh yes, I remember'. That was reassuring. 'What can I do for you?'

Now for some more lies. 'I am involved with a small group trying to launch a new social science journal, something that has a greater interest in theoretical issues than the existing ones – and maybe you might want to get involved at some point - but for the moment I had a particular question. We are intending to have an editorial in the first issue that looks at the way theory has been received, or rather perhaps not received in British social science. And, well, the treatment of your research student Connelly keeps coming up as a key moment....'

There was silence at the other end of the line. McBride said nothing.

'I was wondering whether you could put me in touch with Mr. Connelly.'

The silence continued, Staverley decided to wait.

'Not my finest moment,' McBride said at last, 'and very painful even now, for me, and even more so for Ian, Connelly. I am not sure he would want to talk about it.'

Staverely was thinking as quickly as he could. Serial lies were a new area of expertise for him and he was not sure he had the right skill set. He pressed on.

'I can understand that, but given Layton's death, you must know about that, perhaps Connelly would want to say something. Could you at least give him the option of saying yes or no himself?'

McBride was obviously also thinking.

'I can see what you are saying, but I have no idea if Ian wants to revisit all that happened.'

'Could you ask?' Staverley said.

Another silence.

'Alright, I'll ask, let's see what he says. Give me your number.'

Less than an hour later McBride phoned back.

'Ian says yes, indeed he says he would be pleased to talk to you, I can't think why but there you go. He said I should give you his number, OK?'

'Thank you, that's brilliant.'

Rawlins was not so easy to pin down. Staverley phone six times before he got an answer at the extension he had been given. The teaching commitments in

Polytechnics were heavier than in Universities and Rawlins probably had little time to spend in his office, if he had an office. As it turned out he did have one but he shared it with two colleagues and after a quick exchange he suggested that Staverely phone him at home that night, which he did.

'Dr. Rawlins, its Staverley, we spoke earlier.'
'Yes, ok, I didn't really grasp what it was you wanted.' Rawlins responded.
'Well, I want to come and talk to you.'
'Me, why? About what?'
Staverley launched in with a new set of lies.
'Well to be direct, about Alan Layton.'
Rawlins made a noise that was half laugh half sigh.
'You must have read about his death.'
'Of course', Rawlins said, 'It brightened up my day no end, my whole year in fact. But why do you want to talk to me about Layton and why should I talk to you, he is not my favourite subject, as it seems you know.'
'I do know, and that is exactly why I want to talk to you. I am working on an editorial for the first issue of a new social science journal and its going to focus on Layton's death as a turning point in the discipline. It will be a kind of anti-obituary, not a tribute but an account of the man's stultifying influence on the development of the social sciences. It will be controversial and wont go down well with Layton's acolytes but we feel that something honest has to be said over and against what are likely to be a lot of sycophantic drivel in the mainstream obituaries'. Staverley hoped he was getting to tone right, something that would appeal to Rawlins, but perhaps he was overdoing it. He went on.
'We want to elicit some other voices, critical dissenting voices. We want to bury Layton not to praise him.' That was a nice touch. He hoped all of this would appeal to Rawlins need for redress. There was another one of those long silences.

'I might be willing to be a voice but I don't know that I want to be quoted. Layton and his cronies have caused me enough difficulty already, I don't want to lose another job. He may be dead, thank God, but his influence wont go away that easily. There are too many vested interests, people he helped get on or whose research he got funded or published, or both. Dead or alive his inheritance is going to last and if you publish along the lines you say I wouldn't give good odds that your journal will survive the backlash. There will be people making their careers on Layton's coattails for years to come. I am a humble Poly lecturer, it may not be what I had envisaged but I am good at my job and some days I actually enjoy it. I don't want to jeopardise that, I can't start again. Can you understand?'

'I can,' said Staverley, 'of course I can'. He decided to take a risk.

'Perhaps I should not have phoned and I should let you get on with your evening?'

'Perhaps, but if there is anything I can do that might harm Layton's reputation or undermine his legacy, without harming myself, I would be willing.' Rawlins responded.

Staverley had an idea.

'Did you read *All the President's Men*? Or see the film?'

'Both as it happens, both good. And they got their men.'

'Well you will remember that Bernstein and Woodward were always trying to ensure that their stories were confirmed, cross-checked, but without divulging their sources. And they had their secret informant, deep throat. You could be like that. What do journalists say, anything you care to say will be off the record.' Staverley was pleased with himself. He had also liked the book and the film.

Yet another silence and Rawlins then spoke again.

'On that basis I could talk to you about my experience of Layton, can you come up and see me?'

Staverley arranged a time to meet with Rawlins and mulled over the phone call. Rawlins did not sound like a murderer. He was clear about being pleased that Layton was dead, who wouldn't be in his position, but that was no basis to suspect him of killing Layton. And if he had why would he be willing to speak to Staverley. Unless is was less suspicious to agree than not to. What does a murderer sound like anyway? But any speculation begged the question of how Staverley was going to get a clear sense of where Rawlins was and what he was doing at the time of the murder, if he wasn't committing the murder. Presumably that would be something the police would do, if they decided to interview Rawlins. That might be a way to ask. Did the police speak to you? Did that go well? Anyway he had time to plan his strategy. He had two more calls to make. He decided to tackle the daughter, Monica next.

Three calls this time before anyone picked up.

'Monica Sayers.'

Not Layton then, Staverley thought. Maybe she was married, the newspapers did not say.

'Erh. Yes. My name is Staverley. Lionel Lewis suggested I speak with you.' This is another lie and perhaps not a very sensible one, she could check. 'He's my Head of Department.'

'Oh, how is the Lion?'

'What, sorry?' Said Staverley.

She laughed 'Never mind, what do you want?'

Staverley decided on directness again.

'I want to talk to you about your Father.'

Monica was direct in return.

'No sorry! I have no interest in talking to you or anyone else about my Father, in fact I have no interest in my Father full stop.'

Staverley was disappointed and flummoxed. He had to come up with a different approach.

'Not even if I were to buy you dinner?'

Monica laughed, which could be a good thing he thought. He was not quite sure why he asked. He liked her voice and her candour but boldness with women was not his forte.

'No, not even for a dinner, sorry.'

'An expensive dinner with lively conversation?' Staverley countered.

'Not even that.' She said.

' What could I offer to tempt you?'

She laughed again.

'Look, the banter is fun, but I do not want to talk about my Father to you or to anyone, under any circumstances and certainly not in exchange for dinner.'

Staverley had one more try. As he spoke he winced and held his breath. Not easy to do at the same time.

'What if I buy you dinner but we don't talk about your Father. In fact we studiously avoid any mention of your Father and talk about other things.'

She laughed again. 'Look I don't even know you,' she paused 'but you sound oddly interesting, and I have been virtually locked in my lab for the past two weeks. I don't usually go on dates with strangers who phone me out of the blue but I will meet you at The Green Gallant here in Cambridge at 8.00 tomorrow evening. It's easy to find. This is a one-time offer and I am probably making a big mistake, but if you turn up we shall see. If you look dangerous I will run away.'

She had shifted from reluctant to decisive in one move. It was Staverley's turn to laugh.

'I will be there. How do I recognize you?'

'That's your problem.' And she hung up.

Well that was progress. Or was it? He had just agreed not to talk about Layton. How was not talking about Layton going to be of help? But Monica sounded very likeable. He had a date with an interesting woman, who though he might be interesting, that was progress of a kind. His social life could do with some care and attention. He would be there and hope for the best. He just needed to work on being interesting.

Two down, one to go. Connelly. Staverley phoned after six, as McBride had suggested when he had given him Connolly's home number.

'Hello.'

'My name is Staverley, Ian McBride spoke to you about me.'

'He did indeed.' Connolly said. 'He did indeed. You want to talk about the late and unlamented Alan Clayton – vile man.'

'Exactly.'

'I have been reading about his death in the papers, or his murder should I say. A fitting end to a despicable life in my view and I can imagine that there might be quite a long list of potential suspects given Layton's history with people like me. I might had done it myself if things had turned out differently.'

Staverley had not expected to get into things so directly on the phone, but why not, Connolly was willing to talk.

'What do you mean?' He asked.

'Well, in a round about way Layton did me a favour. When I had finished writing my PhD, before it was examined, I was already applying for jobs in Universities and Colleges, as junior lecturer or researcher, whatever I could find, but the more I thought about what that would involve the less it seemed to be the future I wanted. I enjoyed doing the PhD, reading all those French theorists, but I had said what I wanted to say. I had got out of it intellectually what I wanted and I did not really see myself talking about those things to young people most of whom would probably not be interested, for the next forty years. And doing the PhD gave me some insight into life and work in universities and the more I learned the less it appealed. Too much in fighting. Too much sitting in over lit rooms talking about things of little or no importance. Too much self-agrandising. I might have gone on anyway, if I had found a job, but that would have been inertia rather than enthusiasm, my encounter with the formidable Sir Alan made inertia impossible and over time I have come to see that as a good thing and my life has turned out rather well in fact, different but good. I was devastated initially of course and fought the outcome with Ian's support – he was great by the way. He blamed himself in part but I was the idiot who wanted Layton as an examiner, Ian was never convinced and he was right of course. So I had to think my life differently and a friend of the family offered me a job working for a pharmaceutical company here in Leicester and it's worked out well for me. I am head of the Sales Department, good salary, good prospects, and I met my wife while working here and we have a nice house and two much loved, if unruly and noisy children. In a nutshell and somewhat to my own surprise I am happy.'

Staverley's ears pricked up at the mention of pharmaceuticals given the nature of the murder, and the murder weapon, but in all other respects Connolly did not sound like someone likely to have committed a murder – not enough hate and too much to lose. Or was it all a very clever story, misdirection, playacting?

'Its good to hear that, when you name gets mentioned in relation to Layton, and its still does on occasions by the way, people talk about your career being destroyed and your struggles to cope with the consequences of the exam, but maybe that's all it is, talk.' Staverley was trying to probe.

'Whatever people may think, and I don't deny it was a shock at the time, my life has turned out well as I said, despite Layton's best efforts. I suppose in some way I still hate the man and I did struggle to come to terms with the outcome, I had put four years of my life into the PhD. I had lived and breathed it during all that time like most PhD students. It consumed my thoughts awake and asleep. But I meant it when I said I got what I wanted from it, even if I didn't get a PhD. I even thought for a while of trying to turn the thesis into a book. I could have done that independently. But once I got the job here and met Beth, my wife, all of that became less and less important and the rawness was healed or at least dulled. Dwelling on the past didn't seem to be worth the effort. Beth and the kids are what are important to me. In recently years I have hardly thought about Layton, I have seen reports in the papers and that always stirs up a bit of ire and wrath but cleaning the car or mowing the lawn usually deals with that. I will never forgive and forget or anything like that, and I certainly won't deny that I think the social sciences will be better off without him, and I would even go as far as shaking the hand of the culprit but I won't waste my time bemoaning my experience of him. I am just pleased I never had to deal with him again after the fateful viva day.'

This was sounding more and more like Connelly was an unlikely suspect, but Staverley was not going to take all of this at face value.

'When did you hear that he had been murdered?' He asked.

'I was at a sales conference in Scotland, I heard in on the news the next day. I will admit that I treated myself to a very expensive malt and raised a glass to his passing with my colleagues.'

Colleagues, that seemed to clinch it, an easily checked alibi a long way from the scene of the crime.

'You have been very helpful Mr Connelly, what you have said adds something important to my understanding of Layton.' If asked Staverley was not sure what that understanding would be, but Connelly's story confirmed all of the worst things he had heard about Layton. And he was pleased, if it was true, that Connelly had not been destroyed and had found a life that made him happy.

'Do you know anything more about the investigation than reported in the press?' Connelly asked, Staverley did but he was not going to say.

'No sorry just what the newspapers say and a few groundless rumours.'

He was now unsure how to finish the conversation. Connelly did not seem anxious to get off the phone.

'I did not explain.' Staverley explained. 'I am trying to write something about Layton's untoward leadership of the social sciences in this country, something that is not like a traditional obituary, something more political or micropolitical.' He was getting good at these lies. 'If I have any more questions could I come back to you?'

'You could do that, yes that would be okay. And perhaps when you have written your piece you could send me a copy?' Connelly asked.

I certainly would Staverley thought, if such a thing actually existed.

'Happy to do that Mr Connelly, and thank you again.'

'Jim.'

'Jim, thank you for your time.'

So it looked like one of Duncan's suspicious characters was off the list and Staverley was still not convinced that Rawlins was likely to be involved either but as yet there was the question of an alibi in his case. What did they say in detective stories – motive, means and opportunity. Rawlins had a motive, means were unclear as yet, Connelly might have had means given he worked with pharmaceuticals, Staverley wondered if his company made soaps, he might check. Did Rawlins have opportunity? Well he was going to talk to him but Staverley had another idea. He wondered if Rawlins had a car. But first there was Dr Sayers, Monica. What was he going to say to her? How was he going to spend an evening with her and not talk about her father, or rather get her to talk about her father? He began to make a mental list of possible ploys and stratagems.

CHAPTER EIGHT

In the restaurant Monica was easy to spot. A. She was the most attractive woman
in the room – have you noticed how often that happens in books. B. Staverley had
found a picture of her in the library, although in real life she looked even better
than in the picture. Stunning in fact. Somewhat to his surprise she was wearing a
very fashionable suit, checks, double breasted, big shoulders, big lapels, with a
high neck burgundy blouse, but he noted with relief no Farah Fawcett style big
hair. He did not get big hair, all that back-combing must be exhausting. Staverley
had embarrassed himself on the train to Cambridge as he began to wonder how
womanly or not a woman scientist might be. Pauline would have strangled him,
slowly and painfully if she had known. As it turned out Monica was extremely
womanly, in every sense. He had also decided to wear his suit, his only suit – a
recent purchase about which he was rather pleased – also checks, doubled-
breasted, big shoulders, big lapels and in his case big braces. Very different from
the usual denim he wore to work. They had both taken care obviously.

She was sitting at the small bar in the restaurant foyer looking very much at ease,
chatting with the barman. He was glad he had visited the bank before setting off.
He had promised an expensive dinner and this place looked expensive. The
Carpenters were playing quietly over loudspeakers in the background.
'Dr Sayers? Staverley.' He said.
'Monica.' She said, waited for his response in kind and offered her hand to shake.
'Staverley.' He repeated and she gave in a quizzical look.
'Staverley it is – a drink?'
'A whisky perhaps, no ice.' He sat on the bar stool next to her and nodded toward
the hovering barman. All very sophisticated. When the drink came he asked for
his and hers, she was already drinking what looked like a large gin and tonic, to
be charged to their table.
'So what are we going to talk about?' She asked.
He decided to pursue his recent luck with directness. 'I've made a list. We can
start with childhoods, your privileges against my deprivations, then schools,

your brilliant successes in contrast to my travails, then what's its like working in Universities, we compare your old and revered institution with my brash newcomer, then we get on to what is like being a woman in the man's world of the natural sciences, then football, then why your surname is Sayers and not Layton and we see where we go from there.'

She laughed. He liked her laugh.

'The childhood bit is a little tricky, childhoods tend to involve mothers and fathers and we are not talking about fathers if you remember, so we may have to not do that or do an edited version. Schooling might be manageable but also has some dangerous topics to be avoided but the rest seems okay. I can even do some football, but not much, I did go to see Cambridge United play with a colleague from work, I have to say it was not one of the most fun filled afternoons of my life. And being a woman in the sciences would need more than one dinner and a lot more drink. So given all that, your childhood first please, with an appropriate mix of pathos and witty anecdotes.'

Staverley sighed to himself. He did not like talking about himself but maybe if he showed her his she might show him some of hers. That would only be fair.

'Let's go to the table and I will try to amuse and move you.'

They were shown to a corner table and there were few other diners, about right for an exchange of confidences.

'My childhood was mostly mother only, no father to talk about. He died when I was three. He was wounded in the war and never really recovered. So I don't remember much about him. Only what my mother told me. I have a very vague sense of him being in bed a lot and having nurses visit the house but who knows if that's real or not.'

'I am sorry.' Monica said and touched his arm. Staverley noted the very pleasant sensation that continued the play on his skin well after her fingers had retreated.

'My mother was, is, a good woman and I love her to bits. She worked hard to make up for the absence of my father and was ambitious for me, very supportive of me at school, very strict about homework, that sort of thing. I remember she taught me to read from Janet and John books before I got to go to nursery and used Amami wave set on my hair, which is something I had never previously divulged to a soul. But it was tough for her as a single mum, having to work full-time and look after me. She worked as a shop assistant, for Timothy White's for a long time. It was secure but not well paid, and long hours. All the standing affected her as she got older and now she suffers a lot with knee and back problems. But we managed. We always had food on the table. She always dressed me respectably for school - being respectable was very important to her, she worked hard at it. It came ahead of almost everything else.'

Staverley looked carefully at Monica for signs of boredom but she looked entirely engaged by his story. She smiled at him encouragingly.

'I don't know how my mother coped financially but she did have some kind of pension from the War Office. She didn't have much of a social life though, apart from her sisters, who were very much in evidence. She had a lot of sisters, I have a lot of aunts. And they were supportive in all sorts of ways. There were lots of family events, Sunday teas, Christmases, birthdays. Grandma's house was a regular gathering place for the whole family and I think things like that kept her going. My uncles would take me to football on a Saturday afternoon. But all in all it was a bit of a non-event my childhood – bland and minimalist, of necessity really. But it was okay. I did alright at school. I played football, not well but good enough to be a regular in school teams. I have a chipped tooth and several scars that bear witness to that. I had some good friends – Colin Campbell and Adele Irving were my best friends. I read a lot, books and comics – *The Victor* was my favourite – I particularly liked Ted Tupper the Tough of the Track, he always outwitted his posh rivals. When it was cold or wet the local public library was a favourite haunt and one of my aunts bought me a bike for Christmas one year and I rode it everywhere and was sometimes gone all day, especially in the summer. My mother would leave me sandwiches for my lunch and there was no reason to be at home. I ranged far and wide on that bike. Adele Irving's older brother used to take her and I to the pictures sometimes and also I went to Saturday morning pictures as often as I could – cartoons, shorts and a main feature and free ice-cream on your birthday - so I developed a love of cinema, as I learned to call it later. I still go a lot but not on Saturday mornings. Did you go to Saturday morning pictures?' He asked.

Monica shook her head and seemed to be waiting for him to go on.

There's not much in the way of funny stories in my childhood. I did fall off a slide in a playground once and broke both my arms – that made life a little difficult for a while, and you can probably imagine the funny bits for yourself. As I got older I got interested in girls, as you do, and sometimes they got interested in me, but I wasn't particularly good at girls, too many over active hormones and unrealistic expectations I think. Any funny stories there would be much too embarrassing to share. That's about it really and how I got from there to here is a bit long and convoluted and distinctly lacking in human interest.'

The waiter arrived and they broke off the exchange to order. The restaurant specialized in steaks, different cuts and different sauces, served with rice – interestingly different. Staverley decided to keep his incipient vegetarianism to himself and indulge for once, and feel guilty later. They settled on sharing pate and melba toast to start – Staverley was not entirely sure what melba toast was – a steak a piece and a bottle of wine. Monica did the wine choosing, and clearly knew what she was doing, which was to be explained later, and she did check with him about price before ordering a Nuits St George. Even so she was clearly taking the offer of an expensive meal very seriously. Did she always eat and drink like this he wondered. Anyway he had promised and he was enjoying the experience. The waiter brought the wine and Monica went through the ritual of checking the label and having a sip. She and the waiter exchanged pleasantries and he poured. It was rich and warm and ridiculously chewy. Staverley had not tasted anything quite like it, it was without doubt the best wine he had ever had. 'This will be the first decent meal I have had in weeks, and I don't normally eat like this or dress like this'. Monica said – which answered Staverley's question. 'It's been non-stop at the lab with a big experiment running and I am fed up with wearing my grubby lab coat.'
'Can I ask what it is, the experiment, and what you do?'
'Ah. Thrilling stuff. It involves testing various lithium nickel manganese cobalt oxide combinations for possible use in rechargeable batteries, we are trying to balance safety with high energy density. I am a minion really but I do a lot of the basic efficiency analyses.'

'To be honest I am not sure I grasp any of that, but it sounds impressive and important.'

Monica grinned. 'Don't worry, I am not sure I always understand what we are doing or why. I'll explain it better another time if that's OK. I was hoping to forget about work for one evening.'

Staverley noted the 'another time' and filed it away for further thought. 'No problem, lets get back to getting to know one another – and the topic is school and family, and its your turn.'

Monica took a big gulp of her wine and cleared her throat.

'Just to say, I don't usually do this and I am not sure I know why I am doing it now, and I may regret it, but in the spirit of adventure...' She shrugged her padded shoulders. 'I guess I have to admit that my childhood was pretty privileged, compared to yours, at least in material ways. My mother was French, her family were glass makers, literally, they made glasses, there were several big factories and they were very well off. She came to England to improve her English and met my father, of whom we shall not speak, at some social event at the university, she was almost 20 years younger than him. They married when she was only 18, much too young I think, and she was unhappy with England, and soon she was unhappy full stop. She missed her family, which is huge by the way, and she was very quickly, very unhappy with my Father, although when I was young he was not much in evidence. He was busy making his mark and building a career. He was cold and calculating at work and at home and there were rows, lots of rows, very noisy and very frequent, I used to hate to hear them shouting at one another, and my mother's tears afterwards, but the rows were an ever present part of my growing up. I never really understood what she saw in him in the first place, why on earth she married him. I wish I could ask her.'

Monica paused and looked down at her plate and took a few moments to pile her fork with rice.

'He seems to have insinuated himself into my story hasn't he. Anyway, my mother and I were very close. She was lovely. I adored her. She taught me French, she taught me to cook, and she sang to me – she had had lessons in France and used to sing in a choir there. And she used to take me out on strange outings to odd places, which I loved. "Trying to make sense of England" she used to say. She had her own car and we drove far and wide in search of the weird and the wonderful. But I was young and I never fully realized then how depressed she had become or how much my father suppressed her spirit, he drained the joy out of her life. She was not the kind of career supportive wife that he wanted. I think he believed being young and a little innocent he could mold her into the wife he thought would be appropriate for his lifestyle and his ambitions. But she wasn't, she wanted a life of her own, her own interests and friends and opportunities and he made all of that impossible or at least very difficult. For a while though towards the end of my time in primary school – my mother as a good republican made sure that I attended the local school, despite my father's opposition – she was different, more light hearted, more comfortable, there was less sadness in her eyes. But it didn't last and when I was ten she committed suicide, she drowned herself in a river near to our house.' Monica put a hand over her eyes.

'I am so sorry Monica, that's just so awful. I shouldn't have made you do this. I had no idea. Please forgive me.' He felt really terrible.

Monica shook her head. 'No, don't feel bad, really. Despite what I said before I actually like to talk about her, at least that way I can keep remembering her, the way he eyes shone when she was happy, the way she moved and the way she smelled. Sometimes in the afternoons after our outings we would fall asleep together on her bed, me in her arms and I used to breath her in. I wanted to be like her, to be her, when I grew up. I never properly understood how bad things were for her though and what a short time I would have with her. When she died I was angry with her. Angry because she had left me, abandoned me and even more angry with my father for causing her death, at least that's how I saw it. And after her death my father never talked about her, never mentioned her really and there was no other family in England to explain things to me or to offer consolation. I became a morose and lonely child. The only moments of warm and kindness came from the Lion – Lionel.'

Now Staverley was totally mystified. She had mentioned the Lion on the telephone.

'Oddly in my teens my one solace was science. I liked its clarity and order but I also came to appreciate that in many ways the scientists who inhabited that order did not fully understand it, that the more science knows the more unknowns there are. The combination of order and adventure is what attracted me, does that make any sense?'

'Actually yes it does.' Staverley responded. 'But I have to ask, the Lion, Lionel? Is that Lionel Lewis? I had no idea that you knew him except in passing as one of your father's students. In terms of my relationship of him as a Head of Department and a colleague the idea of him as a warm and kind Lion seems a little far-fetched.'

Monica grimaced. 'Now we are getting into more difficult territory. Why do you want to know this? I am still not entirely clear why you are talking to me at all and why I am talking to you. I should have asked before we started.'

'More than anything, I want to know you.' Staverley said, and that was partly true, even mainly true, but he was also very aware that he was asking these questions for other reasons. He had wanted to know more about Layton and about his daughter and their relationship and Layton's history. But he was also beginning to realise that the more that Monica said about her life and her work and her relationship with her father that she was adding herself to his list of suspects. That was not good, it was not what he expected or wanted, things were not going as he intended – in both good and bad ways. He had hoped to convince Monica to explain to him what made Layton tick, and perhaps who she thought might have wanted him dead, even if there was no shortage of candidates already she might know of some more personal motives. He had not anticipated that she would make herself a candidate and he had not expected to like her, and he was very aware that after just an hour together, he liked her a lot. He could still feel the warm spot on his arm where she had touched him and he urgently wanted to touch her too. He gave her fingers a friendly squeeze of reassurance across the table and they exchanged a smile. He reluctantly, very reluctantly, withdrew his hand. Maybe some more directness would be good at this point. It had worked well up to now.

'As I said to you on the phone, I wanted to talk about your father, I am trying to understand him better, but if I am to be honest, as of now I am a lot more interested in the man's daughter'. Was he being honest? 'But I am also intrigued by the Lion. Its just so unexpected, so incompatible with the Lionel I know.' Monica was silent and breathing deeply, he could see her thinking hard, and she took another mouthful of wine. She had, Staverley realised drunk a lot more than him and the bottle was almost empty. She took an even deeper breath, closed her eyes for a second, sat up a little straighter and started to speak again.

'The Lion arrived when I was about eight. He was my Father's post-doctoral student and general dogs body. He was often in the house, more often than my father sometimes. Father would send him on errands and to sort out domestic stuff, none of which had anything to do with his real work, but if father wanted something done...' She shrugged those big shoulders again. 'He also started to come with my mother and I on some of our outings and he and my mother would make up stories for me about the places we visited. They created a kind of fantasy England of knights and damsels in distress and hobgoblins and wicked barons. I loved it. And I was so happy to see my mother relaxed and light-hearted. The Lion was his name in the stories and it stuck. He was good for her.

At my mother's funeral Lionel was totally distraught much more so than my father, although he had moved on to a permanent job at another university before her suicide and the outings had come to an end. Evidently, so my father said, Lionel's behavior at the funeral was inappropriate, he was livid and Lionel never came to the house again. But he promised to write to me, and he did for years, and a few times a year, when my father was away somewhere, he would come to collect me and take me out. We would go on picnics or to the theatre and we would talk about my mother. And as he talked, and as I grew older I realised that there was more to their relationship than friend and helper and my mother's change of mood in the time before she died had much more to do with Lionel than I had thought. In retrospect I suspect they had an affair, and that that also had something to do with Lionel's abrupt departure and her suicide. But I have never been able to ask Lionel directly about that, it would seem like a betrayal of our time together, the three of us. And whatever else happened I am grateful that he made my mother happy even for a short time and for his support of me afterwards, for being the man my father should have been and never was. Lionel advised me about school and university and he convinced me to spend part my time as an undergraduate in Paris and catch up with my French relations. Both of which were very good for me. He even visited me there a couple of times and took me to hear Dexter Gordon play Jazz in a very disreputable basement club – that was great. He's really an aficionado of jazz, he's seen many of the jazz greats. I still talk with him on the phone, although we now meet less often. He is still my adviser and my guide. I couldn't do without him. He provides a kind of emotional centre I have never been able to find elsewhere. He is the kindness person I know. But I also know that he has probably never quite recovered from what happened to my mother.'

Staverley was trying hard to find a facial expression that would not show his total astonishment with what he was hearing. None of what Monica had said about Lionel made any sense to him. This was not the person he knew and did not like very much. If it was true then where did Lionel keep all of that warmth and kindness and his love of jazz, hidden away. And if this other Lionel existed then why was he so gruff and austere and unsympathetic and difficult with his colleague? And if he had had an affair with Monica's mother then what did that mean in terms of his relationship with Layton, then and now? Why would he countenance having him as an external examiner? Why was he so keen to have Layton come? That did not make sense, unless it made some very horrible sense. The conversation had gone off in a direction that Staverley could not have anticipated. He hoped for more suspects but not ones he knew and worked with. This was turning his research, if that is what he was doing, in a very different direction. And more than that he now found himself in an uncomfortable emotional hinterland somewhere between a person he thought he disliked but obviously knows nothing about, Lionel, and one who he now knew a lot about, Monica, and liked very much – both of whom he was now required to be suspicious of. He was also aware that neither he nor Monica had directly mentioned Layton's death, part of the promise of avoidance, but that was a topic that was now impossible to avoid. It loomed large.

'I know I have been rude and inquisitive Monica, and I have upset you, and I am really sorry, but can I ask about one other thing?'

'Given where we have got to why not, but I reserve the right, as they say.'

Staverley recognised that the wine may be playing its part here.

'It's your name, Sayers. Did you change it or is there a Mr. Sayers I should be wary of?'

That at least got her to smile again. 'There is no Mr. Sayers to be wary of.' She touched his hand again. The effect was the same very nice sensation and it made his whole arm tingle. 'I changed my name when I was in Paris, which is also where I learned about wine by the way, Sayers is a version of the name of my mother's family, it comes from the old French 'to cut', in the sense of someone who reaps or mows – just in case you were wondering. I could have just started using my mother's maiden name but that didn't seem right somehow. But the name change was part of the process of disassociating myself from my father, unpicking him from my life. I have not spoken with him face to face for over seven years, we communicate formally, when necessary, by letter. I hate him from afar. Actually I don't, I don't feel anything for him or about him. I worked hard as a teenager and a young woman to expunge him from my feelings. It was a sort of discipline, an emotional training – not to think about him, care about him, give him any importance in my life. I even stopped thinking about myself as his daughter, and going to Paris and meeting my mother's family helped me with that and changing my name was part of distancing myself from him, casting him off. It helped that my French relations also disliked him and distrusted him and blamed him for my mother's death and they were kind to me. I was able to grieve with them and learn more about my mother's life before the marriage. So, and this is going to sound really cold, and I hope it wont make you think badly of me, but when I heard he was dead I felt nothing but a sense of satisfaction or relief. It was like the end of a chapter in my life. I could at last relax, be myself, I no longer had to work hard at not being his daughter. In a way I was free to get on with my life as someone in my own right. I could just hate his memory and never have to have anything to do with him again. When I saw the news and when the police came it was like hearing about any public figure who died, just a name, nothing

to do with me. I think the officer who came was a little shocked by my reaction.'
Monica closed her eyes again and there was very long silence.

Monica was an extraordinary woman, Staverley felt he had learned so much
about her but that there was so much more to know, so much more to explore, a
bit like the way she had described science. He knew, whatever else happened,
that he wanted to know her better. He could sense some of the pain and torment
that had invested itself in her growing up and the strength of effort involved in
dealing with the things that had happened to her, but he could never fully grasp
it, it was beyond his own experience. It was both admirable and a little daunting.
He could see that the studied objectivity that is supposed to underpin the culture
of science would have its attractions to a young woman trying to manage her
emotions in such a deliberate way. She had in a sense reinvented herself and she
had killed her father but hopefully not in the actual sense of murdering him. The
awfulness of Layton seemed to have no bounds. Staverley could not help
thinking that his death probably made the world a much better place.
'Would you like a pudding?' He asked lamely. Despite all of the thoughts reeling
around in his head it was the best he could come up with as a response.
'No, thank you. In fact I am actually feeling a little woozy, after lots of hard work
and too much to drink, and far too much to say, I think I need to go home. Do you
think you could take me home? I don't think I would be entirely safe going on my
own. Its not far.'
'Of course, yes.' Anything that would mean he could spend more time with her
was good from his point of view.
'I'll go to the bathroom and try and reassemble myself.'
Staverley paid the bill quickly, and tried not to look shocked by the total, he had
promised expensive, and by then Monica was back a little more composed and
ready to go. She steadied herself on his arm as they left the restaurant in search
of a taxi.

When Staverley woke, apart from desperately needing a drink of water, his first
thought was a muddled worry about research ethics – should you be sleeping
with your respondents? His second thought was the realisation that this was not

research, this was real life. His third thought, and by far the most urgent thought, was where in the bed could he find Monica. She had been there when he fell asleep. He turned gently and felt her warmth, then he felt her stir, then he moved closer behind her. It felt good.

Breakfast was a mix of anticipation and slight embarrassment. He was hungry despite the large meal the night before and he needed some coffee. But how do you do breakfast with someone you have just met and then slept with. And he had no toothbrush. But Monica made it easy, she chatted about the work at her laboratory and her colleagues while brewing a pot of very decent proper coffee, in an American style percolator, and making slices of toast from crusty granary bread accompanied by several jars of what looked like home-made preserves. How good could this get? 'My lab partner makes these.' She said, gesturing toward the jars. 'Its wonderful, he lives in the country and his nieghbour has an orchard and he collects the fallen fruit and does this with it, it's one of the wonders of science, I get a new jar every week.' It was delicious, fruity and thick but not too sweet. Staverley heaped a very large spoonful onto his second slice of toast while Elton John played quietly on the radio in the background. His B+B and toothbrush were only 15 minutes walk away but that raised the issue of how to leave. How does one leave appropriately after a night of hectic but totally unexpected sexual activity with someone you have just met and who has told you some very personal things about themselves? It was much more than casual sex, at least he hoped so, but he was not clear what category of sex it did come into. Again Monica solved all that with impressive ease.

'It was good that you helped me get home safely, and not at all what I had expected when you first phoned me. You are a nice man, and really not a bad lover.' There was that smile again. 'But look, you've got to excuse me, when I finish my coffee I have to dash. I have that experiment to check on, lots of data to process and the results to write up. But you don't have to rush. You can stay.'

'No, no problem'. Staverley said. 'I'll walk with you and try to be nice a bit longer, I have a train to catch mid morning. I need to get on too.'

'Ok, sounds good, give me 10 minutes.' She went back upstairs.

While he waited and ate another spoonful of the preserves another of those unsettling thoughts he kept having insinuated itself into his head. This one was, what happens next? What do I say? What does she expect me to say? What will she say? Was this a one off? As he juggled with all of this he was very clear that he very much wanted to see Monica again, and soon. Directness again he thought. Monica was back, briefcase in hand, coat on, ready to go. He stood up and took her hand.

'Monica, can I see you again? Can I see you again soon?' He looked at her and she looked back.

There was a heartbeat of silence. 'Yes you can, I would like that very much. Now let's go, I am going to be late.'

They walked together toward the colleges and parted with a kiss that was just that bit more than friendly but just about appropriate for a morning in public after the night before. Monica had recovered from her wooziness and her revelations and looked fresh and lovely. She was now dressed casually in a skirt and jumper and Staverley felt rather odd to still be wearing his suit. He had a change of clothes at the B+B. He watched her walk away with more than the usual interest one has in someone walking away. There followed a rather stilted encounter with the owner of the B+B, who was somewhat put out that he did not want a second breakfast and appeared to be very aware that his bed had not be slept in. He did not attempt to explain and assumed a sort of worldy air of someone for whom such things were normal.

As he walked to the station Staverley began to confront some of the less happy thoughts about the things Monica had said last night, and in particular about her research lab and chemistry. Chemists knew about, well chemicals and compounds, and research labs were places where compounds or whatever were accessible and could be combined into interesting and dangerous substances, like those which had accounted for Layton's death, for his murder. He would need to find out whether these were just fanciful worries but they raised questions Staverley did not really want to have to confront, very inconvenient and uncomfortable questions. Basically, he did not want to think about Monica being familiar with and handling noxious substances. He wanted her to be someone who sat in a library and thought about science in some sort of abstract way, not someone who wore a lab coat and ran experiments, rather someone who would not know a pipette from a Bunsen burner. Then there was Lionel, the Lion. There had been no further mention of last night's conversation over dinner once in Monica's house and in her bed, they had had other things to think about, but Staverley now needed to think about what Monica had said about Lionel and his relationship with her mother. He needed to think about it a lot and he probably needed to talk to Lionel again and perhaps he would have to add Lionel to his list of potential killers. Or perhaps he just needed to go home and get on with his real work and forget about Layton's death, and concentrate instead on wooing his daughter and thinking about how good her body felt and how wonderful she smelt. It was the latter that provided the main distraction on the train and he became a little hot and bothered as a result.

CHAPTER NINE

By the time the train from Cambridge arrived at Brighthelmstone station Staverley was clear that he could not give up on his research into Layton and his death. Even if he wanted to cultivate his relationship with Monica, simply because she was Monica and he wanted to see more of her, he was not going to be able to do that with the possibility lurking in the back of his head that she might have had something to do with her father's death, even though he really wanted to believe that that was highly unlikely. But she did have a motive, or indeed multiple motives - an uncaring neglectful and repressive father, who may even have been abusive toward her in some way, and who certainly abused her mother emotionally and may have caused or contributed to her suicide. Staverley thought that could be more than enough to want him dead, to plot to murder him. She said not, but if she did blame him for her mother's suicide, murder might be one further step in her efforts to expunge Layton from her life, by expunging his. She had said that she might sound cold, perhaps that coldness extended to calculation and a carefully worked out plot to murder her despicable father. There was a simple solution of course, one Staverley had forgotten to address in the nights cross-currents of revelations and sex. If Monica had a watertight, cast iron, unbreakable alibi like Connelly, then all was well, he could cross her off his list with a joyful flourish of his mental pen. So now he had two clients for his investigation, Archie and Monica, two people to prove innocent by finding the real culprit or by making it clear that they were somewhere else doing something else or even three if you counted Lionel. But even if he succeeded in that, then he would have to find a way of erasing or explaining away his misrepresentation of himself to Monica that would not end up with her never wanting to see him again. And before that he would have to find out if that watertight, cast iron, unbreakable alibi that he hoped for actually existed. That would need some very delicate finessing. The police could ask 'where were you on the night of', but he could not do that without risking Monica's wrath. Given all of that the other thing he was now certain about was that he would have to have some kind of conversation with Lionel about what Monica had told him, but it would be quite unlike any previous conversation they had had and perhaps Lionel would simply not cooperate and remain his guarded, grumpy and difficult self. He would have to beard the Lion in his den. This self assumed research project now consisted almost entirely of impossible conversations. It was not at all like the orderly accumulation of facts and evidence that Staverley had envisaged when he started. It was not about facts but about people and their emotions and their lives and loves and hates and disappointments. This was not the stuff of the social sciences. With all this in mind Staverley felt his resolve weakening again as he walked home but as he approached his flat he remembered that he had arranged to meet with Dr. Rawlins that evening – another train journey and another set of difficult questions, and another set of work tasks that would not get done. He could phone and cancel, bring an end to the whole thing and get on with life as usual. That now sounded like an eminently sensible idea.

On the train to London Staverley tried to work on the revisions of his paper on new forms of overseas tourism and social class. He did like trains and train journeys, they offered both changing scenery and a place to sit and work, with minimal chance of being disturbed, except by the occasional loud talker. The bus journey from Clapham Junction to Rawlins's flat did not take long and he arrived a little early, but he decided to ring the bell anyway and Rawlins was home and did not seem to mind. The flat was in a Victorian red brick block and looked out over Battersea Park. The flat was catching the last of the evening sun, which highlighted the enormous number of books lined every wall, including even some in the kitchen, which Staverley perused while Rawlins made coffee.
'You seem to be an avid reader.' He said.
Rawlins shrugged. 'It keeps me out of mischief and helps with the teaching.'
'Very eclectic, science, social science, philosophy, detective stories and that's just your kitchen.'
Rawlins shrugged again. 'I like to keep three or four books on the go, different books, depending on my mood. It helps me to manage myself. The right book for the right mood.'
'That makes a lot of sense to me.' Staverley replied.

Rawlins handed him a mug of coffee and headed back to the study cum sitting room. 'Cigarette?' He offered as they sat down. He clearly smoked a lot given the smell of the flat and the colour of his fingers.

'No thank you, I don't.' Staverley said, cigarette smoking was something that just did not make sense to him.

'But you didn't come to talk about my reading habits did you?'

Down to business again Staverley thought. Here goes.

'No, as I said on the phone I wanted to talk to you about Alan Layton, and if you felt able, as one of his victims so to speak, to say something about what you thought about his past and future influence on British social science.' It all sounded so reasonable. Lying was getting easier, Staverley would need to take himself in hand when all of this was over and done with. He didn't want it to become a habit.

'And this is for what?' Asked Rawlins.

'It will provide some grist for an article stroke obituary stroke editorial, something different from what the papers have been saying about "the great man of British social science and his legacy", something not written from within his coterie.' Staverley almost convinced himself that this would be something worth doing. Maybe he should write something. It would certainly be a change from his usual more stolid stuff.

'Sounds good to me, what do you want to know?'

'Just about your experience of Layton really, and what you think about his death'. Rawlins seemed okay with that.

'You probably know the story. It's very simple really. As a young academic I was offered the chance by a Scottish social science journal, I did my first degree in Scotland, to review Layton's *Industrial Development* book. His supposed seminal work. My own influences and standpoint had been mainly drawn from versions of Marxism and Gramsci in particular and the book to me read like a very straightforward apologia for capital, an ideological social science, and that's what I wrote more or less. It wasn't written as an attack, I was careful with my argument and my language, I was aware of whom I was writing. It wasn't vicious or polemical it was a reasoned critique couched in a language of moderation. Naively I had no idea of the wrath that would descend upon me. My colleagues at

117

Watermouth were quite clear, at least in talking privately, that my tenure was denied directly at Layton's behest, directly because of the review, and as I later discovered he also intervened to block any possibility of a job elsewhere in the university sector. And nobody, not one of my colleagues was willing to stand up and argue for me, they just folded in fear of Layton and what he could do to anyone who opposed his will. Sad really. It left a very bitter taste. But it was my good luck in the end that he obvious thought that a Polytechnic was not worth his time and attention or I probably would not have got the job I have. I tried to get a couple of research papers published after I moved to EB but they were given short shrift. I had become a pariah and no one who had any concern for Layton's prejudices would dare to take me seriously, and that meant just about everyone. I have had a couple of things published abroad but they don't carry much weight here and no one here reads them. So it looks like I will serve out my time as a teacher in the Poly sector, and as I said to you on the phone I get a good deal of satisfaction out of that. But I do think I could have made some kind of contribution to the social sciences. So to answer your other question, and its obvious really, Layton has been very effective in narrowing the possibilities of social science and the problems it might address. He has made some questions impossible to address or impossible to even think about. And of course he has waged a campaign against theory, particularly continental theory, and both things have impoverished the social sciences in this country, at least that's how I see it. It's good that he's gone, at least I think so, but his effect is not going to dissipate over night, it will take a generation to escape from his malign influence. His followers are dug in deep, they hold key positions and most of them will want to perpetuate his vision of the social sciences when they review papers, and make appointments and evaluate people for promotion. It's pernicious. Is that clear enough?'

'It is,' Staverley said, 'I was pretty sure you would not mourn his passing.'

'And you're right, but I must admit I was shocked to read that he had been murdered. Quite an extraordinary thing really, but he must have had no shortage of enemies, me among them I guess, but it's a big step from resentment and disappointment to murder. Perhaps his death has nothing to do with his academic life and is a family matter or something else, who knows?' This was not something Staverley wanted to hear given what he had learned over the past twenty-four hours. 'That's what statistics say isn't it, most murders are committed by a family member or someone the victim knows well. That's what they always say in the detective stories I read.' He gestured towards the bookcases.

With that Staverley could think of nothing else to ask. Well he could but those were not questions that seemed possible to ask directly, so that was about it. As he got up to leave Staverley hesitated. 'I meant to say to you that as I was waiting downstairs when I arrived there was a young lad doing something very odd to the blue Toyota Celicia parked just outside, its not yours is it?'

'What? No. I wish. Mine's a rather decrepit green Austin Allegro, it's on the other side of the road.' Rawlins pointed out the window.

'Ok, good, and thanks again for your time. You've been very helpful.'

'I'm not sure how exactly but if you say so.' Rawlins showed him out and as soon as he was downstairs and out of sight Staverley made a note of the number of Rawlins's car.

In his office the following morning Staverley consulted his notes and practiced a slightly deeper tone of voice and dialed Rawlins's work number. This time he picked up.

'Mr. Charles Rawlins?'

'Speaking.'

'This is Sergeant Dixon, Wessex Police, Traffic division. Sorry to bother you sir but we are pursuing enquiries into a hit and run accident that occurred on the night of 26th September on the A23 road near Brighthelmstone. We have a partial identification of the car we are seeking provided by a witness. And your car, and Austin Allegro I believe, is one of those that match the partial number plate that we have – that is J 124 BC. Would that be correct sir?'

'It's certainly part of my number plate but I can assure you that I was nowhere near Brighthelmstone on that night. In fact I was not using my car at all, I was in Aldeburgh at a concert with my brother and his family. I can remember it clearly because it is my brother's birthday. And I have already told all of this to the police in relation to another matter.'

'Excellent, just what I was about to ask you sir. Now if you could give me a contact number for you brother I can eliminate you entirely from our enquiries. And apologies for the duplication.'

Rawlins did not seem particularly put out and another quick Sergeant Dixon call to Rawlins's brother and it was done. Rawlins was off the list. But if he was now off, and if Connelly was off, unless there was something else in Layton's past Staverley did not know about then his excursion into the world of crime detection might prove to be a very short one.

The rest of the morning disappeared in a mass of post and paperwork and a steady stream of student tutorials. Staverley tried to remain focused but his mind kept wandering back to soap and suicide and sex, a heady mix, a mix that Staverley could make little sense of. And behind all of that was when and how to speak with Lionel. Should he make a proper appointment with Jean? Or just burst in like he did last time and catch him unawares? Or waylay him in the corridor? Or invite him out for a drink? That would be a very unlikely first. 'What can I get you Lionel and tell me did you have a affair with Layton's wife'? Yes, well, that would not get him very far, he was certain of that. He needed a different starting point. But on the other hand maybe he could resort to what had worked with others, a bit of directness. He rehearsed a few possible phrases and euphemisms to order his thoughts before venturing into the Lion's den.

He knocked on Lionel's door, heard a gruff 'yes' and stepped in.

'Lionel, how are you?'

'What can I do for you? Busy day, busy day.' Charming as usual.

'I wondered if I could chat with you later, just ten minutes, something personal.' He could see Lionel wince at the mention of something personal and was surprised by his response. 'I suppose I could make that work, end of the day? Five-ish perhaps?'

'Great, thank you, see you then, sorry to disturb.'

Well, a result, an appointment, just 3 hours of nervous anticipation to cope with and more distractions from proper work needing to be done. With some effort he focused his attention on practical tasks that required little thought and the time passed. An MA student came to request an essay extension and he reviewed the dissertation titles that had been submitted. At five he tidied his desk, packed his briefcase, girded his loins and walked slowly along the corridor to Lionel's office. He knocked – silence. He knocked again – nothing. Perhaps Lionel had forgotten and gone home, he wouldn't have to do it after all, he could give up on the whole idea.

'Staverley.' Lionel called from behind him, he made Staverley jump. 'Sorry, had a meeting, it ran over. Let's go in.'

They shuffled into the office and Staverley was waved into the visitor's chair.

'I'll just sort these papers.' The wait while Lionel put papers away in his filing cabinet was excruciating. There was still time to make an excuse and run. Finally, Lionel sat down. 'Well, you wanted to speak to me.'

'Yes, I did, I do. Yes.'

'Well'? Lionel already sounded irritated.

'Yes. Well you see its Layton.'

'Of course, the new external, I have some ideas, you?'

'No it's not that exactly.' said Staverley. 'Its about Layton himself, or rather its about Layton's daughter.'

A series of contradictory expressions formed on Lionel's face as he appeared to be selecting among a number of possible responses. His face settled into a mix between perplexity and exasperation.

'Layton's daughter? I really don't see....'

'I went to see her, I talked to her'. Among other things, Staverley thought.

'You did what? Why would you do that? Do you know her?'

A new set of expressions crossed Lionel's face. He looked like he was uncertain which was appropriate or possible. He was clearly not sure where the conversation was going.

'I didn't, I do, sort of... That's what I wanted to talk to you about. When we talked, she and I, well we talked about you, you and her.'

Lionel's face fixed into unmistakable outrage. 'This, that, she, and I, are none of your business. I think you should leave now.'

'I can't, I mean I wont. I need to talk to you, I really do.'

'Well I don't need or want to talk to you, not about things that are entirely personal, that are nothing to do with you, that are nothing to do with anybody.' Lionel began to get up from his chair, Staverley wondered if he was about to be physically ejected from the room.

'But they are things that might have something to do with Layton's death, don't you think Lionel?'

The outrage reverted back to perplexity.

'What do you mean? Don't be stupid. Why would you say that?'

'I say it because of what Monica said to me. I say it because what she said led me to certain conclusions, conclusions I admit that might be entirely wrong, that I very much want to be entirely wrong, but if she says the same things to others, like the police, that might lead them to similar conclusions, right or wrong.' That sounded very confused, but it had the right effect. Lionel sat back heavily in his chair and seemed deflated, the outrage was totally gone now and his eyes flickered from side to side as he tried to think through what Staverley had said. Then he spoke again.

'And what conclusions might those be?'

Now came the crunch, would he say it or not.

'That you or she, or the two of you together are in some way involved in Layton's murder.'

'Don't be absolutely ridiculous, that's the most ridiculous thing I have ever heard. It's outrageous. It's insulting. I am not listening to any more of this.'

Again he began to get up.

'Lionel, I don't say these things lightly, I don't want to say them at all. I like Monica, I like her a lot, but if the police find out about the things she told me at the very least they will want to question her and you further. Your relationship with Layton was not what it seemed, at least not what it seemed to me, and your involvement with his family could well be seen as pertinent in relation to his death.'

Lionel sat back again. 'But why? Why are you involving yourself in these things.'

Staverley tried to explain. 'Since I found Layton in his room, in his bath, I have tried not to think about it, but with suspicion falling on Archie I wanted to help, to do something to make sense of what I saw and what people told me about Layton, and I admit the more I learned about him, the more fascinated I became by his ruthless awfulness. Fascinated is the wrong word, but the man and his effect on people were extraordinary. Really, I am not surprised that some one or several some ones would want to murder him, he was a monster. He damaged people, he ruined lives and not just in the cut and thrust of academia but at a personal level. He was ruthless and vindictive and apparently unstoppable. And I am beginning to think that he may have gone someway toward ruining your life as well as many others, unless I am missing something.'

'I don't want to talk about this Staverley.'

'You might not want to talk to me, fine, and maybe the police will not come, fine, but Layton's death is not going to go away until the police find their culprit and the more stones they turn over the more people are going to be hurt, like you and Monica. Even in his death Layton is wreaking havoc.' Staverley still felt that what he had said made little sense but he hoped that Lionel's skills of argument might be a little dulled by the emotions of the moment.

'Alright, suppose something of my history with Layton and with Monica comes to light, how does that affect her in any way?'

'Well, if I look at it like a policeman I see a young woman who hated her father, although it was perhaps different from hate, more than that in some ways, a young woman who blames her father for the death of her mother, who she adored, and who is also a research chemist who works in a laboratory with access to poisons and the knowledge how to use them, like integrating them into a bar of soap. It doesn't take a major leap of imagination to see Monica as a real suspect.'

Lionel looked as though he had stopped breathing. 'And me?'

'Well a young man who may have loved Layton's wife, who may have had an affair with Layton's wife, who also blames Layton for her death, who probably loves the daughter and its aware of the harm Layton did to her as a child, who has looked out for her all these years, and whose own life may have been blighted by the events of the wife's death. That sounds like a prima facie motive for murder if I ever heard one. And if you put you and Monica together then a conspiracy to murder does not seem that far fetched. You arranged for him to be here, she organized the soap, somehow it was delivered to his room and a lifetime of wrongs and regrets are avenged. What about that?'

As he laid out his thinking Staverley was beginning to convince himself. Which was not what he really wanted, it wanted it all to fall apart, to sound far fetched, to be easily dismissed with a couple of deft rebuttals, but it was not. Lionel appeared to have stopped breathing, he was very still.

'And what if I say, that all of that is rubbish, fantasy.'

'Well I really hope it is, I want it to be, but I would say, prove it to me. You do that, then you can find a way of sacking me, you can ruin my career like Layton ruined other people's.' Staverley paused. 'So, do you have an alibi for that night, that would put a big dent in my hypothesis, wouldn't it?' That would really shut me up.

Lionel shook his head slowly. 'No, I don't. What I told the police was a lie, and not a very good one. I was actually with Monica that night. She is my alibi and I am hers. Given your hypothesis that doesn't help much does it?'

It was Staverley's turn to be shocked, more lies, more lies.

'What! I have not had the courage to ask her but I assumed Monica was in Cambridge that night and I was hoping she would have some way of proving that and show me up as an idiot.'

'She was there, I assure you, but I am her only proof. She was in her lab all night, minding an experiment, and for at least part of the time I was with her. I drove up that evening and back in the early hours.'

'Well, if you can prove that, if someone saw you in the lab, if you bought petrol, had a meal, anything. Then you are okay. Monica must have signed in and out or something, or there should be records of the work she was doing.'

'Nothing like that I assure you'.

'Well maybe her word and your word would be enough. Why didn't you tell this to the police.' Staverley asked.

'Maybe we could or should but given your hypothesis that would beg certain questions. And at least to some extent your hypothesis is correct.'

Again it was Staverley's turn for shocked silence. This was not what he wanted to hear. He wanted a calm and rational dismantling of his worse fears and absolute reassurance that neither Monica nor Lionel had anything to do with Layton's death so that he could return to sparring with Lionel in meetings and work on his relationship with Monica without doubts and suspicions to spoil things. Lionel looked at Staverley very intently. His eyes narrowed.

'You see we were conspiring.'

'No Lionel, no, please, I wanted to be wrong, I really, really wanted to be wrong believe me.' Lionel raised his hands to stop Staverley's protests.

'Listen, yes we were conspiring but we weren't conspiring to murder him. We were conspiring to bring him down, to ruin his reputation, to humiliate him, to put an end to his career, to show him what it feels like to be manipulated and hurt. Oh God, I am going to have to explain what we did. And why shouldn't it be to you? But you have to promise me Staverley that you will not use anything I say to harm Monica in anyway. If you did... Well I don't know what I would do.'

'That's an easy promise to make. Harming Monica is the last thing I want to do. You have no idea.'

'In that case. Over the past five years Monica and I have been systematically collecting material on and about Layton. Among other things Monica has been stealing and copying his papers. She still has access to the family home and he is away a lot so its been relatively easy. It started when she went to collect some legal papers about her legacy from her mother that were kept in his study. He had told her by letter where to find them and left her to it. But they were not where he had said and in looking around what she did find was a set of his personal journals and boxes of letters and other materials he had saved from various points in his career both in universities and in government. She did not mean to or really want to but she thought that reading to journal might help her to understand her father better, his coldness, his cruelty, his relationship with her mother.

She thought she might understand better her mother's suicide but what she found was not that. Instead she found a record of illicit arrangements, personal exchanges of favours, deliberate subversion of procedures, vendettas against academic opponents, the mis-use of positions and influence. There was nothing criminal, no real financial gain was involved, just a history of mundane bad faith and deception and double-dealing, all of which contributed to Layton's ascendance and dominance and his control of people, institutions and ideas. It was extraordinary, an insidious and systematic connivance that went on year after year, that drew more and more people into his sphere of influence, in most cases to their benefit as well as his. He also kept information on people he distrusted. There were copies of letters sent to block certain people from certain jobs, always with vague threats or warnings to those involved in making decisions. There was even some records of papers reviewed for his journal where unequivocally positive recommendations had been ignored or changed. Perhaps worst of all he used his contacts with the civil service to report suspicions about Marxist academics to MI5, which led to some of them being put under surveillance and certainly scuppered some careers. He would go to any length to eradicate potential threats to his view of the world. He made Machiavelli look prudent and gentle. These were the corrupt actions of a morally corrupt man. He was the exact opposite of a real academic in a way, a man who would countenance no criticism or counter argument, who used interpersonal attacks and underhand methods to fend off other standpoints rather than engage with them and dispute them in proper scholarly fashion.

When Monica showed me some of what she had found I was astonished. I thought I knew more than most what Layton was capable of, and I also knew some of the stories about people like Rawlins and Connelly. But this was different. It was wicked. It was evidence of a distorted mind at work. We decided we should do something, but neither of us thought that this was some kind of public duty, we both had our own reasons for exposing him, in many ways the same reasons and its sounds like you know about those. We both had much to despise him for. So we began to plan, to systematically collate the material Monica found and as I said, steal and copy documents. I don't know why he kept these things, he was to be a keeper, there were all sorts of other things that a biographer might find very interesting someday, but he never returned to check on anything or throw anything away or hide anything, he felt invulnerable I suppose. I don't know what he thought would happen to it all after his death. Maybe he didn't care. The journals were full of details of everything he did, almost every meeting and event, and he must have had a current version somewhere. I also did some background work and very circumspectly talked to some of the people who appeared in the journals or to whom letters were written or who had been written about and while some people refused to say anything there was plenty of confirmation and the refusals were also telling in their own way. Rawlins and Connelly were just the tip of the iceberg. But the problem was that this was personal and academic, there were few sensational revelations, the general public and the newspapers would probably have had little interest in what we had found. It might have caused a kerfuffle of sorts but probably nothing he could not ride out or smooth over. It would be a big issue in the social sciences but we were unsure how we could get people to read the stuff we had accumulated, how could we make it widely known? We couldn't think of a way of publishing it through the normal channels. Journals wouldn't touch it. And that's when we came up with the plan. The idea was to get Layton appointed as external examiner here - that is why I was so adamant in pushing the appointment through. The examination board is an official committee of the university with minutes that are available publically. What we intended was that once the meeting had opened and Layton officially welcomed and that was minuted, I would raise an objection to his appointment as someone unfit and inappropriate for the role, enter a summary of the material we had collected to support this and propose a vote to have him sacked as external examiner. With those present around the table there would be no way that what had happened would not spread like gossip wildfire and the man's career of turpitude would be open for anyone to read. His adherents would be in no position to hush things up. The great man would be brought down, his perfidies made public, Monica and I would be very happy – well maybe happy is the wrong word. But we would have done something to counter what had been done to us and what we had had to live with for so long.'

Staverley was stunned, amazed, fascinated. This was very different from anything he had begun to imagine, but most importantly it was not murder.

'Lionel that is incredible, and wonderful, but it didn't happen, obviously.'

'No, someone had a different plan, a more dramatic and decisive one. Monica and I met to finalise everything in Cambridge that night, we met in her lab and spent hours making sure everything was organized and going through exactly what I would say at the meeting and I returned here in the early hours ready to do the deed and Layton did not appear. To tell the truth in one way I am disappointed. I don't regret is death but I so much wanted to see him humiliated. I wanted to see the look in his face when he was voted out. I wanted him to know what it was like to be conspired against. I wanted people to pity him, laugh at him, talk about him, remove him from his honorary positions and memberships, withdraw his awards. I wanted him isolated and shamed.'

'You can still make the papers public.' Staverley suggested.

'We can do that yes, and we have talked about it and probably will. But it wont be the same. It wont get to him, he wont know, it wont cause him any distress now, will it? It will taint his memory, which is something, it might send his cohorts and accomplices running for cover but we wanted more than that, much more. We wanted him.'

'I can see that, and I think a lot of other people would have been pleased to see his fall from grace. Not just those he worked against but maybe also some of those drawn into his conniving and made to collude with him. And the other good thing is that you can show to the police your Layton dossier and explain your meeting together and put an end to any suspicion of involvement in his death.'

Lionel chuckled, which was unlike him.

'You think so. I don't think it changes the basis of your hypothesis. It's only our story of how things were supposed to go at the meeting. Equally the dossier as you called it could be seen as part of a conspiracy to murder, part of a motive on top of the things you have already listed. And it does not exactly show either of us in a good light, searching through Layton's study, purloining personal papers. We might have been intending to publish after his death rather than before. We still have no alibi except each other. It probably makes things worse.'

'But I believe you, and from what I know about Layton and Monica and you, it just makes sense, its believable.' Staverley argued.

'But maybe that's because, as you said before you don't want to believe in the other possibility. I could even be making things up now, concocting a narrative that would account for our actions but not implicate us in his murder.'

Staverley could see the point. Lionel was now arguing against himself.

'Well I am not going to the police. I am not going to repeat to anyone what you have told me. You have to believe me, and what I said before about not doing anything to cause harm to Monica or you for that matter that's still very much the case. We may not always get on, and you may not always be an easy man to work for but I bear you no malice, and I want Layton's real killer found. And that's what I have been trying to do. I don't want to make you tell me things that are painful and difficult for the sake of it. I know I should not be making you say these things, and I cannot even begin to imagine what Layton did to you and to you life but I do not believe that you murdered him, I really don't.'

'I appreciate that, and I know that I am not an easy man to like but I was not always as you find me now, I am not always as you find me now, not when I am with Monica. But just as you described and we found Layton left a trail of devastated lives behind him, and mine was one. My loathing for him was, is, well indescribable, it's visceral. I am not a violent man, I have never committed an act of violence but I have been in rooms with Layton over the years, at events and conferences and I had to stop myself from being physically sick and from doing him bodily harm. So many times I wanted to walk up to the podium and knock him down while he was speaking and to beat his face with my fist until he could not speak anymore. But I didn't, I knew that it would not be enough, it would be fleeting, and as I was arrested and taken away he would still be there, he would still be who he was. And I think I knew that if I waited that the right moment would come, and it did, or so it seemed.'

'I know from Monica that you have good reason for those feelings, but she does not know what really happened between you and her mother and Layton. She said that for her to ask you would be some kind of betrayal.'

'I suppose that's right, we both wanted things left unsaid, we wanted to remember the good things, the happy moments that she and her mother and I had together. And there are some things that she does not know, that perhaps now she should know, I am not sure.' Lionel shook his head, he clearly did not know what was best or right or sensible, and his relationship with Monica was clearly the most important thing and he was not going to do anything that might jeopardise that.

'Would you tell me'? Staverley asked. 'Perhaps that will help you decide what is best?' Even as he said it Staverley was not sure whether that was true. Perhaps he just needed to know, to have the whole story. He felt a little like a voyeur, but he could not stop now.

Lionel blew out a long, slow, ragged breath.

'I never thought I would talk about Monica's mother to anyone but Monica. I certainly never envisaged such a conversation with you Staverley.'

'For what it's worth neither did I. And I would totally understand it if you wanted to keep things between the two of you."

'I don't know, maybe it's like that cliché in detective stories when the culprit confides in the detective because they need to tell someone 'or they will go crazy.' I have never been convinced by that in books but I am beginning to think that it may have something to it. I don't think telling you is going to make me feel better, whatever that means, but it might help me be clearer about what I have to do next. So, it goes like this... ' Lionel sat up straighter and clasped his hands together. 'Monica may have told you that I was Layton's post-doc. I was over the moon when I got the post, there was stiff competition, and at that point I had no idea what it would be like working for him. As it turned out the post was more about his needs rather than mine. I was at his beck and call, not just doing work for his research, drafting reports and papers, library searches, collecting data on British industry, but things for him at home, arranging for repairs, paying bills, even collecting his cleaning. That's when I met Monica and her mother, and I liked them both immediately. The mother was beautiful and had a wonderful easy manner and the daughter was charming and funny and clearly very bright. I enjoyed talking to them and spending time with them. We drank tea. I started staying on for lunch. Layton was never at home. And then I started to go out with them on their trips around the countryside and to nearby towns and villages. Monica's mother clearly found the English and Englishness baffling, she was confused by people's reactions to her, she was often upset by even simple exchanges with tradesmen, she said or did the wrong thing and everyone got confused. So she came up with the idea of searching out the meaning of the English in their history and folktales, not the big history of battles and kings and queens but the quirky little histories of local legends and characters, out of the way places, ruins, enchanted woods. And it was perfect for Monica, she wanted to spend as much time as she could with her mother and she was entranced by these strange places and even stranger stories, and I will admit that her mother and I did somewhat embellish and elaborate on whatever glimmerings of truth we came across. And I thoroughly enjoyed it too.

My parents never really did adventures, they were good parents but down to earth, very focused on the practicalities of life. This was different, it was a joyful fantasy life. For me it was like being a different person. The seriousness of the social sciences and the social problems it addressed could be firmly bracketed away and I was able to explore my imagination. It was like being a child again myself. At the same time the more I got to know Monica's mother the more entranced with her I became, it was like falling up her spell, and the better I got to know her the more I wanted to fall. While all of this was going on I was also realising that things between her and Layton were not good, and that he treated her badly, not physically or at least she never suggested that, but he was oppressive, controlling and verbally abusive and at the same time totally neglectful. He would forget her birthday, or say he had, I think he forgot things like that to deliberately upset her. He constantly undermined her, and tried to stop her from seeing her family, and was utterly dismissive of her child, their child Monica. He was turning a vibrant outgoing joyful young woman into a frightened shadow.

I don't know now the exact point at which our relationship changed but I began to pop into the house in the mornings after Monica had left for school and we talked and then we kissed and then we would spend hours in bed. For a young man with limited sexual experience it was a revelation. It was unreal and very, very real and potent at the same time. She completed my transformation from someone rather reticent and unworldly into an exuberant lover, into someone who was willing to take risks and enjoy life. She re-made me. She made the world look different. I thought about her all the time. I dreamed about her, day-dreamed about her. I counted the minutes each morning until I knew Monica would have left for school. My future was no longer one of being a dour university lecturer and single-minded careful researcher it was one of being in her arms, hearing her laughter, watching her undress, and watching her dress again after we had made love.'

As Lionel spoke his face changed, the care-worn irritable face that Staverley was used to was replaced by something younger, softer even, the face of someone in love.

'We just never thought that Layton would find out. He never came home during the day. But one time he did and he found us.' His faced changed again to one of deep sadness.

'I won't rehearse the scene, you can imagine it. It was not very edifying. Layton was a mix of cold indifference and controlled rage. He wasn't hurt by his wife's betrayal like most men would be he was affronted, his dignity was at stake not his marriage. He made us dress and waited for us down stairs and then he presented a simple ultimatum – the affair would end, we would never see each other again and I would move on, he would find a post for me elsewhere. If not then he would ensure I never worked again in a university, he would not divorce his wife and the two of us would have to face the consequences if we continued our relationship. I have re-lived that moment in my mind hundreds of times and each time I have responded differently from the way I actually did. I have tried to explain it to myself, to excuse myself – the force of Layton's personality, my naivety, the shock of discovery – but the stark reality is that I was a coward, I was the betrayer, I betrayed her, us. I agreed to the ultimatum. I can still see the look of her face. It was the most awful thing I have ever seen in my life. The light went out of her eyes and at the moment my life changed forever. I became the man I am now, the one you dislike, and I don't blame you. I dislike myself, I have disliked myself everyday since that day. I think perhaps at that moment I realised who I really was, no fairytales, no enchantment, the man I really was, was the craven coward. I might have pretended to be something else, I may have believed that I could love, but I was really as cold and calculating and self interested as Layton. Ever since, I have eschewed emotional and personal relations, anything that might remind me of, or re-envoke in me, the feelings and experiences of that relationship. So I am just an empty shell, a vacuum. Then I don't have to feel, I can just remain numb and guarded. The only times that I can be something else, that I allow myself to be something else, something half human, is with Monica. I have come to love her, perhaps in the way her father should have, but I also feel responsible for her, partly because of what I did to her and her life and to her mother. She could have become my daughter. It wasn't Layton who killed her mother, it was me... I never for a moment imagined that she would kill herself, but I know I was the cause, whatever Layton may have done, I remember the look on her face that morning, it was me.

Lionel stopped, his body settled and he shrank a little, his jaw set and the self-loathing he lived with was clearly visible in his eyes. He stared into space, remembering. Then suddenly he began to speak again.

"We could have run away, we could have gone to France, taken Monica with us, I am sure that her family would have accepted us, we could have made a new life, I could have sold glassware, attended seminars on existentialism, anything. I would have been with them, I would have been a real person, a whole person, a husband and a father. I could say that in making my life and making me what I am now Layton in fact destroyed my life, or the life I could have had, but really I did that to myself. If I was a religious man then I might think of the life I have lived since that day as a penance, a suffering for what I did. And there is even more, if Monica ever found out what happened, if she knew what I had done, what I am capable of, then I am sure she would reject me, despise me, and there would be nothing left, I would become less than nothing, a dead space. But I know, I have always known that one day I would have to tell her.'

Staverley really did not know what to think. He certainly did not know what to say. Should he feel sorry for Lionel? Should he also blame him? Was Lionel wrong to blame himself? More than anything he felt a deep sadness. A sadness for the idea of what one moment could do to change the lives of three people, four if you counted Layton, surely he was not totally unaffected by his wife's death. As

Lionel said the only going back was in the mind, the replaying of possibilities, of outcomes and consequences but always knowing that what was done, was done. Staverley could not contemplate himself living with that, living like that, with a total reliance on one thing to make it worth living, on Monica, and with the fear and knowledge that at some point she would find out what had happened that morning and Lionel's decision. It was not just that Lionel was responsible for her, she was responsible for Lionel, for the possibility of Lionel, for making his life as it was liveable at all. He was also astonished to have got to the point of sitting in this chair listening to Lionel's distress. He had started out by wanting to find one truth, the truth about Layton's murder, and had ended up confronted by another very different, the truth of Layton's wife's death and its consequences for Monica and Lionel, a truth that now oddly perhaps seemed more important and immediate. But a truth that he would also now have to carry with him – like a confessor. At the same time he realised that the idea of sharing Lionel's burden was a fallacy.

There was nothing he could do to help Lionel except not give up on his research into Layton's death, that now he was responsible for proving the innocence of three people rather than just one. But Staverley was also very aware that if he believed Archie, if he believed Lionel, and if both Rawlins and Connelly had alibis that he had run out of suspects. He had no one to investigate, no one to ask questions of. In his eager activity he had also lost any sense of what the police were doing. He was surprised that he had not come across aspects of their activities, he knew they had spoken to Monica and Rawlins but not what conclusions they may have drawn or where what had been said may have led them. He knew that they had spoken with Lionel, and that he had lied to them, but the lie had stuck. He was without an alibi just like Staverley. However, also like Staverley, as far as the police were concerned, without a motive. He also knew that they had spoken with Archie, and that he had also lied to them, and those lies were also still in place. Perhaps they where 'following other lines of inquiry' as police detectives said on television. He needed to find out. He should talk to Mellmoth. And like the police, or he assumed like them, he needed to focus more on the mystery woman who had had dinner with Layton on the night of his death. But perhaps they had identified her already, eliminated her as a suspect. He felt like a very inadequate detective.

Lionel and Staveley now both sat quietly lost in their own thoughts and also exhausted by the emotional weight of Lionel's revelations. Staverley felt he had to leave, but that was easier said than done. Could he leave Lionel in this state?
'Lionel what do you want to do?' Lionel looked frightened.
'What do you mean?'
'I mean now, do you want to go home? Do you need a drink? Can I do anything?'
'Oh'! Lionel looked relieved.
'Yes, yes and no'. He reached down and opened a drawer in his desk and produced a bottle of Johnny Walker whiskey and two glasses. This was something else Staverley had never seen before.
'Do you want one?'
'Thanks no, not now'. Said Staverley. 'I need a clear head. But there is something I can do for you.'
'What's that?'
'I can find out who did kill Layton. I may not have done a great job so far but I am not giving up. There are still things I can do.'
'Maybe I should go and talk to the police'. Lionel suggested.
'I wouldn't do that, not yet anyway. Let me find out what's going on, what the police are doing and thinking. Let me do that Lionel.'
'Alright, if you think so. I don't really know what's for the best. Maybe there is no best.'
'And please believe me I am not going to say anything to Monica about what you told me, at least not the part about you and her mother. I think I will have to talk to her about your conspiracy even as only a way of explaining myself to her and getting her not to give up on me. You are not the only one who does not want to lose her. I know its not the same but Monica is the most important thing that has happened to me in a long while.'
Lionel sipped his whiskey and visibly sagged in his chair.
'And perhaps we could speak again, there maybe things that you know about the arrangements for Layton's visit that could be useful, is that okay?'

'Okay.'

'And I don't know what you are going to feel about sitting opposite me in meetings or discussing course reviews or whatever, I don't know how I am going to feel but I think I can be normal, I will certainly try hard. I don't expect what you have said to change anything in our professional relationship. I hope that that will be possible for you too.'

'Okay'. It was clear that Lionel had said enough and had run out of words.

'Please be careful getting home.'

Staverley got up and with a last glance back at Lionel still slumped in his chair with his glass in hand he returned to his own room. He dug around in his brief case and came up with the scrap of paper he wanted, and dialed the number on it.

'Sergeant Mellmoth?'

'Speaking.'

'Hello, this is Staverley, remember from the hotel and from UME.'

'Of course. How are you?'

'I'm okay thanks, and I was wondering if you fancied that pint we mentioned, and if you were free now, I am just leaving work.'

Staverley could almost see Mellmoth looking at his watch on the other end of the line.

'Me too, it's been a day, I am up for it.' Said Mellmoth. 'I could meet you at the Brewery Tap, do you know it?' He was obviously looking at his watch again, 'In twenty."

'I can do that, perfect, see you there.'

'And I do have a couple more questions for you.' Mellmoth hung up.

Staverley was not sure he wanted to be asked more questions.

CHAPTER TEN

The Tap was quiet but the beer was always good. As the name indicated the pub
was attached to the local brewery, an old established and independent firm,
1790 was the date over the brewery gates. They made a set of traditional
unpasteurised English cask ales, and Staverley was particularly partial to the
best bitter. And the pub also offered a range of very tasty, homemade pies with
flaky pastry toppings and Staverley was hungry. The conversation with Lionel
had been demanding and he needed sustenance. He beat Mellmoth by a minute
or so and was standing by the bar when the Sergeant arrived, he asked what he
wanted and whether he was up for a pie. Mellmoth also went for the bitter and
they consulted the blackboard. It was mainly meat again and Staverley's
transition to vegetarian status was going to suffer another setback, he would
have to try harder. He went for the mincemeat and onion, at least there would be
no lumps of flesh to deal with. Mellmoth chose the steak and kidney. They
retreated to a table near to the open fire which was producing more smoke than
flame and needed a good poke with a fire iron.

'Cheers.' He said. 'Good to see you.'

'Cheers and you.' They both sipped, or perhaps they were more than sips.

'So let's do those questions shall we?' Mellmoth got right to the point.

'We have spoken to several of your colleagues but I wanted to get clear who
exactly would know Layton's travel arrangements and that he would be in that
hotel that night?'

That was an easy one, Barnaby had already asked.

'Any number of people, at least the hotel - the members of the board at our end,
admin staff who made the arrangements, and even students perhaps, and given it
was Layton, the great man cometh, any of them might have told others. It was
common knowledge around the department, maybe not the details of where he
was staying but The Paine is where we always put important visitors, the more
lowly get a B+B'. The travel arranagements would probably only be known by
Lionel and Jean and her staff, and maybe Lionel would not know that.'

'I thought that might be that case. And we always ask this but is there anything you have thought of since we spoke previously, anything that's not in your statement, that you have remembered from that morning, or the events leading to Layton being invited?'

That was more tricky, Staverley now knew a lot more about the night of Layton's demise and the background to his appointment than he should in normal circumstances, but he shook his head. It seemed less of a lie that way.

'Anything about the room?'

'I don't think so, I have thought about it, but the thing I remember most is the shock of seeing him in the bath and the state he was in. It's an image I don't want to hold onto, you saw him as well, it was bad, very bad. As I said there were piles of papers on the table in the bedroom and some had slipped onto the floor, and there was a lot of cigarette ends in the ash tray, thinking back I suppose it did seem a lot for one man in one evening, and he was down stairs part of them time. But there was nothing that looked like there had been a struggle or a break in, but you would know better than me. I guess that's not likely anyway in the circumstances.'

Mellmoth smiled. 'Well spotted about the cigarettes, there was more than one brand of in the ash tray, which would suggest someone else had been in the room, but we know that already for other obvious reasons, and they were common brands and no telltale lipstick or anything of that sort that would take us any further. I am sure Sherlock Holmes could have made something of the tobacco residues, but we can't. You realise I am speaking quite freely here, I am assuming that none of this will be shared, certainly not with the press, or your colleagues.'

'Absolutely, I certainly don't want to hinder your investigation.' As Staverley said this he wondered whether that was exactly what he was doing.

'Another question then. I was wondering about those papers. We've looked at them of course, but we were looking for things that might relate directly to the crime – enemies, threats – you know the sort of thing, and there aren't any. To us they seem like the boring and ordinary paperwork that academics write and write to each other, or to themselves. Reading through them reminded me of some of those early morning mind-numbing lectures at UME. Do you remember?'

'I certainly do.' Staverley said with a broad smile.

'But maybe you didn't find them mind-numbing, I mean that is your world now.'

'No, my mind was numbed back then with the best of them. The first year economics course was just way beyond tedious, I regularly fell asleep, although the lecturer could draw amazing diagrams on the blackboard. That was a real skill.'

They both laughed. 'What I was wondering was whether you might take a look at the papers, to see if anything strikes you as out of place or significant or odd, or even something that should be there and isn't. We don't know how the papers got onto the floor. Maybe someone took something and that's the key to the murder. A specific motive is proving elusive, although it is clear that the man was not well liked. But it's a long way from being unpopular to being murdered.'

Staverley was elated, he had wanted a way into the police investigation, to know what was happening and here it was on a plate, he was being asked to help.

'Of course, I would be pleased to, anything I can do to help. I feel like I have a vested interest.'

Mellmoth reached under the table where he had put his brief case, rummaged for a moment and came up with a brown folder which he placed in the table in front of Staverley.

'I need to remind you that this is evidence in relation to a serious crime and that I need these papers returned in tack and as I said before nothing can be shared, with anyone, OK?'

'Understood, I'll start tonight.' Staverley tried not to sound too enthusiastic.

'Tomorrow would be more than fine, to be honest with you I am not expecting you to turn up anything, but we need to look at all the angles.'

'Should I take that to mean that the investigation is not going well?'

Mellmoth hestitated, very deliberately.

'If it were anybody else asking that question then the answer would be that we are pursing several promising lines of inquiry and anticipate an arrest in the near future. As its you, and given previous provisos, the answer is you are right is not going well. We have one obvious suspect, who I assume you know about, someone who visited Layton that night, although the question of timing is complicated by the cause of death. But that person does not seem to have a motive or the means, and is in some ways too obvious, although there maybe developments there, we are digging into his background a little more.'

That was Archie, of course, and the digging into background comment was worrying. If Mellmoth knew what Staverley knew then Archie being 'too obvious' to be taken seriously, might change very quickly.

'The real problem and one main focus at the moment is a woman who Layton had dinner with'. Mellmoth did not know that Staverley knew about her already from Nick, the hotel manager. 'We have had no luck in identifying her or tracing her movements. We have descriptions from the waiting staff but they are vague, she was always facing away from them, spoke very little, arrived and left without being seen, and all that could have be deliberate of course.'

Staverley nodded, trying to look as though all of this was new to him.

'We have two people who may or may not have seen the same woman in the street after she left the hotel but the timings are different and each one reported her as going in a different direction, one toward the station and one away from it. No one saw a car in the Hotel car park, at least not one that was not still there the following morning, she did not take a taxi and while there was a train about the right time the station ticket barrier is unmanned at that time of night. Three people might have got on according to the train guard but he's not sure and then there were people getting on and off along the rest of the line with an interchange stop at Haywards Heath. Tracing passengers has proved almost impossible. The one or two we have found were certainly not our woman and don't remember seeing such a woman either on the platform or the train. So that's it. We're still working on it.'

'And then there is me of course.' Staverley suggested with a carefully constructed wry smile.

'Yes, there is you. Young Barnaby has been following up on your interview and as you said yourself evidently corroboration has been difficult. Barnaby said that you were very adept at picking holes in any alibi that you might have.'

Staverley listened and looked very attentively at Mellmoth, and as said this and there was the hint of a smile. But perhaps that was his imagination.

'We are not eliminating any lines of enquiry but you are not high on our list of priorities at the moment – motive and means again – and from what Barnaby has ascertained you were telling the truth when you said you had never met Layton. Barnaby is new at this but his already well-developed detective's gut reaction is that you are probably not a serious suspect.' Now he did smile and was clearly enjoying teasing Staverley, which was reassuring. And surely he would not trust Staverley with Layton's papers if he was the subject of any real suspicion.

'And the soap?' Staverley asked.

'Yes, the soap, that is definitely something I wouldn't be talking to you about if it weren't for the leak to the press – 'A Clean Death' was one of the headlines, I despair sometimes of the 4th estate, and if I find out who leaked, and I will.... My well-developed detective's gut reaction is that it was someone in forensics and not one of our lads. Some readies being exchanged for information. But the soap is a bit more promising. It's an unusual murder weapon to say the least and the forensic lab people are working on it. The murderer would need access to equipment and to some not easily available materials – the poison was some kind of organophosphate, if I remember the word correctly, a form of ricin. But I am out of my depth with this stuff, I only have O-level chemistry and biology to rely on, and I failed chemistry, and I must have been absent on the day we did how to make poison soap. But evidently this ricin stuff can kill both by entering the blood stream via any scratches or abrasions on the skin, and Layton did have a significant cut on his hand, as well as via vapour or mist, and given he was in the bath... And as far as the pathologist can tell if it didn't get him one way it got him the other – over kill you could say, if you had that sort of sense of humour – its actually less dangerous if is ingested. Which is odd. I am still trying to bone up on the stuff. But that might be the key – follow the soap.'

Staverley had no idea about any of this. He had never heard of ricin, but there would be people at the university who would, and Monica might – that was a thought, but maybe an unsettling one.

Mellmoth went on. 'Ricin comes from beans, would you believe it, castor beans, as in castor oil. My mum used to make me drink the stuff, errgh! Ricin is part of the waste that remains when the beans are processed and the purified toxin is highly dangerous. The forensics people would have had us all in protective suits at the crime scene if they'd known at the time.' Mellmoth stopped suddenly and blanched. 'Damn it, did Barnaby get back to you?'

'No, why?'

'The idiot, and I'm an idiot. How have you been feeling? Have you felt unwell in the last few days? Have you seen a doctor?'

'No, why?' Staverley could sense the seriousness of Mellmoth's questions.

'Thank god for that. The thing is you might have been affected by the ricin, you went into the bathroom, the vapours can be deadly and I think you touched the body if I remember rightly. Barnaby is in for a major rollocking, I can tell you. But look it sounds fine, from what I have gathered you should have been feeling some nasty effects before now if you had breathed the stuff, and the water was cold by the time you went into the bathroom, so there should not have been any significant vapours left. And the hotel manager and staff are all fine. They've been checked. I am really sorry, you should have been made aware of this as soon as we knew. Everyone involved was lucky, apart from Layton of course, and even if you were affected they tell me that if you survive five days, given you are young enough and basically healthy to start with, you should be OK. But you only need a tiny amount of the stuff like a few grains of salt in vapour form to polish off a whole room full of people. It kills the cells evidently, what ever that means and there is no antidote. Normally it takes days rather than hours to kill but given Layton's age and the cut and vapour from the hot bath water and the fact that he was in the bath for several hours, and his age and health, then the lab says it makes sense. And even if he had been alive when you found him it was very unlikely that he would have survived. Its nasty, as you saw, a nasty way to go, the post mortem report makes grim reading, it must have been someone who really had a problem with him.'

'So wouldn't the murderer be putting themselves at risk, carrying the soap around, handling it?' Staverley asked.

'Not really, not in a solid state, as I said it's the vapours that release the poison into the air. The person who planted it was probably long gone before there was any danger.'

'And where on earth would someone get the toxin? Surely its not readily available to any Tom, Dick or Harry?'

'No, quite right, we're are working on that and also trying to find out whether it is possible to pin down the source, whether there is anything distinctive about the particular batch that was used. The only thing the lab has come up with so far is the possibility of an American connection but that remains a bit vague at the moment but really we're are pinning our main hopes for some progress in that direction.'

That was grim as Mellmoth said, but the rest of the evening continued on a lighter note with more reminiscences of their time at UME and some of the characters and friends they remembered. As it turned out neither had much ongoing contact with people they knew from that time. Mellmoth talked about the experience of being regarded with suspicion by fellow students because he was police and by fellow officers because he was a student. He had considered jacking it in at times but on the whole enjoyed it and felt he had benefited from it. It had certainly widened his vocabulary and writing police reports were now a doddle after struggling with essays on Keynsian economics and Schumpterian theories of history. They finished their pies and had another half each and called it a night. Neither felt up to a long drinking session, both had things to do and to think about. Staverley undertook to report back on Layton's papers within three days at most. He was eager to look at them.

On his way home on the train Staverley could not help thinking about what Mellmoth had said about the ricin and whether he did feel unwell or not. You don't usually think about feeling unwell, unless you feel unwell. Did he feel unwell? He didn't think so. He tried to work around the different bits of his body, a sort of health audit. The beer and pie were going down well. His head was as clear as it could be after a pint and a half. His legs felt stable and his heart seemed to him to be beating more or less normally. But the idea of being exposed to a deadly poison was disconcerting. As he worried about himself less he began to worry about Lionel more. Should he have left him as abruptly as he did? Would he be ok? Would he do anything foolish? But then whatever state he was in Lionel was a survivor, he carried on – bitter and broken he carried on, and his sense of responsibility for Monica would ensure, Staverley believed, that he would be at his desk as usual in the morning. He was almost sure.

Staverley had hoped to look at the papers when he got home, but was too tired. It had been a very strange and very hard day. His whole sense of what he was doing with his Layton research project and why he was doing it had shifted profoundly. His head hurt from thinking about it and more than anything he needed to sleep. He did not always sleep well when preoccupied and anticipated a disturbed and restless night, but in fact he fell into a deep dreamless sleep that left him rather groggy in the morning. Two large strong mugs of coffee and a bowl of cornflakes with slices of banana and a scattering of sultanas got him feeling a little perkier. He poured a third mug and opened the folder of papers. It was mostly, as Mellmoth had suggested a disappointment – routine, make-work stuff – a couple of sets of committee minutes, one from a government research group, but nothing there vital to national security, he would read them properly later, the agenda for the examination board he was supposed to have attended, with some gnomic doodles in the margins, some rough notes for a talk he was to give to some business organization, which given the handwriting were virtually impossible to read, a letter from his lawyer about Layton's pension and some related investments, which suggested that he was decently well off, and two requests for references – now here was something interesting. Staverley was a bit taken aback, one of the requests related to Liana his ex-wife- the University of the West of Ireland wanting Layton's views on her suitability for a post as Professor of Health Economics. Staverley remembered that she had mentioned something about it when they last spoke on the telephone, he did not always pay full attention when she was in career-making mode, which was most of the time. He would ask her about it. He had not known she had crossed paths with Layton. But it could well be one of those situations where Layton was consulted irrespective of his direct knowledge of the candidates – just because of who he was. The other request was for a comment on lowly lectureship appointment at a Welsh university, referring to someone he had never heard of. He would check in the library. Then there were various bits of ephemera – notices of events, invitations to attend meetings or speak at them, and a request from a German journal to review a new book on European economic policy.

There were also two personal handwritten letters. One, very short, from a colleague in the US, at Springfield University saying that he had followed up on Layton's suggestion with an appropriate outcome, but neither the suggestion nor the outcome were specified. The other from someone who might have been a cousin asking about Layton's health and offering to meet for tea in London. He would check further on those as well as far as he was able. Finally, there was another set of notes, covering two foolscap pages, that were no more than scribbles really, and consisted mainly of names and places. Staverley recognised some of the latter as British and US universities, but the names were unreadable. He thought he might try them out on Pauline, she had the knack of being able to read even the most impenetrable handwriting – probably a skill taught to undergraduate historians as part of their tradecraft. He had been embarrassed once when Pauline told him that one of his students had asked her to translate his written feedback on an MA essay. He had resolved to make his handwriting clearer after that but the resolve quickly faded. Readability was one advantage of the word processor despite its unreliability. Which reminded him, if he needed reminding, that a morning at the keyboard was inescapable if he was to make any impression at all on the long and increasingly daunting list he had made of outstanding tasks. He would go to university in the afternoon, a short stint in the library to follow up on the papers, then meetings with various students, a chat with Pauline, if she was there, and check up on Lionel, discretely. Then back home for another session on the BBC and some preparation for the seminar he was teaching tomorrow. He would also telephone Monica. The number of things to do was depressing but 'when the going gets tough...' he said to himself and got dressed to leave.

The library offered some help with loose ends from Layton's papers but nothing of much interest. At least he was being thorough. The meetings with students went well, they were all doing what they were supposed to be doing and none had 'problems'. Student 'problems' were always a pain. He also popped into Jean's office and after an exchange of banter he asked if Lionel was in. He was, but tied up all day with appointments and meetings and unavailable. That was all Staverley wanted to know, Lionel was up and running, he was not looking forward to seeing Lionel again. He did not know how they would be with one another after the revelations of the previous day. Pauline was in and up for coffee and cake. She was happy to have a look at Layton's scribbles but a bit miffed when Staverley would not tell her what they were, where they came from or why he was asking. He made some vague reference having applied to join MI5 and this being a test, but she just laughed. Her efforts yielded a couple more names and places but these did not seem to point to anything significant. She also quizzed him about where he had been for the past few days and he invented various excuses. He felt bad about that because Pauline was normally a trusted confidant on almost everything and he always felt he benefited from discussing things with her but now he was carrying around in his head confidences from Archie, Lionel, Monica and the police none of which he could share with her. Even so as they chewed their pieces of cake he did have a strong urge to share and get her views and opinions, and advice, but he realised that too many assurance and promises would be broken if he spoke about what he knew. They did indulge in some idle speculation about the police investigation and the newspaper stories about the deadlysoap but beyond that Staverley remained stum. He anticipated some point in the future when his friendship with Pauline would be tested if she found out what he had been up to over the past few days.

A bit of deskwork, a couple of telephone calls and he retreated home. He made himself a rather impressive cheddar and beetroot sandwich which he took to the wordprocessor. He promised himself an hour of writing before phoning Monica. He made it to fifty minutes before he could not wait any longer but when Monica picked up, he had her home and lab numbers now, she asked him if she could call back in half an hour while she attended to something complicated and scientific that could not wait. That gave Staverley a bit more writing time and he had crafted another 436 elegant and precise words, according to the machine, the number not the elegance and precision, before she phoned back.

'Monica, how are you, I've missed you, you know.'
'Well much to my surprise I think it is possible I may have missed you a little bit too. Not much you understand.'

It was good to hear that laugh again. And it was good to speak to her without having to think at the same time about the possibility of her being a murder suspect.

'Well given that I was wondering whether we could meet again, maybe quite soon, I could come to you or you could come here, what do you think?' Various interesting scenarios were forming in Staverley's head.

'I'd love to come to you, see where you hang out and whether you hoover regularly, but for the next couple of weeks I can't, I still have a lot follow up to do from the big experiment, we still don't know if it produced anything useful, so I could come after that, or I would love it if you could come up here again. I am sure I can squeeze in a few hours of down time, and I owe you a dinner. I might even be persuaded to cook for you, but don't set your hopes too high, cooking is not one of my strong points.'

'It works for me, what about the weekend?'

She thought for a moment, there was a rustle of paper.

'Saturday would be good, perhaps late afternoon?'

Staverley was pleased, he was smiling rather inanely to himself.

'What about this, what if you do what you have to do, give me free rein in your kitchen and I cook for you. I could even do my signature dish, celebrated among Europe's top chefs and epicures.'

She laughed again. 'That sounds, great, perfect, I can hardly wait, what's the dish?'

'You will have to wait and see.' Staverley said.

'Oh that's mean, but I suppose I could survive a few days without knowing. The speculation will keep me sane while it work through pages of lab results. Why don't you come by the lab when you arrive and I'll give you a tour of my domain, that's my workbench, and give you my house keys.'

'That, Monica, sounds like a plan. But I need to warn you, I have to ask you something again.'

He thought he could sense her tense.

'It's nothing to do with families, although actually it is, but not in the way we talked last time. I want to pick your professional brain about ricin.'

'What? Why on earth do you want to know about ricin? What are you planning? Should I be worried?'

'I will explain, and it might be a little upsetting but it's the science I am interested in.'

'You are being mysterious again, but I can do a bit of checking, its not something I'm immediately familiar with but I could offer a quick tutorial if you make it worth my while. It's not the most romantic of subjects.'

'I can certainly make it worth you while, there is the cooking of course, and did I mention dessert.'

'What like ice cream, you mean?' She asked.

'No nothing like ice cream, I had in mind something tasty we could share after dinner, or even before, although as I think about it ice cream could play a part.' They both laughed.

'I'll let you know what train I am catching, see you Saturday.'

They hung up.

Staverley spent a few moments in pornographic reverie considering the various non-culinary possibilities of ice cream. He was enjoying himself until an awful and very much unwanted thought insinuated itself into his mind. Okay he thought, Monica may have been with Lionel in Cambridge when Layton's deadly carbolic was planted, but the maker of the soap and the deliverer did not have to be the same person. What if there was a third-party involved, the mystery woman or the visitor? Perhaps it was a re-run of *Murder on the Orient Express* and everyone was involved. Staverley's reverie faded and his very good mood evaporated. With a single flourish of logic and suspicion he had just re-instated Monica as a possible suspect, at the very least an accomplice. Damn, damn, damn, damn! Could she possibly be part of another conspiracy alongside that with Lionel, or even also with Lionel as a part of it? He tried to think of ways in which that would not be possible but could not. It was not likely but it was possible, unless there was something about the ricin itself that would point in a different direction. How could you have such strong positive feelings for someone and consider the possibility at the same time that they are involved in a murder plot? Perhaps there was something wrong with him. Yet again he began to regret getting involved with trying to make sense of Layton's murder but at the same time he knew that if he had not gotten involved he would not have meant Monica.

The time until he got off the train in Cambridge on Saturday did not pass in the haze of delicious anticipation as he had initially hoped and expected. His erotic imagination was not entirely inactive but ricin related doubts tempered his libido. Monica had given him directions to her laboratory building but it proved far from easy to find, Cambridge was a confusing labyrinth of small streets. He pondered as he walked that the Cambridge Colleges looked as silly in their own way as the buildings on his campus but their silliness was blunted by age and ivy. There was press button intercom on the laboratory front door and Monica released the door to let him in. He had to go to the third floor she said and she was waiting at the top of the stairs. Any doubts he was juggling with about his feelings for her were swept away by a long and lingering kiss that also overcame any shyness that might have crept into seeing one another again after one dinner, one breakfast and one night in bed together. Monica took his hand and led him through a series of doors into a large, complicated and very messy laboratory that extended over half the floor space of the top floor of the building. The space was packed with machines of various kinds and sizes, there were very few of the test tubes he had been expecting, and no odd smells or naked flames. Some of the machines were clearly at work, humming or in one case vibrating rather violently.

'So this is it.' Monica said. 'This is where I do my thing, or to be honest this is where I am told by other people far more important than me to do their things for them. But I do have a sideline of my own that I am rather pleased with that I might tell you about when I know you better.' She kissed him again briefly. 'And that's it really, that's the tour, I could offer some boring explanations about what all these machines do but I think you have something to ask and then you are going to cook me a wonderful supper while I finish up here, yes?'
'Yes. Exactly.' He said.
'So ricin, why an earth do you want to know about ricin?'

'Well, anything I say you cannot talk to anyone else about, I am going to tell you things the police told me and I am sworn to secrecy and now you are too. Ok?'

'The police, why are they telling you things?' She asked.

'That's a long story, can I get to that later?'

'Go on then, ricin!'

'That's the unpleasant bit. I don't want to upset you but it seems that the soap that killed your father, the soap that was in all the newspapers, was laced with ricin.'

Monica looked sort of shocked and her mouth twitched several times but Staveley could not really pin down her response. Given her feelings about her Father she was hardly going to breakdown in tears, but even so she would now know from her reading that ricin was going have very nasty consequences. That was always assuming that ricin and its effects were new to her, which was Staveley's determined assumption unless proven otherwise. He pressed on.

'The police have explained some things about ricin, including the possibility that I might have been contaminated – which I haven't, at least I think I haven't - but I would like to know more about it. I don't really understand what it is and what it does and where it comes from, apart from knowing its castor beans.' He was aware that the possibility of being affected made his interest in the poison seem just about reasonable.

'That's terrible, are you sure you're ok? Have you seen a doctor?'

"Really, I am well, honestly.'

Monica did not look entirely convinced.

'From what I have gleaned the toxicity of ricin could well have affected others in the same location, although being carried by the soap as a medium might have limited the distribution.'

She switched quickly into professional mode.

'Ricin acts as a toxin by inhibiting protein synthesis. What that means is it prevents cells from assembling various amino acids into proteins according to the messages it receives from messenger RNA in a process conducted by the cell's ribosome, that's the machinery that makes protein and at the most basic level of cell metabolism. That is essential to all living cells and thus to life itself.'

Staveley was already struggling.

'Normally, if untreated, within 2 to 5 days of exposure, effects from ricin appear in the central nervous system, adrenal glands, kidneys, and liver. The consequences are catastrophic and symptoms include edema of the eyes and lips, asthma, bronchial irritation, dry, sore throat; congestion; skin redness and blisters, wheezing, itchy, watery eyes, and chest tightness. A combination of those effects are likely to have serious secondary consequences for anyone who is not in perfect health to start with, which I assume would include my father. He might have died for any number of the primary or secondary effects of the ricin.' That bit Staveley could follow and he thought back to seeing Layton in the bath and the dreadful state of his body. Monica continued.

'An antidote has been developed by the UK military, but it has not yet been tested on humans, the American's have done some very limited human testing. Basically ricin is very bad news for anyone who is exposed to it directly.'
'I understood a little of that. But I also wanted to know where it comes from. I know it's a bi-product of castor beans but what's is for, who uses it?
'Well first and foremost it's a chemical and biological weapon, it was weaponised by the Americans and the Russians in World War two, they had designed cluster bombs to deliver it. It was never actually deployed but some people have accused the KGB of using it on a small scale, and do you remember Georgi Markov the Bulgarian who was murdered in London in 78?'

Staverley nodded. It had been big news at the time.
'Well that was ricin, but its now been overtaken by sarin as something of military interest but in the US it's carefully regulated as what they call a selected agent and internationally its outlawed by the 1972 Biological Weapons Convention. But basically it's not that difficult to make, the Castor plant, *Ricinus communis*, can be grown at home and castor beans are the source of castor oil, laxative of choice in many a childhood, and it has a variety of other medicinal uses like softening corns and bunions, and castors seeds are used in paint-making. I haven't been able to go into the processing of the beans very carefully but my impression is that chemically it's not that difficult to produce purified ricin, at

least on small scale. Here.' She gestured to the lab. 'It would be relatively easy but a basic chemistry set might do.'

These were things Staverley did and did not want to hear. The fact that a laboratory was not essential meant that there was no strong reason to suspect Monica rather than anyone else but the coincidence of means and motive remained. She also said she did not to know about the production process. But it is easy to deny that you know things. Nonetheless, he decided, at least for the time being, that everything in Monica's demeanour and her candour meant that all of this was as new to her as it was to him and that she was not a secret manufacturer of purified ricin.

'Well you are certainly a useful person to have around when it comes to the world's deadliest poisons, and lovely with it.' He squeezed her hand and she squeezed back.

'So are you going to tell me why you want to know all of this? Are you intending to wage war, commit your own murder, or what?'

His response was an approximation to the truth. 'It's just curiosity really, given what the police told me and what I saw in that bathroom, and the possibility that I might have been affected as well, I needed to know a bit more about this stuff and what I had got involved in. It all seems so extraordinary, the idea that someone can be killed by a bar of soap seems crazy. You've helped me understand a bit more about that. Thank you.' He hoped that would suffice and Monica seemed to take it as satisfactory.

'I do appreciate the trouble you went to finding all of this, I really do. But I think I know more than enough now about poisons and what I need to do is some shopping and acquaint myself with the eccentricities of your kitchen.'

Monica looked a little dubious but handed over her keys and offered a goodbye kiss that started out as perfunctory and escalated to something much more exciting. Staverley began to wonder where in the lab Monica spent her nights when she was duty machine minder but she ushered him down the stairs and went back to her work.

Staverley's plan was for a chicken risotto. He loved risottos and made them often, usually vegetarian ones, but Monica he thought was probably a devoted meat eater and he did not want to disappoint her. The right rice was a little difficult to find but a back street Italian deli came to the rescue, the rest was easy and he carried his bounty back to Monica's house, buying a bottle of Italian wine on the way, and began to familiarise himself with the kitchen. It had something in common with her laboratory in as much that it was well provided with gadgets and suggested despite what she had said that she did a lot of cooking and might be good at it. He hoped he would find out in due course. The preparations did not take long, the thing about risottos is tending the rice while it cooks, adding the stock bit by bit until the rice is soft and creamy and all the favours have blended. He fried the leeks, added the rice, flooded the pan with the first spoonful of stock and turned it off to be finished later when Monica was back. He broke up the chicken breasts and fried them gently in another pan, leaving them aside to be added later. Then he washed up the pots and pans he had used, found plates, glasses and cutlery, laid the table, and went to explore Monica's record collection. He was not surprised to find a high proportion of the albums were Jazz, the usual suspects Davies, Coltrane, Mingus, Parker, Baker were all there as well as some more esoteric US imports. Mixed in with the jazz were some classical pieces, mainly choral, and a smattering of soul and blues. He put on a Bill Evans record and sat down. He knew little of Evans, apart from his involvement with Miles Davies and his part in the *Kind of Blue* sessions, probably the best jazz album of all time, and certainly the best selling. Evan's tunes were improvisations based on jazz standards and he liked it and thought it set the right mood for the evening. Monica was due back soon and Staverley had a few minutes to think about her and their evolving relationship while Bill Evans explored various interpretations of Our Love is Here to Stay.

To say that the evening went well would be a bit of an understatement. Monica arrived on time and changed. The outcome of the change, a white silk blouse and black leather skirt with a zip that ran most of the way up the right thigh was a lot more alluring than the stained lab coat she had been wearing earlier. The zip was open a couple of inches when she came down to dinner, it was open a lot more by the end of the evening, and what she was wearing underneath, although there was not much of it, was stunning. Staverley was profoundly stunned. The meal went down well and perhaps not surprisingly they did not get back to the question of ricin. That did not arise again until late next morning after breakfast. They were both a little sleepy still.

'So you have fed me, had your wicked way with me, eaten my breakfast, had your wicked way with me again, I have had my wicked way with you, tell me more about ricin, the police and what you are up to.'

Staverley had been dreading this moment.

'The police bit is difficult, I can't say too much. The use of ricin has not been made public, and that has to stay between us. The 'what I am up to' is trickier. My interest in your father and his daughter came about partly as I said yesterday because I was the one who found his body, I feel involved somehow, and I feel a responsibility to find out what happened, or help in the finding out. But it's also about my colleagues, who like Lionel, are involved in different ways, and there's one in particular who may well be the primary suspect, but who I am sure is innocent. In complicated ways I owe him and want to help him and finding the real killer seems the best way of doing that. So I have been doing what the police do, talking to people. You were one person I wanted to talk to, and Lionel was another and there have been a few others.'

Monica did not look happy.

'I am confused here. Us being here now, is this still a part of your personal investigation into my father's death? Is this about clearing your colleagues and feeling responsible?'

'Yes and definitely no.' Said Staverley, he wanted to be as honest as he could without jeopardising what has happening between Monica and him.

'Those are the reasons which led me to be here, but that's not why I am here. I am here because of you Monica, not because you are Layton's daughter or because you can tell me about ricin. Does that make sense?'

'Maybe, say more.'

'What I am trying to say is that I convinced you to meet me because I wanted to know more about your father, things that may have helped me be clearer about his death, but I am here now because I want to be with you, because you are an incredible woman, and because I could not possibly stay away.'

Staverley was struggling with this, to make himself clear and dispose of the half truths with which he had started. If he was honest with himself he was still unsure where his feelings for Monica had got to, they were certainly way beyond 'like' or simple lust, in very murky territory that he was just not ready to name. He was also uncomfortable about not being able to explain that, for a time at least, he had regarded Monica as a suspect for her father's murder, and that even now, although he was almost certain that she was not involved, there was still a lingering logical possibility that she was. Logic and emotion would just not fit together. He noticed that Monica had pulled the sides of her dressing gown into a more respectable arrangement, which seemed like not a good sign. He had been enjoying her attractive dishevelment.

'I might need to think some more about you Staverley, and about what we are doing here. It seems to me that you know a lot more about me than I do about you, despite our exchange of histories over dinner. I need to consider how much I can believe you and trust you. I am not ready to get into something that will end up leaving me feeling let down and used. Perhaps it would be better if you made your way home now and give me some space to think. I may not be mourning my father but there are a lot of emotions going around in my mind and I may not be making entirely sensible decisions here, I need to be absolutely sure that you are what you say you are and that I am not letting my libido mislead me.'
That was not what Staverley had been hoping for but appeared to be inevitable in the circumstances.
'Can I phone you tomorrow then?' Staverley asked.
'No, I will phone you, in a few days.'
That was definitely not what he had been hoping for.

Once home Staverley pottered about feeling miserable and stupid. He could not stop thinking about Monica, and the possibility of not seeing her again was unbearable and he could not settle to anything productive. Their relationship had only come about because of Layton's death, but it was also blighted by his death. He decided on a long walk, possibly followed by a film, something continental would suit.

The following morning Staverley organised some notes based on what sense he had made of Layton's papers and telephoned Mellmoth. In fact there was little to report. He clarified some of the documents and explained the things he had followed up on. The only loose ends were the American professor and the cousin. Mellmoth said that he would try and contact the cousin and asked Staverley to check further on the professor. Staverley did not mention that one of the reference requests was about his ex-wife. After he hung up the phone he wondered whether he should have. Perhaps Mellmoth knew already. That worry was like some kind of premonition, just as he was ready to leave for the university the phone rang.

'Its me, Liana.' She said. As though he may have forgotten. She sounded relatively subdued. Staverley was never sure how she would be when she phoned.
'Good to hear from you.' He lied. Lying was becoming something he did a lot and he was getting good at it.
'Well we haven't spoken since your big day.'
'What big day?'
'You, Layton, the body, Staverley on the spot. Once I read about it in the newspaper 'Lecturer finds dead professor' or whatever the headline was, it didn't take long to work out who the lecturer was. I had this inkling that you might be involved somehow. A bit of a shock finding him dead, I would imagine.'
All of this was very empathetic by Liana's standards.
'It wasn't a good moment no. He was in a terrible state. It's an image that going to stay with me for a long time. I didn't know him, and I don't think I would have wanted to, but it was not a good way to go for anyone, no matter how unpleasant they were.'
'Unpleasant,' Liana snorted, 'that's an understatement, he was disgusting, a horrible man.'
'I didn't know you had even met him Liana.'
'Oh, our paths crossed. If you work in the social sciences and want to get on with your career then inevitably at some point you cross paths with Layton.'

'I know what you mean. In fact I came across one of those crossings a couple of days ago. The police asked me to look through some of his papers and you were there, it was a bit of a surprise, Layton had been asked to comment on your application for the Irish chair. You mentioned that to me last time you called.'

Liana snorted again. 'Well, that's one reference he wont be writing, thank good ness.' She had shifted from subdued to noisy and excited.

'I assumed it was just one of those routine, lets ask the big man's opinion things.'

'It might have been that, I certainly didn't ask him. He had written a reference for me before but things didn't turn out well.'

This was all new to Staverley. Liana knowing Layton, him writing references for her.

'So what happened?' He asked.

'Do you really want to know?' An unusual question coming from Liana, her normal mode of functioning was to assume that anyone she spoke to would want to know anything and everything about her, and especially about her career. She did not wait for a reply.

'Well, he was involved in the post I applied for in the States. That job should have been mine. I spent two months there making an impression. He had recommended me for consideration and I was invited to do some summer school teaching, which went really well, and give a faculty lecture, as they call it, before a final decision was made. There I was thousands of miles away, giving a lecture that I had spent weeks preparing, there were people there from all over, and a few asides about the weaknesses of methods of analysis in British social science, an illustrative quote from Layton's dreaded tome and its all over. Layton's mates report back, he feels affronted by my inappropriate criticisms and general treachery, as he quaintly put it, letters are exchanged and the post goes to some dud American economist who would not know and original idea if he fell over it in the street. The bastard.'

Staverley had never heard Liana swear before.

'A hateful man he was. You have no idea. But he can't stop me now, can he? But in the meantime there I am with a short term contract in Staffordshire of all places, on a ridiculous and boring research project looking at social class patterns of engagement with NHS out-patient services. Very dull, me, can you imagine. And I am already practically running the project. The Director has no clue. Layton had a lot to answer for, but with him out of the way the Irish thing should be done and dusted. I know they are tremendously keen on me, and the department there needs some energy and impetus, and it will be a good stepping stone to something more appropriate, somewhere I can make a mark, without the bastard getting in my way, weaving his evil spells.'

Liana's self confidence and strategic vision for herself never failed to amaze Staverley, no matter how many times he heard her speak like this. But her involvement with Layton was all new to him and seemed to be no end to the list of people who were pleased that he was dead or wanted him dead. Staverley wondered whether he should get Liana to tell him more about the debacle in the US. Perhaps it had something to do with the letter from the Springfield University professor. He would probably have to meet her to do that properly. On the other hand, since their divorce Staverley had been careful to avoid any face-to-face contact with Liana. He found it difficult enough to manage on the telephone. Maybe he would think about it. But he had to accept that in all other ways his research into Layton and his death was stalled, like the police he had now had no clear suspects, no clues, no obvious direction. At least that meant he could get on with the work he was supposed to be doing.

'Listen Liana, I have to go, I am running late for work. You must tell me more about all of this, and what happened in the States and your plans, and good luck with the interview in Ireland. You have an interview I assume.'

'Of course, it's the end of next week. Must go and get these research people sorted. Bye.'

And she was gone. As usual Staverley was relieved that the conversation was over. Sometime ago he had realised that whatever other feelings he had for Liana, he was actually a little frightened of her. Getting in her way, as he had in a sense as her husband, was not a good idea.

CHAPTER ELEVEN

As was always the case when Staverley was running late the train was also late and he arrived at the Social Sciences building with no time to get to his office before the Programme Leader's Meeting he was supposed to be attending – an important meeting following Layton's passing. They now had no external examiner for the new degree.

There was as usual a queue for the lifts and the floor lights gave no indication of movement, a sure sign of the porters' continuing disgruntlement. He turned to the stairway and began his long ascent at speed two steps at a time. By the time he reach the 7th floor he was reduced to a plodding pace one step at a time and was breathing hard. It is recovery time that is important he told himself but the sweaty patch in the middle of his back was sticking to his shirt and he felt in need of a shower and his knees ached. He could see people moving along the corridor, the meeting was convening. He hurried into the room and found a place in the corner where he could cool down and allow his breathing to return to normal. It was gloomy outside so the lights were on in the room, basic strip lights that he found oppressive and which often gave him a headache. That and problems with the BBC screen had made him begin to think he needed an eye test – something else to find time for.

Feeling a little better he looked around the room. Pauline slipped into the chair next to him and smiled. Roger and Duncan were in animated conversation with Daniel Dalgliesh. Daniel was wearing as always his red velvet jacket, he was the resident, card-carrying Marxist, although his views about education and politics always seemed distinctly at odds with his ideological commitments, and as he wrote very little it was never quite clear how those commitments translated into an actual framework for analysis. But he was politically active in other ways though and acted as a sort of political conscience for the department. Mary Marsh sat opposite to Staverley, between Lionel and Archie. Mary was a psychoanalyst, a very small, very quiet woman, with very long blonde hair. She also had a very hesitant manner and very quiet voice and rarely spoke in meetings. But she was capable of insights, sometimes a little odd but often interesting, into the conduct of meetings, if not necessarily about what the meeting was about. Staverley sometimes wondered if she regarded her colleagues as research subjects, although like Daniel she wrote very little, so it was difficult to know. What she did write was about troubled children. Perhaps that was how she viewed her colleagues, as difficult and quarrelsome infants - it would not be too far off the mark.

It was very strange to look around the room now – post-Layton. Everyone was affected, directly and indirectly by the death, either personally or in relation to work or both. As far as Archie and Lionel were concerned the affects were enormous but invisible to most people. Their lives were changed. However hard he tried Staverley could not sit in the room with a sense of business as usual. He now knew things about Lionel and Archie that he could not un-know. No matter how normal things may seem, he knew what he knew and they knew that he knew and they knew he knew. For him they were different people now, realer people, flawed people with difficult and complicated lives. Both bore their histories stoically. As he looked around the rest of the room he wondered what other secrets and what other pain and regrets had made his colleagues the people they were. He had his own history but the revelations over the past few days made his problems and regrets seem relatively insignificant and he tried to be grateful for that. But lives and the way we experience them cannot be weighed and compared so easily. Possibly we all make the best of our history but some are better at doing that than others.

Lionel called the meeting to order in his usual manner of gruff efficiency.
'Well colleagues, the main item of business for this meeting is to move forward in finding a new external examiner for the undergraduate degree in the light of recent unfortunate events.'
Staverley was surprised that Lionel could sound so calm and matter of fact.
'I have given the matter some thought but I am very open to suggestions from colleagues. Archie I believe has something to say, Archie.'

Staverley studied Archie carefully. Was it his imagination or did he look a little younger or maybe less careworn than of late. He must still be worried about the police investigation but he exuded a greater sense of energy than he had for some time, and he had had a haircut. He looked oddly well groomed and presentable.

'Thank you Lionel, my point was one of strategy rather than having a specific person to put forward to the meeting. I would like us to consider a change of tack and rather than seeking an old hand, a senior figure, as we had previously, we might consider a less senior appointee, someone who represents the future of the social sciences rather than its past, someone whose name would compliment and reinforce the innovative nature of the degree.'

There was a moment of thoughtful silence and then Lionel spoke again.

'I must say that I am rather sympathetic to that idea. If we want potential students to view the degree as something different from what is already on offer at longer established more traditional universities, and that I think is very much the case, then such an appointment would signal our intention to teach the social sciences differently, and to teach a different social science.'

This was rather a major change of position from Lionel but Staverley knew now that he had pushed for Layton's appointment for reasons other than academic ones. It was good to see the two senior members of the department in agreement for once and what Archie had proposed was clearly a good way to move on from and away from everything associated with the murder and the dissension surrounding Layton and his appointment. There was a general murmur of approval around the room, and Roger, probably sensing the direction of the meeting added his two-pennuth. 'Sound, very sound.' Both Des and Mary nodded enthusiastically.

'In that case, unless anyone has any immediate ideas.' He paused but no one spoke. 'I would suggest that Archie and I perhaps with Roger, Mary and Staverley', he looked to each of them, and each nodded, 'get together quite quickly to draw up a short list for further discussion by the meeting. Agreed?' There was more of that incoherent murmuring that regular committee goers immediate recognise as agreement. For Staverley this had been a perfect meeting, it was quick and focused and there was consensus, no rambling, no pointless tangents, no histrionics - rare and worth savouring.

Staverley was hoping for a quick exit and a bit of time in his room before teaching but was waylaid by an unusually ebullient looking Roger. But when Roger spoke it was in a conspiratorial whisper.

'I was thinking about you'. Roger said. Staverley did not like the sound of that.

'Really.'

'Well you and your ex.' Staverley did not understand what Roger was talking about.

'You mean Liana?'

'Of course, the lovely Liana.' Roger's schoolboy grin, a joyless thing at the best of times, made Staverley wince.

'What about Liana and me?' He asked.

'Well seeing her around I assumed that there were, well, you know, developments.' He grinned again, making developments sound obscene. Staverley winced again and edged toward the door.

'You've lost me here Roger, I haven't seen Liana face to face for months. We talk on the phone but that's it, and that works for me.' He edged further away.

'Oh! Sorry, my misreading of the situation obviously. When I saw her the other night I just assumed she was meeting you. Maybe she had another assignation.' If he grinned again Staverley thought he might do something drastic but in this case assignation was a matter of pedantry rather than innuendo.

'Being divorced usually means not seeing one another Roger, that's how it works, that's what its for basically, getting out of each other's lives and not seeing one another. But anyway when was this, she never mentioned coming when we talked on the phone last night? Are you absolutely sure it was her.'

It is her life Staverley thought, and she was in perpetual motion most of the time, but odd that she had not mentioned it. He really wanted to get on.

'Quite sure. I was on my evening run, I am up to 80 kilometres a week you know.' It sounded a lot. Roger would not have mentioned it if it were not. Staverley wondered how far that was in miles.

'It was near the station in town, she was rushing, catching a train I assumed. Past me before I had time to stop and then she was gone. So that would be my B intinerary – I have three routes. Keeps it interesting, change of terrain, slightly different muscle groups, variety of breathing patterns.' Staverley did not want to know any of this.

'So…' Roger was thinking and counting in his head. 'This is the 19th, so it must have been September the 26th. That sounds right, around 9.00 pm I would estimate. I cut over 30 seconds off my PB for that route that night, so I remember it clearly. Haven't got close since for some reason. I am thinking that I need to research circadian rhythms – that maybe the answer. Do you know that…'

But Staverley cut him off, hoping to avoid another lecture. 'PB?' he asked, trying hard not to sound exasperated.

'Personal best.' Roger looked at Staverley with a how could anyone not know that look. Roger had the uncanny ability to make him feel stupid.

'Right, yes, good to know. Nice talking to you Rog.' Roger did not like people calling him Rog, so Staverley made a point of doing it at every opportunity.

'I have students.' He said and turned away abruptly.

There were students. Two were waiting outside his door. More were due. They were coming to agree essay titles. He got through eight of the twelve fairly painlessly but then the ninth began with the dreaded. 'I can't decide what I want to write about.'

That usually meant a circumlutory account of the student's every thought and inclination for the past week, leading to no firm conclusion and Staverley was not in the mood.

'I tell you what Cormoran, why don't you go to the library do a bit of browsing, look at the journals, make a decision and come back tomorrow. We can then agree a title and discuss the essay.' If you don't decide, he wanted to say, then don't come back, but he did not.

Cormoran looked dejected but shuffled off and as he left Archie's head appeared around the door.

'What about a bite of supper tonight chez nous?'

Staverley was pleased. It was a long time since he had been invited to supper at Archie's. He took it as a sign that things might be changing for the better between them.

'I'd love to. What time?' He asked.

'Can you come at 7.00?'

He could and he passed the rest of the day in an efficient good humour and for the first time in weeks he had a sense that he was managing to make some inroads into his backlog of work and extraneous tasks.

On the train home he crossed several things off the long to-do list in his notebook. Having done that and enjoyed a moment of satisfaction he began to think back to the conversation with Roger and as the train juddered into the station he was struck by a very disturbing realisation. September the 26th was the night of Layton's murder. If Roger had not imagined seeing Liana, and Roger had little imagination, then she was somewhere near his hotel heading for the train station at a key time. She may have seen something, or someone, or…. The second 'or' was difficult to get beyond. The second 'or' would mean that Liana's presence that night might in some way be directly related to Layton's death. Other reasons for being in that place at that time seemed unlikely. Staverley became aware that everyone had left the carriage and the train was beginning to fill up again for the return journey. He did all of those things you read about when people are trying to process unpalatable thoughts. He swallowed, closed his eyes momentarily and rubbed them with his hand and sighed deeply. None of that really helped, he was still faced with the looming possibilities of the second 'or'. He tried to resist its implications but ended up on the other side of it with the inevitable conclusion that yet another person he knew, or thought he knew, had become a suspect – at least as far as he was concerned. How many potential murderers were there out there? He had managed to get to the age of 31 without encountering a single murderer or murder suspect, he was now surrounded by them. They were everywhere and they were all people he knew or had got to know. The sense of calm that had developed during the day, something he had not experienced much of since Layton's death, was gone again. He had another difficult decision to make. He could and probably should phone Mellmoth as soon as he got home or, another one of those deceptively innocent 'ors', or he could speak to Liana first and see what she had to say for herself. Perhaps Roger was wrong and it had not been her, and she was in fact in Antwerp or Warsaw, or perhaps Liana had a perfectly good explanation for why she had been there which had nothing to do with Layton. But Roger was annoyingly rarely wrong and if Liana had been there when he said, why had she not said anything. Even in her very self-centred world she would have realised the significance of the date and the time. And those thoughts were inflated and inflamed by what Liana had said about Layton and his interference with her career plans.

Staverley phoned her from his flat and got her on the second attempt.
'Liana, its me, Staverley.'
'We may be divorced but I still recognize your voice.' She responded tartly.
'Liana I need to see you.'
'Really, but I thought you didn't want to see me. I seem to remember you saying that quite loudly the last time we met. I thought that was why we only spoke on the phone, so we were less likely to say things loudly.' All of that was true. They had a meeting with a solicitor to arrange some financial disentanglements and the coffee afterwards had degenerated into something rather unpleasant, and loud. Staverley shuddered at the memory.
'All of that is true.' He said. 'But this is different. I need to ask you something. Its important, and its nothing to do with us, and I will not speak loudly I promise.'
'Alright, I don't know what could be important but I will agree not to speak loudly either, but only because I am in a good mood. When is this momentous coming together going to take place?' She asked. Staverley thought she sounded odd, her good moods were very few and far between, he was wary, but pressed on.
'What are you doing tomorrow? It's a bit far but if I set off early I could come up and see you.' He suggested.
'No need, I am in London tomorrow. I have a meeting and a lunch, but I could do tea. I will be at UCL in the afternoon, what about that bookshop tearoom place near the British Museum we used to go to. I like their cakes.'
'Perfect, 4.00 okay?'

'It is, *a demain*, bye.' She said and hung up abruptly. Staverley scoured his smattering of schoolboy French, he had failed at O-level, and finally understood what Liana had said. Her good mood was very perplexing.

There is nothing more he could do now until they spoke directly so he had a quick shower and shaved in readiness for supper with Archie and family. As he looked at himself in the bathroom mirror he thought again that he might have his hair cut, and smarten himself up a bit. He might grow a moustache. With all that in mind he avoided jeans and found a reasonably well-pressed shirt tucked away in his chest of drawers. If he left straightaway he would have time to pop into the off license and buy a bottle of wine to take – but definitely no Blue Nun – nail polish remover - or Lambrusco – sugar water - or Le Piat Dor, that definitely tasted of strepsils. An Australian chardonnay would serve, lots of oak and butter. Valerie liked it he remembered.

The daughters were definitely more friendly this time, although they were all quickly gone – cinema, friend's house and 10 pin bowling respectively. That left the three of them for supper in the kitchen and remembering Staverley's growing suspicion of meat Valerie had thoughtfully made a fish pie, to which the chardonnay was a perfect accompaniment. The pie was rich and creamy with a crispy topping of cheese and potato. The conversation was light and cheerful and despite the continuing uncertainty around Archie's relationship with Layton, as far as the police were concerned, he was less burdened than Staverley had seen him for a long time. He said he was considering a clear out of his study upstairs, which made Valerie laugh out loud and Valerie talked about her latest role in her amateur dramatics society. She had the leading part - Staverley had seen her in plays a couple of times and knew she was good. She could turn her hand to anything – musicals, farce or serious drama. He was no theatre critic but he thought she might be very talented. This time she was playing a man, or rather playing a woman who passed as a man – Albert Nobbs. Albert, she explained, worked as a butler in late-19th-century Dublin and although biologically female, spent over 30 years living as a man. Staverley would definitely go when it opened the following week. There was some football banter and then Valerie sent Archie and Staverley to talk the sitting room with the last of wine while she tidied. Staverley offered to help but was ushered away.

He did not want to spoil the mood but could not resist asking Archie whether he had heard anything more from the police. Just a phone call Archie explained to re-check his movements that night. There had been no one at home that evening when he left home nor when her arrived back to corroborate his account of the timing of his visit to Layton's hotel. Valerie was at rehearsals and got back late, and the girls were also out doing whatever it was they did in the evenings after finishing homework and were also late, and got into trouble for it. But as yet the police had no reason to question the reason Archie had given for his visit. As far as they were concerned he had no motive, despite his opposition to Layton's appointment, and he had given a plausible account of his meeting with Layton. He had explained his opposition as an academic matter rather than a personal one. They did not, as yet anyway, know the real history of their relationship and that would not be easy to recover. But he had been in the right place at the right time and was as yet the only person the police had identified who might have placed the soap in Layton's bathroom.

'Are you still alright about being my accomplice?' Archie asked.

'What do you mean?'

'Well you know now that I lied about why I went to the hotel that night and you know about how I felt about Layton. Are you still okay about keeping that to yourself?'

Staverley did not hesitate. 'I am Archie, I believe absolutely that you had nothing to do with his death. You might have wanted him dead but so did plenty of others it seems. And wanting and doing are very different. I have no problem about keeping what you told me to myself. In a way it's a kind of privilege, a burdensome privilege, but I am grateful that you felt you could say those things to me. To be honest I really missed our friendship and times like this with you and your family. You are important to me in ways that are difficult to explain.'

They both looked at their feet. Stavereley's surety was heartfelt and firm, they were both appropriately embarrassed. Archie nodded and curled his chin but did not say more. They talked further about the murder and other possible suspects and Staverley felt bad about not sharing the other things he now knew about some of those involved but the conversation moved on to the Department and the change of collective mood that seemed to have come about, which pleased them both. Valerie rejoined them and Staverley asked her more about what it was like to act being a man.

'I like it.' Valerie said. 'Its not like anything I have ever done before. You have to learn to do everything differently – talk, obviously, but stand, sit, walk, hands, even facial expressions are different. I am having trouble with some of that, much more than the lines, you men are such funny creatures - I wonder how you manage. I have spent some whole days at home being Albert and I have been out in role a couple of times and no one stares or points, so I take that as a sign that I am getting the hang of it. I need more practice.'

'So you must be deep into the rehearsals now?' Staverley asked.

'Yep. It's been every Tuesday to Thursday for the past six weeks and it's tiring and for me the dressing and make up take ages – I do a lot of the makeup myself now. I just want to get on and do it on stage with an audience.'

'Well I will be there definitely. I am sure you are going to be outstanding.'

And it was time to go. Staverley had enjoyed the evening and getting back to something like his past relationship with Archie and Valerie, and he walked home feeling more positive.

But he did not sleep well. There were just too many dark and difficult thoughts eddying around in his mind. He tried to focus on some more benign work ones but as soon as he began to drift toward sleep his brain reattached itself to the ones he did not want to think about in the middle of the night. He gave up eventually, had a quick breakfast and left early for the university. He tried to fit a whole days work into a morning. Cormoran was back and had reluctantly chosen a topic to write about and appeared to have a sensible plan for his essay. Back to the station and then a connecting train to London, and an hours work en route. He arrived at Victoria just before 3.30, time enough to get to Bloomsbury punctually.

Liana was waiting, reading a book and sipping a cup of tea. She was dressed as though for a business meeting, dressed to impress. Her long black hair was gathered in some device at the base of her neck and she was wearing makeup. She had lost weight he thought. She had an odd ability to look and be different depending on the occasion. Staverley was not sure what this occasion was but he was certain that she had not dressed this way or worn make-up for his benefit.

'Sorry.' She said 'I was early and couldn't wait for my Earl Grey.'

She never drank ordinary tea, or coffee, always Earl Grey.

'That's alright.' He went to the counter and ordered a pot of tea and a cheese scone. He had missed lunch in the rush to be on time.

'So.' Liana said 'What is this about? Nice to see you by the way, I think.'

She was still in a good mood. He threw all caution to the wind and launched in.

'Liana, what were you doing near The Paine hotel the night Layton was killed?'

'What! Who says I was?'

'Well Roger actually, he saw you.'

'Roger, puh! Was does he know? Silly man.'

'So he's wrong, you weren't there.' Staverley was preparing to be mightily relieved and enjoy his scone and go home.

'I didn't say that.' Liana said.

'So you were there?'

'Maybe I was. It's possible.'

This was exasperating.

'Liana don't mess about, were you there or not? This is serious. It really is. If it was you that Roger saw the police have been trying to identify you, they have devoted a lot of time and effort to tracing a woman who was seen walking from Layton's hotel to the station on the night he was killed.'

'I am not responsible for how the police allocate their resources. If they can't find me that their incompetence.'

'So I was you?' Staverley asked again.

'Maybe it was.'

'Liana.' He said, in frustration. Staverley realised that he was beginning to speak loudly and he had promised he would not do that. Their conversation was also attracting the attention of some of the other tea drinkers. He lent forward and spoke quietly.

'Liana, tell me please, were you there or not? Was it you that Roger saw?'

'I suppose it was. I was there. I am the mystery woman.' She still seemed playful and was not taking Staverley's questions seriously.

'I was there and I met with Layton – I had dinner with him. So there.'

Staverley was astounded.

'You were that woman. You were the one he had dinner with. Why didn't you say something? Why didn't you tell the police?'

'Well that would be a very stupid thing to do wouldn't it.' Liana said.

'Why would it be stupid?'

'Well then they might think that I was involved in Layton's murder, and I would not want them to think that would I, because, well, I was.'

Staverley could not think of anything to say. His mind froze in a blank space that contained no words. He knew he needed to say something, he wanted to say something, but there was nothing there, nothing was coming. This was not something he had anticipated. He found it impossible to respond. He just stared at her. Liana filled the silence.

'I don't see a problem. He was a despicable man, who did despicable things and would have done more despicable things if someone had not stopped him. Lots of people are pleased that he's dead. He deserved to die.'

Staverley did find response to that.

'He may have done some awful things but killing him, why would you do that, I don't understand. Are you really telling me that you did it? Why you? What reason did you have for wanting him dead?'

Liana laughed out loud and various tea drinkers looked their way again.

'I had several reasons in fact. Retrospective reasons, prospective reasons and very immediate ones.'

'What on earth do you mean?' Staverley asked, getting more exasperated.

'Well, alright, because it's you and you will understand. I will explain, and then you will see that what I did was right and necessary – in the public interest.' She laughed again. Her revelation heightened even further her good mood. Indeed he began to think that Layton's death was the reason for her good mood. Staverley had always found her difficult to read. It was one of the problems in their marriage, he often got things wrong and would infuriate her with his inappropriate responses, too often he took trivial things too seriously and did not recognise when she was saying something she thought was important. Now he could make no sense of her at all, she had admitted being involved in Layton's murder, whatever involved meant, but seemed to think she had done a good thing. What had she said? 'In the public interest.'

'He may have got away with his plotting and manipulations with other people but he was not going to get away with it with me. It was him that put a stop to me getting the job in the US. That was my job, I wanted it and he took it away. It was because of him that I am working in that godforsaken, back of beyond, third-rate university on that ridiculous research project. And then he was going to do the same thing with the Chair in Ireland. He told me that they had written to him and he told me what he would say, unless I could convince him otherwise. And that's why I was there that night, I was there to convince him otherwise. The dinner was just a precursor; the convincing would come later in his room. And he was very specific about what would be involved in him being convinced. He told me what I should wear and what I would need to do to convince him, and it was disgusting. He was an ugly revolting perverted old man. I even thought very fleetingly about doing what he wanted, giving him what he expected, but I am ashamed of myself for even contemplating that. He couldn't be trusted and he certainly wasn't going to get the better of me. So I decided on a different course of action. I decided that he should die or at least be very, very ill, and that I would get on with the rest of my career and he would never get in my way again. I hate it when people under estimate me. That's one thing you never did.'
That may have been a compliment but Staverley ignored it.
'But how did you do it? The soap, where did that come from and how did you get it into his room? The people in the hotel said the woman he was having dinner with left abruptly and if you got the 9.05 train how was there time to plant the soap? Did you do it before?'
'Well I might have done that early mightn't I. But I am not telling you anything more about that.'

'Why not? If you are telling me you planned it all why not tell me what the plan was? And where did you get the soap?' Staverley asked again, and he looked around to make sure they could not be over heard.

'Well, that's where Dirk came in useful. He is very fond of me. He made it for me.' Staverley was confused for a moment and then remembered the new American boyfriend she had mentioned.

'He researches chickens and has been working on a new kind of feed which includes castor beans and very helpfully he explained to me the issues with ricin as a waste product of the manufacturing process and with a few falsehoods and a lot of encouragement and promises of even more encouragement to come he made a very professional, very lethal bar of soap for me. Probably the best present a man has ever given me, and that includes you Staverley.' Her jollity was as disconcerting as her revelations.

'But that's horrible.' Staverley said, and then stopped to think.

'But Layton was in his room when his dinner guest arrived, so how did you manage to put the soap there?'

'You are very annoyingly persistent, but I have told you everything I am going to tell you. You will have to work out the rest for yourself.'

'I don't want to do that. I don't want to work it out. I want you to explain it to me. And what are you going to do now?' Staverley asked.

'What do you mean? You don't mean going to the police and making an emotional confession or some such? Absolutely not.'

Again she laughed. She had laughed just about as many times during tea as the whole of their marriage.

'You could turn me in of course, as they say. But I don't think you will. You will just have to cope with the fact that you know I was involved in doing away with Layton, and that you don't know exactly how it happened, and you are not going to be able to tell anyone. Just keep thinking about how improved academia is already by Layton's absence. Think about all of the people who smiled when they read about him in the papers. Think about the collective sigh of relief. And think about your ex-wife on trial and in prison and you having to give evidence. Think about those things, and weigh them up. A while you do that I have a train to catch.'

Liana stood up and collected her coat and bag and took a step toward the door. She then turned back and smiled broadly at Staverley.

'It was good to see you, it really was. Can you pay for my tea?'

Staverley sat for a while then paid and left, his cheese scone only half eaten. He walked in a daze. It cannot be real, he kept saying to himself. He embarked on this investigation or quest of whatever it was to help a friend and ended up finding that the woman he had been married to, who he had lived with for two years was a murderer. That was not how it was supposed to turn out. It was supposed to be someone else, anyone else, very specifically someone he did not know, and certainly not Liana. It cannot be real, he kept saying to himself. He stopped walking and realised he was in the Charing Cross Road. He would normally have browsed the bookshops there, he liked browsing, but now was not the time. He was not in the mood. But he needed to stop saying things to himself, and he need to do something that would give him a bit of distance from what had just happened. He needed to get beyond shock to be able to think properly and think about everything Liana had said. He decided on a drink and a film – hiding in a bottle and then hiding in a cinema – two distractions might be better than one. He diverted in Long Acre and ordered a double malt, a Talisker, in the Kembles Head, a pub he had visited before and that was still not much changed from its nineteenth century origins. He did not often drink spirits but the whisky had a welcome numbing effect on his brain. The nearby Lumiere cinema was showing *Local Hero*, which seem to promise the right sort of distraction and despite everything he enjoyed the quirky charm of the film. When he re-emerged into St Martin's Lane it was dark and he was hungry. He found an Italian café nearby and ate a pizza. It was very good.

By the time he got home Staverley had thought of a long list of questions he should have asked Liana and without her answers he had made little progress in resolving the dilemmas she had left him with. Liana's revelations were now added to the other secrets and confessions that he was carrying in his head and guarding - Monica's and Lionel's plot to discredit Layton, and Archie's history with and hatred of the man. He felt confident that keeping those things to himself was right because he was also convinced that they were not murderers, but this was different. Unless this was some sort of bizarre fantasy that Liana had conjured up then she was a cold-blooded killer. She had carefully plotted to eliminate Layton, or at least to disable him. She had involved her lover by getting him to make the soap. And she clearly thought that it was a good thing she had done, for herself and for others. He should have phoned Mellmoth immediately, but he had not, and Liana's absolute confidence that he would not give her up was as disturbing as it was infuriating and apparently she was right. How was it that she seemed to know him so much better than he knew her? Their relationship had been tumultuous, some of their arguments escalated into shouting and pointing, but there had never been a hint of anything violent. Liana tended to participate in the arguments through the medium of ironic and barbed comments, which Staverley hated. He did learn by the time that it was clear that the marriage had irrevocably failed that not to respond to the barbs was the best way of dealing with them – but all too late. He supposed, in a way, Layton's death was not violent as such, it had been calculated and planned but was once removed from the perpetrator in the sense that she was not there when the poison took effect, she did not watch him die, it was even possible as she intimated that he might not have died – as he had learned people do survive ricin. But what of the cut on Layton's hand? He hadn't asked about that. Each time he replayed what Liana had said, as she calmly sipped her earl grey, he became more and more aware of the careful wording of her confession. She was 'involved' she had said, more than once. She did not say in any straightforward way 'Yes, I did it.' Or 'Yes, it was me.' She had said 'Yes, I was involved' and had refused to explain how the soap was placed in his room. What did all of that mean? What was involved? Clearly, one thing it might mean is that she was not acting alone, that someone else or more than one other person were also 'involved'.

Maybe this was *Murder on the Orient Express* and everybody did it. That might even make some sense, at the same time as it was a very stupid idea. There was obviously something significant that Staverley was missing, and given Liana evasiveness he was meant to miss. Perhaps her evasiveness was just a ploy? If she left doubts in his mind about the nature of her involvement, and who else might be involved, if anyone, then he would be less likely to rush off to the police without knowing more. Perhaps this was just another of her clever manipulative tactics to create confusion. If so it was certainly working. But in another way it was not like Liana. To a degree, thinking about it, he was not surprised that she had confessed, she liked to take credit, she liked her intellect to be on display, she would enjoy people knowing the complexity of the murder plot and the careful appropriateness of the ricin – serving up an appropriate mix of agony and humiliation. Even the fact of having Layton die in his bath was a touch of gory creativity, although even that begged questions. How did she know that he took a bath every evening before bed and why the uncharacteristic coyness about being 'involved'? All of that brought him back to the same problem – what to do with what he did know? It was late now, but he could phone Mellmoth anyway or he could wait until morning and hope that somehow during the night, awake or asleep, he would come to a clear and firm decision about what was the right thing to do – a decision he could defend, at least to himself, and live with.

CHAPTER TWELVE

It was very late by the time Staverley had finally got to bed and he slept surprisingly well, exhausted by the day. But there was no revelatory dream that solved his dilemmas and he awoke to confront the same questions and uncertainties he had wrangled with the night before. The proper thing to do was obvious, he should tell the police what Liana had told him. He owed no loyalty to Liana after all - they were divorced, she had treated him badly during their marriage, at least that's how he saw it, their current relationship, such as it was, was strained and decidedly one-sided, and now she was taking him for granted and manipulating him. So why did he not reach for the phone? Well, it was just not that simple. He did have some sense of duty of care or some such for Liana. He felt a kind of responsibility for her. Or was he just being stupid? Then also there was still that irritating and disturbing word – involved - that was getting in the way, making things even more complicated and unclear.

He finally admitted to himself that he wanted to know what that word meant before he took action, or took no action, and had a better sense of what the consequences of either might be. It could well be that this was just Liana's way of seeding doubt and confusion as he suspected but he needed to know for sure. If there was or might be someone else involved he should revisit his list of suspects, both those about whom he retained doubts as well as the ones he had crossed off – he might have missed something. He also needed to think again about the events of the night of the murder, that's what Peter Wimsey or Sam Spade would do, he was sure. He now knew the identity of Layton's dinner guest but the other visitor, the one who had stopped at reception, remained an unknown. He had a good sense now of who that could not be, if he believed everything he had been told, but perhaps he was being gullible. One real possibility was that if someone else was involved then that person was the visitor and that in some way or other it was the visitor who had planted the soap. If that was the case it was equally possible, even likely, that the visitor was yet another hapless man who had come into Liana's thrall, like Dirk, the Dutch

American. That would probably be someone Staverley knew nothing about and Liana was simply protecting the identity of her acolyte.

Even so, over a breakfast of muesli and banana and a very large pot of coffee, Staverley began to draw in a notebook a table of people, times and events – as he had done many times in his research. It was a way of organising data and looking for connections and omissions. He decided to eliminate no one in the first instance and started with the names of everyone who had any dealings with Layton, however tenuous, both personal relationships and professional ones. He included all of his colleagues who had been involved in the decision to invite Layton and the people who had made the arrangements for his visit or knew of them. It was quite a long list and he knew that some people would quickly be erased but he was determined to start by making no presumptions. He then planned out the day of Layton's death with the timings of his arrival, dinner and discovery and any comings and going's he was aware of. To this he added the people who he knew had visited to hotel – Archie, Liana and the mystery man. Finally, as best he could, and using the notes he had made of the various conversations he had had, he tried to plot who was where at the key times, although alibis were thin on the ground and those in place might need to be tested further. He assumed that this was the sort of thing that the police would do, but also that they had a lot more information than he, and resources, although of course he also knew a number of very important things that they did not. He was searching for anomalies or inconsistencies and was beginning to trace one niggling inconsistency and carefully re-reading a section of his notes when the telephone rang.

'Hello.' He had stopped giving his name when answering the phone at home a couple of years previously when a slightly unbalanced female student had found his number and rung him several times and tried to initiate inappropriate conversations. She had been served with a restraining order organised by the University solicitor and eventually been whisked away by her embarrassed parents.

'It's Sergeant Mellmoth.' Staverley noted the use of the rank and was nonplussed to hear Mellmoth given the uncomfortable time he had spent last night and this morning trying to decide whether to ring him.

'I need to ask you to come down to the station, this morning if possible, its something I cannot discuss on the phone, but its important.' Mellmoth said. This sounded serious, perhaps Mellmoth had found out about Staverley's interviews and he was going to be charged with withholding information or perhaps his own whereabouts at the crucial time were still an issue and he would be facing another session of questions. He tried to keep a level voice when he replied.

'Of course, if I make one phone call to do some rearranging at work I could come now, would that suit you?'

'The sooner, the better.' Said Mellmoth, which ramped up Staverley's nervousness several notches. The phone went dead.

Staverley could not help himself and he looked from his kitchen window to the street below just to check there was no police car waiting to intercept him. He phoned Jean and asked her if someone could put a note on his door to say he would be late, assuming of course that he would be able to go in at all and not end up languishing in a police cell. He was getting himself into a state and tried a few deep breaths. He hurried down the stairs and set off on the short walk to the police station. As he walked he thought that he had never actually been inside a police station, not beyond the counter that is. He had once turned in a lost dog when he was a student and a couple of years ago had found a wallet in a telephone box but certainly had no experience of an interview room apart from what he had seen on television. As it turned out he would have to wait for that. Mellmoth collected him from the front counter and led him to a large office full of untidy desks, only one of which was currently occupied. Mellmoth got him sat down and pulled out a brown folder from the tottering pile of other brown folders that took up most of his desk space.

'Right, there is a degree of formality to this. There are certain things I need to go over with you, and I need to remind you that anything said today cannot in any circumstances be communicated to a third party. Ok?'

'Ok.' Staverley found himself rather sadly focused on the word degree, 'degree of formality', maybe not a caution or charge then.

'I have to tell you that at 5.45am this morning my colleagues from the Staffordshire Constabulary raided an address in Tamworth. They were seeking to take into custody a Liana Highsmith, whom I believe you know.' There was a space for Staverley to assent. His mind had gone into some combination of meltdown and overdrive and he struggled to find the right thing to say.
'Liana, yes of course.'
'Your ex-wife I understand.' Mellmoth stated, it was not a question.
'Yes, that's right.' What else to say, Staverley wondered? He was trying to regain some kind of control of his brain and come to terms with what Mellmoth had said. They knew, they must know. He needed to explain.
'We were married for two years and divorced about two years ago. It was a bit messy but we stay in touch.' He offered, and then quickly realised that he needed to be seen to ask what was happening, not to do so would probably seem very suspicious.
'But sorry, I am a bit taken aback here. What is Liana supposed to have done? Why would the police go to her house? Does this have something to do with Layton's murder?' He asked.
'It does indeed. We now believe that your ex-wife may well be responsible for Layton's death or at the very least conspired with others to bring about his death.'

'But that's incredible, it's unbelievable.' Staverley was aware again that he needed to cover himself here. He could not be seen to know too much, or anything really. He had to appear to be shocked, but that was not difficult.
'It makes no sense. I didn't even know that Liana knew Layton. Are you absolutely sure about this?'
Mellmoth hesitated for a second.
'We now have considerable evidence which points to your ex-wife's involvement in Layton's death.' There was that word again. 'The exact extent of that involvement remains for the moment somewhat unclear. We had hoped to

discuss that with Ms. Highsmith but she was not at her address in Tamworth and the initial assessment of my colleagues is that she left fairly recently in a hurry taking at least some of her possessions with her, a bag or two at least maybe more than that. In other words, in police parlance, she has done a runner. Does she have a car do you know?'

'Sorry I have no idea, I don't think so.'

Staverley was collecting himself somewhat. He knew he still had to be careful.

'So you have evidence that suggests that Liana may have killed Layton or helped someone else kill him, you, or rather the Staffordshire police, tried to arrest her but she was gone, she's run away?'

Mellmoth looked a little peeved. 'I think that's what I just said.'

'Sorry, I'm just having trouble processing this. What is the evidence against her, can I ask that?'

'I will get to that.' Mellmoth said. 'But first I need to ask you when was the last time you saw your ex-wife and whether you may have any idea of her current whereabouts?'

Staverley had a quick decision to make, how many lies to tell and whether those lies would be robust or fragile.

'I met with her yesterday, in London. That was the first time I had met with her face to face since soon after the divorce, but we used to talk on the phone every few months. She would phone me. To be honest I wasn't entirely enthusiastic about keeping in contact. Our marriage did not end well. But she phoned a couple of days ago and asked me to meet her and talked me into it, she said she needed to ask me about something important. But when we met, we had tea in Bloomsbury, she just complained about her current job and talked about an interview she has coming up form a job at a university in Ireland, the one that Layton had been asked to comment on. She actually didn't ask me anything or have anything important to say and then left rather abruptly, but she can be like that. Perhaps she intended to say something and changed her mind. There didn't seem to be anything unusual about her, or her manner, not by her standards, in fact she was in a good mood, and she certainly didn't say anything about going away, apart from that she was already planning the trip to Ireland, so I have no idea where she is now.'

Staverley had never imagined himself in this situation, systematically lying to the police about a murderer. Well a half-baked mix of truth and lies to be accurate. But he really did not know where Liana was or where she might have gone. With every twist and revelation his lack of understanding of her and what she was capable of was made clearer. He wondered whether perhaps she was unstable, suffering from some kind of mental illness, or maybe she was a psychopath or sociopath – he wasn't sure of the difference. It was possible that her certainty about Staverley not betraying her to the police was just bravado and she had run just in case but he could not think where she would go or to whom. Nonetheless, here he was not divulging her confession, for whatever good that might do. He had the horrible feeling that all these lies and omissions might have consequences. But given he had not told anyone about what she had said over tea in Bloomsbury there was also the question as to how the police had identified her. Staverley wondered whether Mellmoth would be willing to tell him, or in the circumstances it could be that their previous friendly relations were on hold.

'Philip.' Staverley decided to try out Mellmoth's first name rather than sergeant, 'would it be inappropriate to ask how it is that Liana has become your main focus of interest? I am still having problems reconciling the Liana I know with being part of a murder plot or working out why she would do such a thing. What was her relationship with Layton, apart from the reference request you found in his papers? Surely someone would not commit murder over a reference for a job.' Staverley might have believed that before Liana had spoken to him, not now, but he thought he should ask. Mellmoth was also clearly having some problems with exactly what kind of encounter this was and what the limits were to its degree of formality. Several possible responses seem to form themselves into different facial expressions and he sniffed.

'Look, I shouldn't be saying anything more to you, especially given your relationship with the suspect, but as you have been helpful in the investigation I can tell you this. It was the soap, or more precisely the ricin. We have had considerable help from the Americans both the FBI and the CDC.'

'CDC?' Staverley asked.

'Sorry, Centre for Disease Control, its in Atlanta. Both them and the FBI are twitchy about ricin and they were more than willing to help. Both have labs that could do a breakdown analysis of the remaining poison we were able to send, far superior to anything we could muster here, and the science is beyond me to be honest, but basically they were able to trace the source of the ricin to a research lab at Cornell University, something to do with chickens of all things. Anyway a quick visit from the FBI and questions to the research team and the poison maker owned up and implicated your Liana. Evidently she sweet-talked him into making it for her with some story about an abusive partner and teaching him a lesson and the idiot fell for it, and for her. The FBI is now considering what charges they should bring against him. The upshot of all that was a teletext to us last evening and the subsequent request from us to the Staffordshire lads to pick her up. If, as you say, she was in London yesterday afternoon either she rushed back to Tamworth to pick up her baggage or she was already on the move when you met with her. Did she say what she had been doing earlier in the day?'

'Not at the time.' Staverley said 'but when we spoke beforehand she mentioned a meeting and a lunch, but I didn't ask her about them. She was always meeting people, developing her social network, getting herself known in ways that may be helpful to her future career. I gave up asking a long time ago. She was a strange creature Liana, obviously even stranger than I had appreciated. I used to think strange and wonderful. Does this make any sense to you, do you have a theory about what she has been doing?'

'Nothing more than we have discussed before, there is that letter obviously, but as you said that hardly seems to be a motive for murder. But it is possible that we are not dealing with an entirely rational mind here. We are exploiting our newly established relationships with the FBI to find out more about the time she spent in the States and given the ricin link they are pursuing it for us. We'll have to see.

They are also going to speak to the professor who wrote to Layton, you remember the letter?' Mellmoth explained.

Staverley added a little something. 'Well she was there for three months earlier in the year, at Leyland, and it looked as though she would be taking a permanent position she said but it didn't work out for some reason, I don't know what happened.' He was lying again.

It did not seem like a good idea to know too many things and if the FBI contacted the professor then Liana's link to Layton and her motive for murder would probably become clearer. He felt bad about keeping things from Mellmoth and spinning these lies and evasions, but if he said any more then he might put himself into a very difficult position. Again he felt the burden of the confessions he had elicited and the emotions with which they were invested. He felt tired and in a way dirty – a sort of moral tainting. He was finding about things about people he knew and finding out things about himself – things he was not sure he liked very much. He had never thought of himself as a liar, at least not beyond the sort of social lies that keep bits of everyday life going, but these were big lies, important lies. He was again opening himself up to possible prosecution for obstruction or accomplice after the fact, or some such.

The only good thing in all of this, and not that good, was that he no longer had to struggle with deciding whether or not to reveal what Liana had told him, that was no longer necessary, apart from the details of Layton's connivings and his ultimatum and what happened over dinner, the police knew as much as he did. They already had one motive and if they were able to track down Liana he was in no doubt that she would regale them with all of the sordid details of the night, although there was still the matter of that word 'involvement'. Liana had used it and so did the police. Maybe she would be more forthcoming with them than she had been with him. But the word was not going away. It recurred, it loomed. There was something missing. Nonetheless, he did not want to get into discussing with Mellmoth who else, if anyone, could also be 'involved'. He thought back to his table of times and places and people and the anomaly he thought he had found but he was also very aware that it could easily be explained away. He would find out.

'Staverley?' Staverley had drifted off into silence.

'Sorry, I was trying to work things out and getting nowhere. Perhaps the FBI will be able to shed some light on the backstory to all of this. I'll tell you this has thrown me. The idea that my ex-wife might be a murderer is chilling. We had our difficulties and ended up realising that we were, what's the word, incompatible, but it's a long way from falling out of love with someone and ending up disliking them to the idea that I could have become a practice run for Layton. You must have plenty of insights into the criminal mind or whatever but I am just at a loss here, I think I am going to have to spend a lot of time re-thinking our marriage and re-thinking Liana.'

'Well, I can't be much help. I have seen a lot of nasty things and nasty people in this job but I have also come across people who have led ordinary blameless lives and then committed acts of incredible violence which have shocked everyone - wives, husbands, parents, friends. We use psychiatrists and conduct interviews and all of that but sometimes its just inexplicable, or its just one trigger that turns ordinary people to violence and ruins their lives and other people's lives. There is even a matter of chance in some cases, if a word had not been spoken, if a turning had not been taken, if a knife was not to hand, then nothing would have happened. The courts and society generally want things explained, put into a category or a type, it makes us all fell safer and gives us a sense of being in control, but sometimes stuff just happens and to try and subject it to rational explanation distorts its craziness. Sorry, this is beginning to sound like one of those seminars at UME, evidently I was paying some attention.'

Staverley smiled. 'No that's useful, I do know what you mean, and the social sciences feed into that, and feed off of it. It is an explanation business. In part at least research is about constructing plausible explanations of the social and we forget that more often than not those explanations do injustice to social complexity. We simplify things to make them sensible, leave out bits that do not fit, smooth over exceptions. People don't want to know that the world is complicated and that perhaps there are large chunks of it that we cant understand and certainly can't control.'

He was more confident talking abstractly like this with Mellmoth than trying to maintain his feigned ignorance and skirt around what he did and did not know about Liana and could and could not say.

Mellmoth returned to the matter at hand.

'We may need to speak with you again, and if there is anything that occurs to you in the meantime about where your ex-wife might be, and obviously if she contacts you again, or you remember anything else, then please contact me immediately. And I'm sure I don't have to remind you that anything I have told you today cannot be discussed with anyone else, to do so could compromise the ongoing investigation.'

With that they shook hands and Staverley left both relieved and upset. He had agreed with Mellmoth about it sometimes being impossible to explain things and he knew well now that he was not good at explaining Liana, but there was something else going on here and he needed to try and work it out.

As Staverley sat on the train he gnawed away in his mind at the anomaly he had hit upon earlier and began to construct a version of events that might make some sense of it. It was a horrible sense, worse perhaps than any of the other possibilities he had contemplated while asking questions about Layton's death. But he was now tired of thinking, or at least thinking about murderers and alibis and means and motives and by the time his train arrived he had convinced himself that he was wrong, that he was joining up things that had no connection at all. He was also certain that he wanted to be wrong but equally that he would have to ask, he could not, not ask. There were no musings about the university's bizarre architecture this morning although he did notice that yet another round of roof repairs had begun, and the lifts in the Social Sciences building were working – perhaps the porters had settled their industrial dispute or were just feeling benevolent The Rovers had won at the weekend and relegation might be averted, that might be it. Staverley needed to speak with Archie. He checked his pigeonhole on the way to Archie's office and there were a few disturbingly fat envelopes and a telephone message taken by Jean. He recognised the return number as Monica's and for the first time that morning there was the possibility of something positive to think about – wasn't there?

Staverley knocked on Archie's door, who said to come in, but he was with a PhD student.
'Sorry, didn't mean to interrupt.' Staverley said.
'No problem, we're done, just winding up, come in. So Becky you have your deadline for Chapter 4 and your outline sounds solid, so press on, get it written. I'll look forward to seeing it. The thesis is really coming together excellently.'
Becky beamed, nodded enthusiastically and collected up her papers, stuffing them into an enormous canvas bag.
'Thank you Archie, very helpful.' She said and was gone.
'Morning Archie, I just wanted to ask whether you might want to stop off at the student bar for a beer on the way home, about 5.00?'
'Oh, great idea, but I can't I am teaching a late seminar this evening, the part-time MA. Maybe tomorrow?'
Staverley tried to look disappointed. 'Of course the MA, I had forgotten, let's do it tomorrow then.' He said. He had not forgotten about the MA. This might be a bit easier than he had anticipated.

He now had the rest of the day to worry and to return Monica's call. He was surprised how nervous he felt when he got back to his room and sat in front of the telephone. The events of the last couple of days had kept thoughts of Monica at the back of his mind but Staverley had been almost constantly hoping that she would ring. He had thought of ignoring what she had said and calling her but he knew that would be a bad idea, so he had waited. Now he could ring. Should he think of something to say? Something that would convince her to give him another chance or perhaps this would simply be Monica telling him that she did not want to see him again. He knew he was being stupid, the only way to know was to ring, he began to dial the number, it was her laboratory he thought – there was no answer. He called twice more in the next half hour but Monica did not pick up, nor did any of her colleagues. He decided to find himself some lunch but tried once more before setting off for the cafeteria adjoining the university bookshop – they had a book for him that he had ordered. This time she answered after one ring.

'Monica, its me.' He said, hoping that she had not forgotten his voice.

'Hello, you.' She said, which he thought sounded friendly at least.

'How are you?' She asked. He did not want to do social formalities, he wanted her to tell him why she had called. Nonetheless.

'Well, not good, it's been a difficult couple of days, I have a lot to tell you about but its very complicated, too complicated for the phone really.' She was silent for a second, it seemed longer to Staverley. He realised how important, this, she, was to him.

'Well if I were to come down there and see you, you could tell me what's been happening...' Staverley was ecstatic.

'But...' Oh dear, a but. 'But, you are going to have to be especially nice to me and ply me with fish and chips and ice cream and maybe even a stick of rock.'

He was so relieved. 'I can do that, I certainly can. I would be pleased to indulge you with all of the culinary delights our small seaside town can offer. When can you come?'

'What about next weekend? I need to check a couple of things but I think I could travel down on Friday afternoon. What about you?'

He did not need to think, anything that got in the way could be changed or ignored. 'That's perfect. Let me know what train you will be catching and I'll meet you at the station.'

'I'll call you on Thursday then.' She said and was gone before he could say goodbye.

His day had taken a definitely turn for the better and he set off for the bookshop and lunch more lighthearted than he had been for sometime. But that did not last long.

Staverley left the university just before 5.00 and was in the town centre before 5.30. He walked to the seafront and turned right. He tried to pay attention to the state of the sea – rather flat and grey – but spent the walk trying to prepare some questions that would allow him to disavow his suspicions if the answers were the ones he hoped for. He was soon standing at the door and only then did it occur to him that there might not be anybody in, he should have telephoned. Perhaps he should go home and come back another time. Before he could decide the door was opened.

'I could see someone lurking on the doorstep through the stained glass, Wally always knows when someone is going the ring the bell, he growls. Why are you lurking Staverley?' Valerie asked.

'Oh sorry, I didn't mean to lurk. I was just passing by and thought I might say hello and then I thought I would be bothering you, I was trying to decide whether to ring the bell or not. What should I have done?'

'Ring of course.' She said. 'Come in, Archie's at work, but I can make you a cup of tea and I have just made flapjacks. They are an experiment. I had one the other day in that health food café near the pier and I thought I would give them a try. I think mine are just as good.'

'Sounds like an offer I can't refuse.' Said Staverley.

They settled around the kitchen table and Valerie made the tea and put a plate in font of him with the flapjack. He tried a bite and it was delicious.

'This is great Valerie, so moist and chewy. I really like it.'

'I am so pleased, you are my guinea pig. I might let you take one home.' They both sipped tea and chewed.

'How is the play coming along, it opens next week?' He asked.

'Yep, two more rehearsals and then the curtain comes up on Tuesday. I haven't been so nervous about anything like this for a long time. Its not just being the lead, it's the amount of time I am on stage and the unusual demands of the role. I told you about that.'

'So just one Wednesday and Thursday evening left, I think you said Tuesdays, Wednesdays and Thursday for rehearsals?'

'That's right. Its scary.'

'So do you ever do additional rehearsals, if things are not working out?' Staverley asked with care, trying to sound innocently interested.

'No, we cant do that. It's all so complicated with the cast and all the back stage people. There are nearly thirty of us. There's a schedule set well in advance that everyone commits to and changes are impossible - most of the time, especially in the later stages everyone has to be there. It's quite logistically difficult. I'm pleased I'm not on the production side of things.'

That was not what Staverley wanted to hear. He had to press on.

'I was thinking about you and the play and all of the things that have been happened to Archie.' He left that dangling.

'Well I did think about dropping out when it was clear that Layton was coming and then again after what happened to him. But Archie was adamant that I should carry on, and to be honest it's been a help for me, a distraction, and somewhere I could channel some of my surplus emotions. Who knows, it may have even improved my performance. I did worry about leaving Archie alone so much, I know he has talked to you about Layton, and I am grateful that he did. It's something that he and I have shared for many years and it's a sort of relief that someone else knows, and I know he feels better about it all - apart from the fact that Layton is dead. That's like a shadow that's been lifted from our lives.'

'Archie does seem different.' Staverley added. 'It's just a shame that the police are still interested in him.'

'I know, but I am sure that won't last much longer.'

'I was thinking about what Archie told me about that night. It's such a pity that there was no one at home on that Monday who could confirm his comings and goings more precisely, in a way that might satisfy the police, but no girls and you were at your rehearsal he said.'

Valerie's face froze and her colour drained and in an instant he knew she knew he knew. She must have realised that his questions were not as innocent as they appeared and where they had led.

'You've worked it out haven't you?'

'I think so.'

A tear formed in Valerie's left eye and rolled slowly down her cheek.

'I thought I had been so clever. No one really paid me much attention, all the focus was on Archie and your colleagues and given the police did not know about Archie's problems with Layton...' She wiped her cheek with the back of her hand. 'What was it that made you think about me?'

Not for the first time Staverley wished he had never started all of this, and just left things to the police. He really did not want to know about all of these secret lives and people's fears and drives. He liked the Valerie who baked and acted and sang and organised Archie and their daughters. He did not want to know Valerie the murderer and he certainly did not want to have to confront again whether or not he should tell the police what he knew, he had just avoided that once with Liana, and Valerie was very different. He liked Valerie a lot. She was kind and gentle and she was a mother and a wife. Layton was ruining lives in death as much as he had when alive.

'It was a lot of small things. You told me the other day about your rehearsal nights but then Archie had said you were at rehearsals on that Monday. It started to bother me.'

'I told him it was a costume fitting, and he never checked of course, why would he, and of course he was distracted by everything else going on.' Valerie said.

'And then there was Albert, your alter-ego, and you mentioned your outings in role, and I know how good an actress you are and I could easily imagine you being able to be a man and as you said when you tried it people didn't realise. The person on the hotel reception certainly had no idea except for a sense that there was something odd about the visitor.'

Another tear was making its way slowly down Valerie's cheek. She looked so crushed and vulnerable.

'The last thing was what Liana said to me. I haven't told you about that but yesterday I met with her in London and she confessed to what she called her involvement in Layton's death. She wouldn't say more than that, and certainly never mentioned you, but it made me think again about that night and how the soap got into the bathroom. She could not have put it, she never left the dining room and Layton was still in his room when she arrived. Reception called him. It had to have been someone else and the only real possibility was the visitor. And once I started to wonder about Albert and the problems of being a man and being manly, I also remembered how well you and Liana got on together, how unusually at ease she always was with you. And then you both had reasons for hating Layton, she for what he was doing to her career and you for what he had done to Archie. It was all so tenuous, full of holes and big assumptions and logical leaps but it also made a horrible sense. It didn't want it to make sense Valerie, you've got to believe that, I was really hoping that you were going to explain it all away so that I could enjoy my flapjack and go home and be happy that I was stupid and wrong. I don't want to be talking about this with you. I should have let it go before now. Why did I have to carry on asking questions?'

Valerie gathered herself a little.

'Its hardly your fault, Archie said that you were asking questions because you wanted to help him and he was pleased about that. You weren't to know how things would end up and where you questions would lead you. Its like a full circle, it started here and now it's ended here. I had better speak to Liana.'

'You can't.' Said Staverley, 'or I don't think you can, unless you know where she is now. The police tried to arrest her last night. They traced the soap poison back to her from the US. But now she's gone, she's run and they are looking for her.'

Valerie was shocked and clearly had not heard about the police or Liana's flight.

'Do you know where she is?' Staverley asked.

'Not a clue, we haven't been in contact since before that Monday, that was part of the plan, that we should have as little contact as possible before and none at all afterwards, and if either of us were caught then we would claim responsibility and leave the other one out of it. We realised that there were flaws and problems in our plan but we also thought that we would be unlikely suspects because of a lack of previous involvement with Layton, me especially, so even if things went wrong then there was always a chance that one of us would be ok. I had never spoken to or met Layton before that night and Liana had only spoken to him on the telephone.'

'God, that must have been odd, meeting the man who you knew so much about from Archie.'

'It was and he was as unpleasant in real life as Archie had described him – arrogant and rude, and there was so much I wanted to say to him, I wanted to scream at him, I wanted him to know what damage he had done, but I realised that he wouldn't care and would probably enjoy it. So I stayed in role and hid my loathing as best I could. I told him that I had been sent by the department to explain a change in the arrangements for the following morning and then asked to use the toilet before I left. 'If you must' he said and waved a hand at me. He was already in his dressing gown so it was prefect timing. I just had to switch our soap for the one already there. It was so easy. I had no idea then that Archie had already been to see him, he told me when I got home, we only just missed each other. It would have been very odd if we had coincided. And difficult to explain.'

This was a side of Valerie that Staverley had never seen, and he was impressed, if that was the right word given the circumstances. Perhaps it was all a part of her acting abilities, being able to remain calm and control her feelings and carry on, according to the script. A murder mystery translated into real life.

'Staverley, I need to ask you something, or several things. I have no right really but I have to ask. Will you give me time to tell Archie about all of this and explain to the girls what is going to happen? There are some things I need to sort out and arrange for them. The girls are old enough to manage the house with Archie, but its going to be very difficult in all sorts of ways.'

Staverley was shocked by Valerie's request, and for a moment he was not clear why he was shocked. Then he understood.

'You don't think I am going to tell all of this to the police do you? Unless you decide you are going to tell them then everything we have spoken about remains between us.' He said. And as soon as he said it he was sure it was the right thing to do, or not to do. There were no writhing doubts, no hesitation. It would be added to the pile of other secrets he had been accumulating over the past few weeks. And to his surprise this was a secret he was happy to keep even if it implicated him further in the conspiracy around Layton's murder. He had stopped being an objective investigator some time ago, and now he had become part of the conspiracy, he had a share of the guilt and the worry to carry and he was certainly willing to do that. The alternative was too awful to contemplate. It was Valerie's turn to be shocked.

'But I thought that ...' She began to cry again. There were a lot more tears this time, a mix of fear and guilt and relief Staverley assumed.

'I intend to say nothing, nothing at all. It's entirely up to you what happens now and I can't help much with that. But I think you should say nothing. The police seem to have got nowhere in identifying Albert, and there are a lot of things they don't know and wont know unless someone, you or me or Archie or Liana, tells them. And I wont be the one to come forward, I am very clear about that, and they don't have Liana, and I don't think it will be easy to get her to implicate you if they do find her. You might want to tell Archie, again that's up to you. He may not want to take on a new set of fears and worries but equally I am sure he would not want you to keep all of this to yourself, but that's for you to think about and decide. I wont interfere in that either. All I would say is don't do anything hastily.'

Staverley experienced a sort of peace in his mind. He could now stop. He would no longer be constantly analysing, suspecting, doubting and questioning his friends and colleagues. He had done what he set out to do. He had never thought about what he would do if he did find out who had killed Layton. He supposed he might have rushed to the police station or phoned Mellmoth, all pleased with himself for doing what the police were unable to do. But now he would do nothing. There was all that Philip Marlowe heart searching in the movies when the detective turns over the woman he loves to the police, serving justice and having to pay for your crime, but he didn't feel any of that. From all he had learned about Layton from the people he had talked to, the people who had been touched by Layton's repellent obsession to control and his willingness to hurt and destroy, he had no sympathy for the man or regrets about his death or misgivings about keeping all he knew to himself. That may make him as bad a person as Liana and Valerie, if they were bad – he wasn't sure about that - but he didn't care, not telling seemed right, it was right.

'You seem to have become the bearer of our family secrets Staverley and you are covering for a murderer. Two murderers.' Valerie said. 'Although, I don't feel like a murderer, I don't know what I feel like. Are you really sure you are Ok with all of this? You are probably committing some sort of crime by keeping quiet about what you know.'
'I am Ok, I really am, although I would rather not know any of these things, and there are other things I have come to know in the course of this that I will also be keeping to myself for the foreseeable future. To be honest, ignorance really

would be blissful right now. I am just so sorry to leave you with deciding what you will do.'

'I was already doing that, trying to decide. There have been so many moments since that night when I have almost explained myself to Archie, but then I have looked at him across the table and looked at the girls and thought about what it would be like if the police came for me and I could not be with them anymore. And I have had times laying awake at night when I felt that I would have to go to the police and confess, because I am an honest person, not a criminal - I know that must sound very strange. – and I have to accept that I have murdered someone or Albert did. We weren't sure that Layton would die, but we knew it was very likely. So for now at least I need to think more about what I have done and what I have become before I do say anything to Archie and I have no idea what he will think of me. I know there is that thing about feeling relieved to be able to tell someone, and it maybe true, but at the moment that someone is you. So I have to think about that as well.' She shuddered.

'And there is that other thing that murders... that people in my situation say, "if I had to do it all again". Well if I had to do it all again, I wouldn't, I really wouldn't. It was awful and terrible, the way he died was hideous, I know that now. But I did do it and I can live with it. I really can. I did it for Archie. You know now what Layton had subjected him to but you probably don't have any proper sense of how much those awful experiences changed Archie and distorted him. I love him totally as he is, he's wonderful as a husband and a father. But sometimes I see glimpses of another man, a man who is carefree and light of heart. Layton's campaign of humiliation destroyed the possibility of joy for Archie. He took something very fundamental away from him, and diminished Archie's life in a way. And though it doesn't sound that much it was a terrible thing. I thought about that a lot during the time I have known Archie and many years ago I decided that if it were ever possible, in some way I would revenge Archie's loss. He would never have asked me to, and he will be utterly appalled if or when I do tell him, but I felt I owed it to him, Layton owed it to him. And Liana in her own very unusual way offered me the opportunity to act on my decision. I know it may seem like an unlikely alliance. It was more like a collision of anger, hers about the job she wanted and mine about the pain that Layton's appointment was causing Archie. And as we talked we began to realise how much we each hated the man, and the lengths we were willing to go to to get back at him, and slowly a common resolve emerged. It's an incredible thing when you realise something like that about yourself, what you're capable of. I am not the person I thought I was, and that's frightening, and even a bit exciting. But would never have been able to do it without her. She had the imagination and the means to get the soap made, and I came up with the idea of how to plant it in his room. And before you ask, she did not talk me into it, if anything I was the one who convinced her that we had to do something, not just talk. We were very much in it together. When one of us wavered the other was resolute, we were a good partnership. She's a remarkable woman and we made a formidable team I think. I will always be grateful to her.'

There was a look of determination on Valerie's face.

Staverley looked at his watch, it was almost seven.

'I think I should go, unless you want me to wait with you until Archie gets back from his teaching?'

'No, no it's fine. You go, the girls will be home soon and I haven't got their supper going yet.'

They both got up and Valerie came round the table and put her arms around Staverley, he put his arms around her, and they stayed like that for a while sharing a sense of relief and both beginning to think about what might come next. They both knew that there was no guarantee that the police would not work out the same inconsistencies that Staverley had, although he doubted that they would, he knew things they did not.

'Will you be alright?' Valerie asked.

'I will, you don't have to add me to your list of worries. And I really enjoyed the flapjack. Can I have one to take home?'

She wrapped a flapjack for him and them walked with him to the front door. He turned as he closed the front gate.

'I am going to come and see you do Albert next week. You're going to be great.'

He said and walked away.

Staverley walked towards home and stopped off at the pub that he called his local, a free house with guest beers, for a pint of Hawkshead bitter. After a first long swallow he sipped the beer slowly and slipped into a kind a reverie staring out of the pub window and half listening to the chattering of the other drinkers. It was a quiet night and most tables were empty. He started to think about the tidying up he needed to do, and the covering up. He was going to have to be very clear about what he could say to whom and what he could not say. He could see the possibility of another list. Then he would be able to begin anticipating Monica's visit at the weekend, and what he should say to her about her father – if anything. He probably would have to explain further about his amateur investigation, but say that he had run out of ideas and was giving it up, leaving it to the police. If other people could have there secrets then so could he. The big question was Liana. If the police found her, and he assumed they would in due course, then he and Valerie would have to rely on her being willing to take the blame on her own. That remained to be seen. Monica was also bound to ask about Liana once she heard that the police were looking for her. He did not know what he was going to say. He would be spending the weekend with the daughter of the man his ex-wife had murdered. He had started as an outsider to everything and was now in some ways at the centre.

By the end of the week the police search for Liana as a suspect in Layton's murder had become a significant news story, not front page but quite a bit of coverage on the inside pages. Someone had leaked the role of the FBI and that gave additional spice to the story and lead to speculation around Liana's lover in the US as an accessory. But of Liana herself there were no sign or sightings. Another call to Mellmoth seemed in order but Staverley failed to track him down. At work he was busy and after the first gush of talk around Liana's disappearance and a whole range of commiserations and condolences of varying sincerity for Staverley, the daily routines of teaching and meetings reasserted themselves and the department was returning to some kind of normality. But as it became more widely known that Staverley's ex-wife was being sought as a murder suspect, teaching sessions became a little difficult to keep focused, the students wanted to ask questions. He also took time to meet with Lionel and without saying very much they seem to have agreed that they would not be saying anymore about Layton or his wife, although Staverley did mention Monica's visit and Lionel's eyebrows shot up, but again he did not say much, simply saying he hoped he would see her. Staverley decided to leave it to Monica to explain things further. The fact that Staverley was himself via Liana part of the murky goings on around Layton's demise, at least second hand, meant that Lionel seemed less embarrassed now about his and Monica's plans to bring Layton down.

Roger did not appear to recognise his part in the whole thing and he had made no effort to speak to the police, he was engrossed in trying to complete his latest haiku and improving the timings of his evening run. Staverley was half-heartedly avoiding Archie but they bumped into each other in the coffee corner and Staverley could not detect any further change in his demeanour so had no idea whether Valerie had told him, but assumed not. They fell into a comfortable exchange about football and the upturn in The Rovers fortunes under their new manager and less comfortably the potentially dire consequences of the Conservative government's proposals for the privatisation of nationalised industries. 'They'll be privatising us next.' Archie had quipped. Staverley made good progress with his 'to do' list and he, Lionel, Mary and Archie generated a short list of new names for the external examiner position.

The postcard arrived at home on Friday morning. It was postmarked Calais and showed a rather dull scene from the city centre. The message was written in capitals.

I KNOW IT WASN'T YOU. DON'T FORGET ME. L.

Printed in Great Britain
by Amazon